*Dedicated to all those soldiers who fell in
the Battle of Stalingrad 1942 - 1943*

INTRODUCTION

I first met the enigmatic Englishman at a militaria fair, held in Dusseldorf, where I happened to be on holiday at the time. I was looking at a Soviet PPSh sub-machine gun, complete with drum magazine, on sale for the bargain price of three hundred euros. Offers considered, of course. I said to my wife, 'that's a weapon with an amazing history, there must have been tens of thousands of these made, they were used in lots of different theatres of war, from Russia to French Indochina. I wonder what it would look like on the wall of my study.' Another man was looking at the gun, studying it intensely, with a look of curiosity on his face. I asked him did he know anything about the PPSh. He didn't answer at first, then said that he had never touched one, but his father had owned one in the war. I am fluent in both English and German, he was obviously English, although he spoke good German, I asked him in which theatre of the war his father fought. He told me the Eastern Front.

We chatted about the gun for a few minutes, I asked the dealer how old it was, then I asked the Englishman the question that I had been desperate to ask since he said that his father had used it on the Eastern front, the war between the Soviet Union and Germany. The English army did not send troops to that area of the war. Which unit was his father in? There was another long pause, I thought at first that he wasn't going to answer. When he did, I was certain that I was hearing things. He replied, 'The Waffen-SS, initially SS-Liebstandarte Adolf Hitler, afterwards the SS-British Freecorps. I was staggered. An Englishman, fighting for Hitler, in an elite SS regiment, then as part of the unit of turncoats and traitors founded by John Amery, son of Julian Amery, the British conservative politician? I pressed him on this, but he was adamant, even slightly angry that I appeared to doubt him. He asked me in an aggrieved tone, did I want proof? It was too good an opportunity to miss. I told him that I was an avid student of the history of the second world war, and if he did have any documentation that supported his statements, I would be very, very grateful for the chance to see them.

I offered to buy him dinner, and we agreed to meet the following evening at 'Im Schiffchen', one of the city's nicest restaurants. He arrived carrying a briefcase full of documents, which he gave to me to read. I was allowed to take notes, but not to take any of the material away. The material was a war diary, the property of SS-Hauptsturmführer Winston Wolf, which my contact said was not in fact his father's real name. There were several maps, a paybook and various decorations including the Iron Cross first class. There were various certificates, awards for sport fencing, together with numerous black and white photographs, in one of which I saw a tall, good looking man who my companion said was his father, Wolf, standing in white fencing kit with Reinhardt Heydrich, Olympic fencing champion and founder of the SS intelligence organisation, the Sicherheitsdienst. Other photos showed Wolf with a beautiful, elegant young woman, several showed Wolf in full SS uniform together with another man, an SS sergeant. I asked the man's real name, but he smiled and refused, saying the war was over, why dredge up the past? His family had apparently suffered badly at the hands of MI5, the Security Service, who gave the family of an English renegade a particularly hard time during the war.

I made copious notes, filling a two hundred page A4 refill pad with written material. I my dining companion what was his first name, he told me, with a smile, it was Winston, like his father. I never had another chance to review the material, Winston left after the meal, packed everything into the briefcase and declined another meeting. He told me he shouldn't have shown me as much as he did, it was just that after all of these years of secrecy, he wanted someone to know about his father. A brave man, the Iron Cross proved that, a traitor, without a doubt. A mystery, certainly.

In view of the dubious reputation of some war 'recollections', I decided to write the story as a novel, using all of my written notes for the basis of it. The 'Hitler Diaries' were exposed as fakes, as have many other supposed true accounts. The post war story of the SS serving in the French Foreign Legion, while presented as fact, is believed by many to be more fiction than fact, despite the truth of a great many former German soldiers, including Waffen-SS, joining the Legion. But as a story, a work of fiction, it makes thrilling reading.

The SS-British Freecorps existed, that is a fact. MI5 did monitor their activities carefully, I afterwards found out, documenting as much as they could about the people involved and their families. The fear of German spies in wartime was a very real one. I believe the story of Winston Wolf, as he called himself, to be essentially true. The events and people that he depicted and wrote about are certainly part of historical record. You will have to make up your own mind as to the veracity of the rest of it, how much really occurred and how much was the rambling fantasy of an English traitor caught up in the cruelty of the most horrific war the world has ever known.

Eric Meyer

SS ENGLANDER

CHAPTER ONE

October 4th 1942

Shells crashed into the ground close to the bunker, churning up earth already turned over and pulverised many times by the incessant barrages. Perhaps it was an exaggeration to call our position a bunker when it was just a stinking hole in the ground surrounded by the smashed and shattered remnants of buildings that once were the pride of Stalingrad, the city on the Volga named after the Soviet warlord in 1925.

The industrial city of Stalingrad had been a centre of heavy industry and transport, once well served by both rail and river and critical to the Russian war effort. The city was no stranger to war, having been fought over by the Tartars, Cossacks and then it suffered the ravages of the White armies in three massive assaults during the Russian Civil War under Ataman Krasnov, the White commander.

There were eight of us in the bunker, but just one ducked as a shower of dust and stone chippings showered down. Perhaps the rest of them were showing what fearless, tough soldiers they were, but I was already numb to the passion and the horror of battle. Quite frankly, living or dying had ceased to be of any particular interest. It seemed certain that there would be only one end to this battle and living was not an option on the table. Two of the occupants, Russian prisoners, were bound with baling wire, ducking was not an option for them either.

"Lieutenant I can see some movement in the department store across the street. I think we are in luck."

The speaker gave me a challenging look. Stabsfeldwebel Lutz Fassbinder was a veteran of Von Paulus' 6th Army, seconded from the 76th Infantry Division to command the group of four Wehrmacht soldiers who acted as my guard. He knew full well that I was an Obersturmführer in the Waffen SS Liebstandarte Adolf Hitler. He used my Wehrmacht equivalent rank in an endless attempt to bait me, to draw me out, probably for his unit's amusement. I couldn't care less. There were of course no Waffen SS serving in the 6th Army, except for me...and Müller.

By rights I should have been serving a life sentence in Germany for murder. Instead, my old fencing partner Reinhard Heydrich had given me the alternative of accepting a commission in the SS-LAH, "a chance to redeem myself", he said at the time. It seemed like a good idea then. Germany was not really fighting England, despite the declaration of war, people called it 'the phoney war'. The uniforms were smart, the girls all loved them, and an SS officer's mess was a major improvement to a prison cell. With my old fencing partner as protégé my future seemed rock solid. Years before we had fenced hard often without protective masks and jackets. Heydrich was as mad as I was, like me tall, athletic, a superb shooter, fencer and reckless with both life and women. Then the offer to fence for the German national team together with his commission in the embryo Sicherheitsdienst, the SD, Nazi secret service of the SS, made him a real celebrity in Nazi Germany, a national hero.

The reputation of the SD was well known throughout the Reich. It had been created in 1931 by Heinrich Himmler and run by Reinhard Heydrich. This early form of the SD was originally known as the Ic-Diensthad and had expanded rapidly with the success of the Nazi regime. The organisation was renamed Sicherheitsdienst (SD) with its primary role now being the detection of enemies of the Nazi leadership and their neutralisation. By 1938 its remit had expanded further, making it the intelligence organisation for the State as well as for the Party. It actively supported the Gestapo and worked with the general and interior administration through its network of agents and informants. A very powerful organisation indeed, Heydrich could do no wrong and I was at that time his protégé. That was of course until Germany went to war leaving me trapped on the wrong side, then Heydrich was assassinated and I was left isolated without favour or influence in the command structure of the Nazi hierarchy.

I picked up my rifle and carefully wiped the sensitive optics of the telescopic sight. The rifle was a Soviet Mosin Nagant 7.62 mm, a weapon I preferred to the Kar98k that was the preferred choice of the high command, and which I had used to win the SS-LAH marksmanship competition in Berlin, spurred on by my mentor, Heydrich. But Heydrich was dead, the high command was not in Stalingrad, I was, and when the dust and rubble, mud and ice prevented the Kar98k from firing, the slightly inferior Mosin Nagant kept pumping rounds into the enemy. The Mosin Nagant model 1891/30 was the standard issue 7.62mm bolt-action rifle to all Soviet infantry.

The sniper rifle variant was fitted with a 3.5 power PU telescopic sight. As found with many pieces of Soviet equipment it had to be modified to work outside of its original specification. Because the scope was mounted above the chamber of the rifle it would interfere with the bolt action. This required the bolt handle to be replaced with a longer, bent version so the shooter could work the bolt without hitting the scope. This made the rifle look like it almost had a broken bolt mechanism. The rifle carried a 5-round non-detachable magazine, loaded individually or with five-round stripper clips. All of this was nothing next to the rifle's single most important feature to me, that of its almost silent bolt-action mechanism. I had taken the rifle from a wounded Soviet sniper left lying like a discarded bag of rubbish, legless and dying in the mud after getting too close to an exploding round from one of the panzers. It wasn't a one-way transaction. I gave him the gift of a bullet from my Walther automatic to send him on his way to the communist heaven, or wherever Joseph Stalin's slaves wound up after death. He was my first killing of the war, a good death, I hoped. But there were to be no more good deaths, this was Stalingrad, men called it 'The Cauldron', a sealed container of hellish butchery.

I checked with my telescopic sight through the viewing slot. Fassbinder was correct, the Ivans were moving around, occasionally showing themselves as they prepared for what would undoubtedly be an attack. Fassbinder turned to his men.

"Get yourselves ready to move, men. When the officer starts firing we won't have more than ten or fifteen minutes before the Ivans start to zero on top of us."

The three Wehrmacht infantrymen, Koch, Farber and Hoffmann, began to pick up their packs. Stuffing their meagre possessions into them, food, dry socks and most important of all ammunition, prior to a rapid exit.

"What about the prisoners, Lieutenant?" Fassbinder asked.

I looked at them dispassionately. One was a Soviet captain, a woman. The second and the most prized capture of all, a commissar. They were ragged and filthy having endured brutal, severe treatment from my men after they were taken. I had to give them credit, they didn't look frightened, although they must have realised their inevitable fate. We were a small, fast moving unit. Prisoners were not a luxury we indulged in. My job was to liaise with 6th Army high command, reconnoitre the battlefield and interrogate prisoners, whilst doing as much ancillary damage to the Soviet command structure as possible. That meant interrogating, or killing, high ranking Soviet officers, then reporting back to Berlin, doubtless to demonstrate the superiority of the SS over the Wehrmacht where matters of conducting a mere battle were concerned. Certainly, Himmler was looking for ammunition to ingratiate himself with Hitler, to show that his Waffen SS could solve any problem that the Wehrmacht was incapable of. Personally I couldn't care less. Like every man here, I would say what was needed to be said, finish up and get out of the ruined city.

I had no need to issue orders about the prisoners. The sixth member of my unit, SS Scharführer Albert Müller was already leering at me in a way that I found increasingly repulsive as the battle went on. Like me, Müller was a member of SS Liebstandarte Adolf Hitler. Unlike me, coerced and blackmailed into joining, Müller was a true fanatic. His God was Adolf Hitler and he worshipped at the altar of cruelty and death. A prison officer before hostilities began the war gave him the opportunity to indulge his deepest psychotic fantasies in the brutal hell of Soviet Russia. He had originally been assigned as my aide on the orders of Heydrich, before the SD supremo was assassinated. So here I was, surrounded by the misery and blood of probably the most violent battle in modern

European history, with a committed psychopath for an assistant, as if the damned war itself was not enough. It was almost a macabre joke, except that I often wondered if Müller had orders to shoot me should he decide that I was less than a hundred per cent loyal. I preferred not to put it to the test.

"Herr Obersturmführer, if I may be permitted to put some questions to the Ivans before we have to move?"

I nodded for him to go ahead. The Russians were both squatting in a pool of filth. The stench was appalling, as if we were sheltering in a cesspit. Perhaps we were, I wondered briefly if it was a Russian cesspit or a German cesspit. No matter, Russian shit, German shit, what the hell, it still stank like shit. The prisoners were secured with baling wire around their wrists and ankles, tied so tightly that it was obvious their circulation had been cut off to their bound limbs. As Müller moved across to them, it occurred to me that their circulation was the very least of their problems. The watching infantrymen had seen it all before, they gathered around now to watch the fun. Koch, Farber and Hoffmann, factory workers, possibly farm boys. Now they were like the crowd in the Colosseum, lusting for blood, for the visceral torment of the hacking, slashing, wounding blows, for the ultimate agony of death. Fassbinder looked at me and shrugged. There was nothing to say or do, only to stand apart and try not to let what was coming spill onto our psyches, to infect and destroy what little human compassion we soldiers of Stalingrad had left.

"Now, my friend Ivan," Müller said to the commissar. "Tell me what you know of the attack your friends are launching. What is their objective, how many men and tanks are they planning to use?"

Surprisingly Müller, like me, was fluent in Russian. Unlike me, he had learned from a brutal Russian stepfather who lived with his mother after finding her bed more comfortable than his berth on a Soviet freighter docked at Bremen. I had learned Russian at university, when I was convinced as a gullible teenager that communism was the way the world would go forward into a golden future. Was that why Müller hated all Russians, his stepfather? But then he hated everybody, except of course his idol Adolf Hitler. He was undoubtedly mad. But weren't we all, in this Wagnerian hell?

"Yob Tvoy Mat," hissed the commissar. "Go fuck your mother."

"Hmm, feisty one, are you?" he said, smiling. "Let's see if I can help you out here."

Müller took his knife out of his jackboot, the prized weapon that he spent hours every day honing and polishing so that it was constantly razor sharp. But he didn't use it to shave. He moved the knife slowly to the front of the commissar's face. Then with a quick slashing motion he literally carved off the man's nose, as if it was part of the Sunday roast. The man screamed out in pain. The woman, the Russian captain, shifted her position, her face now betraying her terror at the sudden brutality.

"Now let's see, my friend, what shall I cut off next?" The knife moved downwards, towards the man's midriff. Then suddenly it slashed up, slanted sideways and took off the man's left ear.

"Anything to tell us, Ivan?"

The Russian moaned, shook his head. As he did so, Müller slashed again, taking off the other ear. Still, the Russian shook his head, twisting against the wire that held his arms and legs to try and ease the terrible shock and agony.

"Right then, still nothing to say to Uncle Albert?" His face had a strange, far away stare. Arousal, I wondered, was he getting off on this terrible torture of a human being? About to climax sexually?

Then his knife slashed down, ripping through the man's waistband and down through his trousers, so quickly that it was a few seconds before his trousers fell apart. He wasn't wearing underwear, so his genitals were exposed, a red line showing where the knife had cut flesh. The men laughed, "Look, no underwear, dirty bastard," grinned Koch. The other two chuckled. But Müller didn't like Koch stealing his limelight. He reached down, grabbed one of the exposed testicles in his hand and slashed across. Blood was pouring down the man in increasing torrents from his multiple wounds.

"Hey, I've got an idea," he said to his audience, looking serious. He slashed again, cutting away the other testicle.

"Man's got no balls." The infantrymen roared with laughter.

"Shut up you men!" I snapped. "Müller, hurry up, we're running out of time."

I pushed the barrel of my rifle through the vision slot and looked through my telescopic sight. A Soviet soldier was clearly in view and in range, it was a worthwhile target, a Russian colonel. Gently, I squeezed the trigger. The 7.62 bullet crashed out of the barrel and in the blink of an eye smashed into the target. I had hit him squarely in the chest. He was either dead or a severe casualty drain on the Soviet medical service. There was another scream behind me. The commissar was still bleeding profusely, semi-conscious in the shock and raw agony of his wounds. Müller had moved his attentions to the woman, the captain. Her uniform blouse was ripped open and her left breast was now just a bleeding hole. She alternately sobbed and screamed. Damnit.

"Müller, for God's sake hurry up and finish it, one way or the other."

"Of course, Herr Obersturmführer. Finding it hard going, Sir?" he said, still playing to his audience. "These are hard times, they need hard methods. The Führer said so himself," a pause, "Sir."

He arrogantly smoked his cigarette, blowing the smoke into the bleeding woman's face.

"Two minutes Müller, then we need to get moving." I refused to show him how disgusted I felt, he would take it as a sign of weakness. Besides, I had not tried to stop him. I was complicit, guilty as much as him and his ghoulish audience. Another scream from the woman as Müller slashed again. Still she refused to say a word. This was a waste of precious time.

"Right, finish it now Scharführer, we're moving! Men, pick up your kit, get ready to go on my command."

Müller slashed once, twice. Two throats opened up in bleeding horizontal lines. I could hear the Russians choking on their own blood, dying but still not dead.

"Müller, finish them quickly, that's an order. Shoot them, damn you!"

"As you wish, Sir." he murmured. His voice was low, hoarse with passion, as if he did indeed have an erection and was about to climax. Maybe he was. I didn't care. I just wanted the screams to end. He pulled out his sidearm, like mine, a Walther.

He put it in each of the Russians' mouths in turn holding their eyelids open so that they were forced to look at him, and down at the pistol. Two shots rang out. Two bodies slumped, their lives extinguished, thankfully the screams stopped. I heard the cheering of a Russian attack launching opposite our position.

"Let's move!" I shouted. "Go, go, go!"

We ran to find another rat hole, maybe another vacant latrine that we could temporarily occupy. We ran fast, darting along a narrow trench that was formed from heaps of rubble either side. I felt a tug on my sleeve and glanced down to see that a bullet had sliced through the material, narrowly missing my arm. As we dashed towards a low building, I briefly wondered whether the bullet was German or Russian. Then again, a bullet was a bullet, the bullets that killed and wounded in Stalingrad were often not fired by the enemy. We saw an open doorway, the wooden door of the building had long disappeared, probably chopped up for firewood like most wooden structures in Stalingrad that could be burned to keep soldiers warm. We burst through and ran straight into a Soviet platoon, there were eleven of them. They had set up a defensive position inside the building, presumably in readiness for a possible counter-attack. We had run right into their hands, into the barrel of a Soviet machine gun, a DP. We were finished, it was no contest. A Russian soldier, speaking in German, ordered us to drop our weapons. The men looked at me, frozen, terrified by the abrupt turn of events. None of us were in any doubt, this was the end. We had just left two Russians slaughtered in our observation point. These Russians were not likely to treat us any more kindly. I gently put my Mosin Nagant rifle on the ground.

"Do as they say, men. Don't give them an excuse to shoot."

As so often happened in my life when faced with a moment of maximum danger, when death seemed to hold out her hand and invite me to come and join her, my mind emptied of all emotion. I didn't fear dying in this place of death. It was an inevitable end that would come sooner or later. Later would be best, though. I began calculating how to deal with the machine gun. There was a clatter as the weapons fell to the floor. I still had the Walther in the holster, my men would have a variety of weapons concealed in their uniforms. I moved towards the Russian, an NCO, a sergeant.

"Are you going to kill us?"

"Russians soldiers do not kill prisoners, fascist. We are civilised." he sneered. "Now, kneel down, all of you. Hands in the air!"

This would be it, kneel down and be executed like pigs in a slaughterhouse, the sergeant was lying. I had seen our own people do it often, I had no illusions. I had also been told of the way the Russians dealt with their deserters. Stripped of their uniform, underwear and boots, so that they could be re-used by another soldier, it was a simple matter of an expedient bullet in the back of the head. A Russian officer stood at the back of the group cradling his submachine gun, a drum fed PPSh, ready to point the barrel and cut us down if we resisted. The submachine gun was a classic example of Soviet wartime engineering. It was one of the most mass produced weapons of its type and gave the Soviet soldier massive short-range firepower. It had a box or drum magazine, and fired the 7.62x25mm pistol round. It was made with metal stampings to ease production and its chrome-lined chamber and bore helped with reliability in combat environments. Because of the similarities between the Tokarev and the Mauser cartridge used in the Mauser C96 pistol, the PPSh was easily supplied with ammunition when captured by our troops. Many of

our soldiers used them. I had often examined captured examples of this weapon, but not from this end of the barrel.

I decided to grab for the Walther as my knees touched the ground, then fling myself flat and open fire. I trusted my men to have a similar idea, there were too many Russians for one small pistol. I felt my knees touch the ground, I whipped my hand down and pulled out the Walther and saw the Russian sergeant aiming at me. Then the building reverberated to the hammering sound of a PPSh, deafening, deadly. I pulled the trigger, again and again, seeing the Russian NCO fall, his body twitching as the bullets struck. I waited for the hand of death to finally take hold of me, for the terrible pain of impact and then the final blessed darkness as the first of the Soviet bullets smashed into my body. My pistol clicked, clicked again, I had run out of ammunition, but I still pulled the trigger repeatedly, like a crazy man, looking for some magic to make it fire again. Then I realised that the only sound left in the building was from my pistol. Click, click. The guns had gone silent, yet I was still alive, apparently unhurt.

I looked up. The Russians were dead or dying. All of them except for the officer, a captain. His PPSh still issued smoke from the barrel. Koch lay dead, his body unmoving. The others, Müller, Fassbinder, Farber, Hoffman, were kneeling like me. The Wehrmacht men were frozen, eyes shut, not one of them had gone for a weapon. Müller, to his credit, had pulled out his knife, about to throw it when the firing started. He was still tensed, arm behind his head, still readying his knife, not sure where to throw it.

"You had better get back to your lines, fascists." the Russian captain said. His German, spoken with a strange accent, was nonetheless understandable.

"Why?" I asked him. "Why shoot your own men?"

He smiled. "You would prefer I shoot fascists?"

I waited. Müller watched him closely, still poised, ready to throw the knife, but I doubted he would beat a loaded PPSh.

"They are not my men. I am Ukrainian, I did not choose this fight," he shrugged. He was a big man, easily six feet four inches tall, with a strong muscular physique. He looked like an Olympic wrestler, which I was

20

afterwards to find out he had once aspired to become. A hard, tough man, it would not do to try and tackle a man like this if you were unarmed.

"I hate these Red bastards," he continued. "The more that die, the sooner I can look forward to again calling Ukraine my home, instead of a Soviet prison. They gave me no option, I had to join their army, but I am fighting my war, not theirs. Now go."

"Who are you?" I asked.

"My name is Vasyl, fascist. And you?"

"Winston. Winston Wolf." I pronounced it in the English way.

"Winston? Like Churchill? Is an English name!"

"It's a long story," I replied. "Why not come with us?"

"Come where, English?"

"To our lines, of course, join us. If the Russians find out what you've done, they'll slit you into little pieces."

"They will not find out," he said. "Besides, when the Red Army takes the city, they would find me in a fascist uniform. Then I would certainly die."

"Take the city?" I laughed. "The Red Army is finished, Vasyl. We'll be across the Volga in a few days."

"You think so, English?" Vasyl laughed. "I say you will not. What you see here is nothing. The Red Army is preparing a counter-attack that will smash your little German army. You think you are fighting the Red Army? You are not. You are fighting just a small piece of it. When Stalin gets down to business, you will undoubtedly lose. Now, you must go quickly, an attack is moving towards us and when it hits you will find out what the Red Army truly is capable of."

The Ukrainian abruptly turned and left through a side door of the building. Müller lowered the knife then put it away. My men picked up their weapons, I scooped up my Mosin Nagant and we found a door at the back that led us out of the building and in the direction of our lines. The firing had intensified, it sounded like a full scale battle was already underway. Fassbinder found a narrow alley that he recognised and led us in the right direction. Through a gap in the rubble I could see the iconic Red October Tractor Factory. Apparently the Russian attack was trying to dislodge Wehrmacht positions that threatened the factory, from literally across the street of the huge structure.

The factory had been established in 1897. After the Bolshevik Revolution the factory became known as Krasny Oktyabr, Red October. The massive building was now almost totally destroyed after sustaining heavy damage from shelling and bombardment. I could see through the shattered walls to parts of the interior. The roof of the building had caved in, burying the machinery underneath it and covering much of the floor space with heavy rubble. Dark areas marked out the many tunnels leading into the building. All over the ground were dozens of trenches, rifle pits and shell holes providing extra cover. Rifle fire winked out from dozens of positions in the rubble, warning us of the high concentration of entrenched infantry throughout the ruined structure. We ran on towards the Barrikady, another huge factory complex, jumped into a trench and literally bumped into a Wehrmacht colonel, accompanied by a company of his men. They had their guns raised, ready to open fire if we had been Russians.

"The battle is the other way, Obersturmführer," he said drily. "I didn't know the SS were invited."

"No, Sir," I panted, winded by the run, "we're not. Special assignment to General Paulus' HQ, evaluate and report to Berlin."

He inspected my uniform, minutely. At that time, I had no medals or decorations.

"One of Himmler's errand boys, are you? Don't want to get your uniform dirty?"

I said nothing. He was only trying to taunt me, an army combat veteran laughing at an SS new boy. His uniform showed the Iron Cross First Class, two Silver wound badges and an array of ribbons that I didn't recognise and frankly couldn't care less about.

"Well, Obersturmführer," he continued, "you're in luck.   Are these soldiers assigned to you?"

"Yes, Sir."

"Very good. You can join us."

He waited for an argument. He was a colonel, a decorated combat veteran, with a heavily armed company of similarly experienced battle hardened troops. Here in Stalingrad Himmler's influence was worth less than a bucket of shit, and we both knew it.

"Yes, Colonel."

"Good." He smiled, was it something of a sneer, did he think I needed to be challenged to prove that an SS officer was brave enough to join the attack? He was wasting his time. Ever since I had accidentally killed a man in Berlin, fighting in a cabaret club over a girl, something had died inside me. Taking that first human life seemed to link me with my victim's death. I no longer cared, live or die, it made no difference. My soul had died with the corpse of my opponent in Berlin. His smile faded, perhaps he saw something of the death wish in my eyes. As a veteran of the Russian front he would recognise the look, share the drug-like deadening of emotions that stripped away fear. Was it better than the sheer terror we saw all around us in this awful place? The white faces. Wild, staring, terrified eyes, constantly looking behind them for an escape. But at least cowards had feelings, I had none, nor I suspected did the colonel.

"I am Colonel Mayer, you are about to join the 94th Infantry Division. We have been ordered to take the Barrikady and drive the Ivans into the Volga." He grinned, then unexpectedly shook my hand. "I'm glad you're with us, Obersturmführer. Take your group to that ruined gatehouse." He pointed to a wrecked building halfway across the open ground that lay between our position and the tractor factory. "You can take a field telephone, my communications sergeant will lend you a spare one. Try not to snag the wire, we're finding it hard to replace. I want you to use your eyes and ears, let us know everything you see or hear. We need to establish their weak and strong points before we go in. Clear?"

"Jawohl, Herr Colonel." I clicked my heels, stood to attention. The soldiers around us grinned at my SS trained response. I could see the message in their faces, "He'll soon learn."

"Right, we'll give you covering fire, when the shooting starts, get going."

"Yes, Sir." I turned to my men, who had been listening. The three Wehrmacht men nodded. Müller was unhappy.

"We are SS, Sir, not army. That colonel can't give us orders, we answer to Reichsführer Himmler."

"Müller," I replied, "if you can get Himmler on the telephone, by all means do so. I don't think the colonel is in any mood to listen to anyone else."

He looked around. A group of Wehrmacht troopers ringed us, casually holding rifles and machine pistols at the ready. I guessed they were indifferent as to whether they shot at the Russians or at the SS. Some of them were smiling expectantly, waiting for the order to fire if any one of us refused to obey the order.

"Well, he'd better watch his step," Müller said grimly, "battles are dangerous places. He could get hurt."

"Leave it, Müller." I said quietly. "He's a combat veteran, he'll eat you for breakfast. And if he doesn't, I will. So let's move."

He looked at me, a hard, threatening stare. Then he turned away.

The firing started suddenly, so that even the most hardened of us jumped at the unexpected hurricane of shots. It seemed as if every soldier had started shooting at once. As if every gun, mortar, machine gun and even pistol had begun their deadly barrage synchronised by some mystical force.

"Get going, get going!" Colonel Mayer shouted. "Watch the wire, be careful. Report as soon as you're set up."

I nodded, beckoned to my men, then ran. Bullets flicked the ground all around us. Müller grimaced as a Soviet round nicked his ear. Then Farber went down, riddled by a Soviet machine gun burst, the cable drum he had been carrying spiralling across the ground.

"Hoffman," I called, "pick up the drum. You two," I pointed at Fassbinder and Müller, "help him." They dashed over to obey, picked up the drum and carried it to the gatehouse, Müller firing his MP38 at the source of the sniper who had hit Farber. The submachine gun fired in a slow clatter, spraying 9mm pistol rounds wildly across the building.

We reached our objective and crouched breathlessly behind the wall of the building. Over the continuous firing and crack of explosions I heard Farber screaming. I looked around, he was inching across the ground about thirty metres away, trying to reach us. His intestines had been ripped out and were dragging along the ground beside him. The pain must have been astonishing, he should have been dead. I was about to use my rifle to finish off the poor devil when a mortar shell hit the ground right next to him, showering fragments of his body over a wide area. Somewhere inside me I could have sworn a spark of emotion flared, a slight sympathy with the soldier's fate. Perhaps it was my imagination,

some distant memory of a forgotten life. I turned to the men.

"Get the telephone working, hurry. Stabsfeldwebel, tell them we are in position, we'll be reporting on the Russian positions as soon as we can."

"Jawohl, Herr Obersturmführer." I noticed that in the heat of the action he used my SS rank, the sneering Wehrmacht rank forgotten. Well, that was progress.

"Russians moving two hundred metres to our right flank, Sir." Fassbinder shouted. I checked, a group of about seventy or eighty Russians were assembling, glimpses of them showing through the shattered walls and broken windows of the factory.

"Call it in." I told him.

Then there was a crash of artillery as a barrage hit fifty metres behind us. Another barrage struck even closer, then a third barrage struck the side of the building and my world dissolved into a dark night of dust, smoke and spent gunpowder. There was no noise, I realised that the explosion had deafened me. I looked around. I was alone. Müller, Fassbinder, Hoffman, they had all gone, or were buried in the rubble. I was covered in dust and mud, almost invisible in the ruined building. There was a loud cheering then scores of Russians ran past me shouting, firing repeatedly into our positions.

Something had gone wrong. The Colonel had not attacked in time, now he was being assaulted by large numbers of Soviet troops. I lay still, waiting for the shout of exposure, the angry Russian faces and the bullet that would end it all. Once again my luck held, my death was delayed still further into the future. I began crawling towards our lines, cutting diagonally away from the line of the Soviet advance. I had lost the Mosin Nagant, all I had left was my pistol and two clips of ammunition. Then I heard a stealthy sound. I crept forward quietly. Two Soviet infantrymen were at work repairing a broken telephone line. They were well hidden from the German lines in a rubble strewn shell crater. Unluckily for them I approached from the Soviet side, so they were not expecting an enemy. I got within four metres of them and paused as I dislodged a stone. They whirled, reaching for their rifles, but I was ready. I shot the first one in the chest, whipped the gun around to shoot the second man a glancing shot that hit him in the shoulder. I fired at him again, this time hitting him in the neck, he went down. I ran up, pistol ready, but both men were finished. Blood poured from the neck wound, seconds later the wounded man keeled over, dead. The other was growing pale, his face frightened, the air hissing out of his lung where he had taken my bullet. He was finished, but to be sure I put the pistol to his head and pulled the trigger. He jerked, then lay still. I carried on crawling.

Eventually I came to a trench that seemed to point in the right direction. I crawled forward then heard a shot.

"Halt!"

"Don't shoot, I'm on your side." I shouted back. "Wolf, attached to General Paulus' staff."

A helmeted head looked over a stone barricade. "Come forward, slowly. Keep your hands where I can see them."

I crawled to the barricade, where willing hands dragged me over the stone wall to safety. There, I found myself staring at the amused face of Colonel Mayer.

"Back from the dead, Herr Obersturmführer?"

"Sir," I replied, "what happened?"

"A total cock up," he replied. "No artillery support, no communications and the Russians jumped off first. We were lucky to only lose twenty eight men. The bloody Luftwaffe was supposed to give the Russians a 'housewarming', but they failed to turn up, as usual." A 'housewarming' was our nickname for a Luftwaffe bombing raid.

"Twenty eight out of two hundred?" I said, appalled.

"You will learn my friend, that in Stalingrad anything less than fifty percent losses counts as a victory. Your three men, Fassbinder and Hoffmann, and the SS man, made it back. The other is missing, presumed dead."

I told him about Farber, he nodded, but it was only one more death in tens of thousands.

"Your men are further up the trench, being fed and their wounds dressed, nothing serious. Headquarters has been looking for you, so I suggest you take your men and get back. Good luck, Herr Obersturmführer." He held out his hand.

"Good luck, Sir." I replied.

As I walked up the trench I heard the scream of incoming mortar rounds. I dropped flat and heard them strike the trench I had just left. I heard screams, then shouts that the Colonel had been hit. I ignored them and carried along the trench where I collected Müller, Fassbinder and Hoffmann and reported back to HQ. This was Stalingrad, the city of death.

I found out afterwards that Colonel Mayer's attack was not the only reverse suffered by the German Army on that day the 4th of October 1942, when the German 6th Army began the attack on the factory complex. Von Paulus combined elements of the XV Panzer, 60th Motorised, and 389th Infantry divisions, but Russian reinforcements managed to stop the German advance dead. Hitler then demanded the capture of Stalingrad by October 15th, putting enormous pressure on General von Paulus. Our German forces managed to drive back the 37th Guards in a daring counter-attack, but the Russians still contested every metre of ground. Later that day Katyusha rockets wiped out a whole German battalion with just one salvo. Von Paulus' losses were a total of four battalions, after which he stopped the attack. We had gained just one block of flats in the Red October Factory housing area.

MARCH 1944

Stalingrad was a distant memory, a visit to hell itself, still etched firmly in my nightmares, as if a mad surgeon had repeatedly slashed a scalpel through my brain, the wounds healing slowly inside my head but still vivid for all to see in the haunted depths of my eyes. The ragged band of men watched me intently, hating me no less than Stalin's hordes in the satanic depths of the ruined city on the Volga. For these were also my enemy. British, like myself, but I was fighting on the opposite side, the side of their enemy. They were prisoners of war, marking time in Stalag III-D, located in the rural outskirts of Berlin. Stalag III-D had been established in 1940 in Berlin-Lichterfelde. The camp consisted exclusively of prisoners of war, all of whom were allocated to sub-camps and work details in the local area. Stalags were intended to be camps for NCO's and enlisted men only, this was no exception. The German prison camp system was complicated and consisted of eight different categories of camp, so much so that I still did not understand it. I just went where I was assigned. As well as Stalags, these camps ranged from Milag camps for merchant seaman, Stalag Luft camps operated by the Luftwaffe for captured Allied airmen to Dulag camps, short for the Durchgangslager, transit camps where prisoners were processed and interrogated. I had seen inside most of them, they were drearily similar.

These privates, corporals and sergeants had been here for more than three years, slowly becoming accustomed to the daily routine of their captors. Outwardly servile, yet the guards had told me of loud cheering when the RAF bombers dropped high explosive and incendiary bombs in an effort to obliterate the city of Berlin. It was one of the prisoners that had made me think of Stalingrad.

"Russians kicked your bloody SS arses at Stalingrad, mate, didn't they?"

He was quite wrong, there were no SS units at Stalingrad. Although I had been there, as had Müller. I had a strange relationship with both prisoners and guards. They knew I was British, indeed, was here because I was British. I had initially been commissioned to the SS Liebstandarte Adolf Hitler, an elite regiment, in 1940. The "Leibstandarte" was originally Hitler's personal bodyguard unit called the Schutzkommando, which was renamed the Sturmstaffel (SS). The LAH had already participated in combat during the invasion of Poland, and then in the successful invasion of France and had an exemplary reputation for combat. I had joined the unit in July 1940 as it was being expanded to a full Waffen SS brigade, preparing for the invasion of Britain. Luckily for me the invasion was cancelled and instead I found my first combat experience to be in Greece, as an observer seconded to Heydrich's SD, although I never fired a shot in anger.

Under a good deal of duress, and after the occasional protest, I had served my SS unit well and carried out my side of the bargain. For my troubles I had recently been transferred to the SS-British Freecorps, a unit of the SS recently created by Heinrich Himmler. My job was to recruit more British PoWs to the Freecorps. Himmler reasoned that because I was British I would empathise with the men and them with me. He thought all Englishmen would want to fight against the Bolsheviks. I was certain that he fondly imagined that secretly all Britons wanted to be Nazis. Perhaps he should come and see this lot. Personally, I hated the prisoners as much as they hated me, if that were possible. They saw a traitor, a treacherous Englishman dressed in the black dress uniform of the Waffen-SS, yet with the Union Jack badge and cuff title of the SS-British Freecorps. I saw a menacing rabble who, but for the presence of armed camp guards, would have torn me into little pieces. Müller was standing right behind me, watching them carefully. Like many of Himmler's ideas, this one was not likely to be blessed with a favourable outcome. I remembered our last meeting.

Heinrich Himmler had a roundish face that reminded me of a weasel, something not helped by his receding hairline and small moustache. As always he wore his customary round spectacles. He had summoned me to his office, a summons that meant dropping everything and reporting at the double. Sat beside his desk, he was both bland and deadly. A squat, neat, black spider waiting to catch any prey that fell into his web. I stood rigidly at attention and waited.

"Herr Obersturmführer, I have decided to assign you to a new post." He looked up at me, quizzically through his trademark schoolmaster's glasses. I said nothing. Orders were not to address the Reichsführer until told to do so.

"You have heard of the British regiment I am raising to fight the communists in Soviet Russia?"

"Yes, Sir." I replied. I knew now what was coming, but still prayed it would be something different.

"I have decided to transfer you as of now to the SS-British Freecorps. We are holding tens of thousands of British prisoners here in Germany. Many of them would surely jump at the chance of joining the SS to fight the communists, rather than rot in a PoW camp."

The SS-British Freecorps was created to fight in the pan-European Waffen SS against the Bolsheviks on the Eastern Front. The initial idea was to create at least a single infantry platoon of thirty men, though other units would be formed elsewhere in the Reich. It was decreed that no SS-BFC member could be part of any action against British and Commonwealth forces, nor could any SS-BFC member be used for intelligence gathering.

31

They would not have to receive the SS blood tattoo, swear an oath of loyalty to Hitler or be subject to German military law. They would receive pay equal to the German soldiers of their rank. All SS-BFC soldiers would wear standard SS uniforms with appropriate insignia.

"I'm sure that's true, Sir." I replied. No, I was not sure it was true. I was totally sure that it was the very last thing those men would consider. Most would probably join the Russians given half a chance, just to be able to take pot-shots at the Germans.

"Excellent. You will find your orders waiting for you when you leave. Dismissed."

I saluted "Heil Hitler", as regulations demanded, about turned and left. The next day, with a Union Jack badge sewn to my SS tunic I reported to my new unit, to Julian Amery, the strange, slightly mad British aristocrat that ran it. My first recruiting assignment was here in Stalag III-D and it was not going well. I heard one of the prisoners say, in a stage whisper designed to show me their contempt, "Bastard is only doing this job so that he doesn't have to fight. Too yellow, piece of shit wouldn't last five minutes in a battle."

That was not strictly true. Yet had they been battles in the real sense, those scrambled, bloody actions in Stalingrad? There were precious few brave soldiers charging forward, bugles, flags, orders shouted military fashion. Not many officers leading their men into action, sergeants chivvying them along. No, it was not like that. It was a war of butchers, fought in cities that had become muddy, rubble strewn butchers shops, where the slaughtermen fought each, tripping over the bloody meat of corpse upon corpse upon corpse. It was a vision of hell named Stalingrad. I wasn't yellow. I wished I was. But I was indifferent, cold to whatever fate life had to offer me. Neither was I brave. I just didn't know how to feel anything. Love, fear, they had all left me long ago. After the Russian Front we all knew that only one fate awaited us anyway, so why worry? And yes, I had survived the butchery that was called battle. It wasn't bravery or indifference that had spared me. It was just luck, fate's temporary pass that would soon expire. I couldn't tell these men I had been at Stalingrad, though. We had lost that one, hardly the kind of propaganda that Himmler would have appreciated.

"Your enemy is the Russian communists." I shouted to them. "They will take over the world if you let them. Germany is your friend. We stand between a free civilised society and the barbarian slaves of communist Russia. We offer you a chance to fight for freedom, for civilisation, to save Europe. We Germans allowed the British troops to leave Dunkirk unharmed because we knew in the end we would work together to defeat the real enemy of our countries."

I didn't believe a word of my script, neither did they, but I had to say it.

"Bollocks!" I heard. "Fuck off."

A stone came from the back of the group of men and hit me a glancing blow on the head. I put my hand up and felt a tiny trickle of blood. I ignored it, but Müller was outraged. He had seen who threw it and called to two of the guards. The three of them stormed into the group of PoWs forcing them to part, their Kar98K rifles threatening. The brutal SS Scharführer bludgeoned two of the Englishmen to the ground, then grabbed a third, the stone thrower. He clubbed the man with the stock of his gun and then the three Germans dragged him around the back of a hut.

"Müller, no, no! Bring him back!" I shouted.

The crowd of PoWs ran around the corner, I followed them. The two guards held the prisoners off with their rifles while Müller laid into the stone thrower. Unbelievably in only seconds he had delivered enough blows to render the man to a bloody pulp. He drew his knife and I knew I had to stop it before there was a riot. I pulled out my pistol and fired a shot in the air. Müller paused, the prisoners turned and looked at me. In the distance I heard the sound of boots running towards us.

"Müller, put him down, leave him alone. Now!" I shouted.

He threw the man to the ground, disgustedly and sheathed his knife.

"You men, you may not like listening to what I have to say, but you will behave! If you attack any member of the SS you will be dealt with severely, as you can see. Next time, I will not call him off."

A troop of guards, guns drawn, ran up to me.

"What's happening here, Herr Obersturmführer?" their sergeant asked.

"Nothing, just a misunderstanding," I told him. "You can stand down."

"Jawohl, Herr Obersturmführer, if you are sure?"

I nodded, and they marched away.

"Are there any questions?" I asked them.

"Just one, mate," a prisoner asked. He was thin, wiry looking. I nodded for him to continue.

"What do you do when you haven't got your tame monkey to watch your back?"

Their contempt was not unreasonable. What would I do without Müller?

Müller, like myself, a survivor of the horrors of Stalingrad, where he had saved my life on more than one occasion. Would any of us ever finally escape those memories that haunted our waking and sleeping nightmares? My mind drifted back to the smoke and stench of Stalingrad.

CHAPTER TWO

OCTOBER 1942

The next morning we got a lift out to Von Paulus' headquarters in Golubinskaya and walked into a mess of chaos and noise. Men ran to and fro, officers shouting orders, radiomen and runners dashing from room to room. The sound of the heavy guns was all too clear in the distance, punctuated by the occasional 'whoosh' of the Katyusha rockets, inaccurate, except that when they did find a target they were deadly. The roads around the headquarters were full of men and vehicles, all in a rush to get towards or away from the carnage unfolding in the city. Hiwis, Russian volunteers, some former captives, were all busy loading and unloading stores and building fortifications.

Apparently we were winning. The Russians were pinned down on a thousand metre long strip of the city with their backs to the Volga. One last push and we would send them tumbling into the river, Stalingrad would be ours. Von Paulus had ordered the 76th and 71st Infantry Divisions to attack the central landing stage on the Volga, with the 295th Infantry Division sent to conquer the strategic hill of Mamaev Kurgan that dominated the city. Control of the hill had become vitally important, as it offered a view of the whole city, a strategic strongpoint. If we could take the summit we would be able to direct heavy weapons from the top and rain down fire onto the defenders below. The Soviets knew this and to defend the hill they had built strong defensive lines on the slopes, trenches, barbed-wire and minefields. To man these defences they had stationed hundreds of infantry.

I reported to the intelligence officer, Colonel von Loringhoven, who sat in his office reeking of brandy, smoking a foul smelling cheroot. Müller and I came to attention, saluted "Heil Hitler".

"Ah, the Waffen-SS are here," he smiled sardonically. "Well, Obersturmführer, it seems your work is not complete. Führer HQ has insisted on a fuller appraisal of the Soviet strength. When I suggested a reconnaissance into the Russian sector, they agreed immediately. We need a prisoner to interrogate, preferably a high ranking officer. I reminded them of your presence and they insisted that you be given the honour of carrying out the mission. Here is the order from Reichsführer-SS Himmler."

He handed me the paper. I was to carry out the reconnaissance and bring back a senior officer, preferably a general, for interrogation. I was reminded to uphold the honour of the SS in the midst of a Wehrmacht operation. Typical Himmler. What he meant was to take suicidal risks to prove that his SS troopers were superior to the Wehrmacht. Perhaps some of our SS lads were superior, but only as long as they were alive. Dead troopers were worthless.

"I will need some replacement for my escorts, Colonel. We lost two on the last operation. Can you give me two good men, preferably with experience behind the lines? I have Sergeant Fassbinder and Private Hoffman waiting outside, both good men, I could do with a couple more."

He smiled at me. "So the SS needs help from the Wehrmacht, yes? Fair enough, I will assign two more men to your escort. Try and bring them back in one piece, Obersturmführer. Now, we need to know unit strength, objectives, morale, any information you can get will help us. Obviously we'll pass it on to Berlin." He paused. "This is not to leave this office, but General von Paulus is puzzled. The Russians are beaten. They've taken an incredible hammering, yet they're still fighting. Are they too stupid to know when to give up, or do they have something up their sleeves? Try and find out for us, Obersturmführer." He hesitated. "Wolf, it is essential that we finish this campaign quickly."

"Because of the Führer?" I asked him. "Because that's what he wishes?"

"That's true. But there is a more pressing reason. Our flanks are being guarded by our allies, Italians, Romanians, Hungarians, God knows who else. They are not as," he searched for the word, "determined, shall we say, as our own men. Besides, they've been hit pretty hard by partisan raids and it's unnerved their morale badly. Their equipment is also second rate, a lot of it is totally obsolete. We need to break the Russians now, before they counter-attack. Between you and me, if the Red Army hits our flanks we're in deep shit."

"Yes, Colonel, I'll do my best," I replied. I was shocked, were we that weak? I remembered the words of Vasyl. The Ukrainian seemed sure that the Russians had huge reserves waiting, that eventually the Russians would mount a massive attack and force us back out of the city. But it didn't seem likely to me. If they were going to deploy reserves, surely now would be the time when they were almost beaten, clinging to a fingernail of the city along the west bank of the Volga. At that time the Russian held area was the central landing stage with scattered forces along the shoreline. This was the heart of the depleted Soviet frontline and it had to be broken before the Volga finally froze and made it easier for the Soviets to cross more troops. Reinforcements and supplies were being brought in to keep the last few units fighting including those on the hill of Mamayev Kurgan, towering above the city and the Number 1 and Number 2 railway stations. The shore of the Volga was packed with demolished and flattened buildings that proved perfect to conceal infantry and snipers whilst blocking armour from reaching their positions. But still, with one more big push we could capture the land up to the Volga and Stalingrad would be ours.

"I'll send your men to you in thirty minutes. Good luck. Dismissed."

"Colonel."

We saluted, turned and left his office. Fassbinder and Hoffman were waiting down the corridor, smoking. I beckoned to them and led the men to the ranker's canteen. Some of the soldiers looked irritated that their sanctum had been invaded by an SS officer, I ignored them. The divide between officers and men was fairly loose in the SS, unlike the stiff-necked military protocol within the Wehrmacht. We drank mugs of steaming hot tea, laced with schnapps. Hoffman went and brought back bowls of steaming soup, meat and potatoes. As we ate, I outlined the

mission.

"The thing is, Ivan is beaten, in total disarray. We go in quietly, get an idea of their remaining strength, hopefully we'll be able to confirm that they're all swimming back across the Volga. Grab a senior officer and bring him back. No noise, no fuss, no shooting. That's it."

"We did that last time, Sir. Farber and Koch were killed, remember?"

"This is war, Stabsfeldwebel. Men do get killed. We've got no choice, let's do it, an in and out job. If we can grab a high ranking officer, we need to get him back here if that's possible. If not, Müller can have a chat with him before we get rid of him."

Müller smiled. I sometimes thought that his little chats were the only pleasure he had in this life. A vicious psychopath, who I would certainly have to deal with one day.

In the afternoon, two Wehrmacht soldiers reported in and saluted, "Corporal Schultz and Private Wagner, reporting for duty, Sir."

I acknowledged their salute. "At ease men, grab yourselves a bowl of stew and some coffee, then come and sit down." They goggled at an SS officer sat in the other ranks canteen, but made no comment. Soon they returned with their food and joined us at the table. I outlined the assignment to them.

"It's a quick in and out job, I don't want to get caught up in some crazy shooting match between their troops and ours. There is a new assault going in tomorrow morning at five am. We'll move to the flank of the attack and try and infiltrate one of their command centres through the cellars. Any questions?"

The two new men looked aghast. So far their service on the Russian Front had been with a huge army. Now they only had a very small group to rely on.

"What if we meet a group of Russians? There are only six of us, what do we do?" Corporal Schultz asked.

"What we do Corporal, is move quietly so that they don't know we're there. Müller will go in the lead. He can use his knife to dispose of any sentries. If we meet a large group of Russians our only hope is to run. Got that? No shooting unless it is a last resort, I don't want to find the Red Army chasing our arses half way across Stalingrad."

There were no more questions, just a few pale faces and Müller, of course, anticipating the next day's killing with that dreamy look in his eyes. I dismissed the men. They went off to find somewhere comfortable to spend the night, possibly their last night on earth. Müller and I settled down in a warm corner of the canteen close to the field cookers, pulled our shelters over us and tried to get some sleep. At midnight there was the sound of bombs exploding nearby. I was instantly alert.

"What the hell is that?"

"Don't worry, SS, it's only the sewing machines," a voice called out sarcastically.

"Sewing machines?" I asked.

"Russian U2 bombers," another voice called over to me, "they're only biplanes, Obersturmführer. They send them at night on nuisance raids. Nothing to worry about, until the bomb drops on you, that is."

I grunted an acknowledgment. Eventually the warmth of the canteen, together with the hot stew and schnapps-reinforced coffee, made me drowsy and I dropped off. I remember wondering if Müller ever slept, or did he wander off in the dark reaches of the night to carry out some awful and bloody ritual.

I woke up again to the sound of the morning barrage which had started at four am. Müller and I grabbed a cup of coffee from the cooks and sat in silence, waiting. Soon the Wehrmacht escort, led by Fassbinder, arrived and sat with us. Normally a military operation started off with plenty of chat, men swapping old jokes, pretending not to be awed by the coming battle. This time, none of us were part of a conventional unit, with all the easy familiarity of old comrades. We were a motley collection of strangers, different armies, both SS and Wehrmacht, brought together for an operation that would be extremely risky at best. At worst lay capture, torture, wounding or death at the hands of the Russians, a lonely fate separated from one's own friends and comrades. Damnit, I realised that my own thoughts were becoming dark and pessimistic. We had a job to do, either we would do it or we would die. Then I heard the shouting, coming from the area of Von Paulus' quarters.

"For God's sake General! If you don't get some clarity from the Führer this front could turn into another Verdun."

"Calm yourself, Colonel Groscurth, the city is almost won. One more push and we'll have our victory."

"Exactly, General, one more push, the slogan of Verdun, as I recall."

Then there was silence, I tried to put the ominous comparison with Verdun out of my mind. The six of us left and carefully made our way back to the front. Trucks rolled past in an unending stream, the evacuation of the civilians from the city. The barrage was deafening, our own guns hammering incessantly, the Ivans' Katyushas occasionally 'whooshing' overhead, their strange sound unnerving. The Katyusha multiple rocket launcher was a type of rocket artillery that could deliver a devastating amount of explosives to an area target quickly, but with lower accuracy and requiring a longer time to reload compared to artillery guns. The launchers were usually mounted on trucks giving them mobility. This allowed them to deliver massive attacks and then to escape before being attacked with counter-battery fire. Many Katyushas were deployed on the west bank of the Volga, using the cliffs for protection. They drove out to fire their missiles, then retreated under cover of the high cliffs. A tough nut to crack.

We came upon units of the 76th Infantry, waiting for the go. I nodded a greeting to their colonel, it was no time for formalities. He looked terrified, his face pale and frozen. I wondered had he forgotten to take the 'Stalingrad ration', the German military issue of Benzedrine and alcohol intended to stiffen the troop's resolve and fighting ability during the terrors of street fighting. We moved out to their northern flank, waiting. Then we heard the whistles blow and men ran forward, supported by the hammering of our MG34 machine guns. Men dodged, ducked, dived for cover, then got up and ran a few steps further. Some did not get back up, the Soviet return fire was intense. I nodded towards a narrow alley in the rubble, barely a metre high, well away from the main battle that was developing a hundred metres away from us.

"Time to go, men. Keep low."

I led them off, moving in a crouching, crabbing run through the alley. Several shots pinged around us, but no-one was hit. Finally we reached a manhole cover. I pointed and Schultz and Wagner ran forward and lifted it, throwing it to one side. I dropped into the evil smelling dark, wondering if this was to be my entrance to hell, my final resting place after meeting a Soviet ambush. The men followed and I switched on my torch leading them deeper into the sewer, further towards the Soviet

lines. We crept forward for almost ten minutes, the stench was appalling, overpowering. I was convinced that Stalingrad had to be the shit capital of the world. Then I heard voices, Soviet voices. I held my arm up for the men to stop and turned off the torch.

"No talking," I whispered, "stay here." I edged forward, around a bend in the tunnel, there was a light. I got on to my hands and knees and crept through the stinking, squelching slime. Part of the tunnel wall had collapsed, so that I could see into a subterranean room. It was some kind of a sleeping area. About fifteen men were lying on beds of old blankets, rags and pieces of uniform. A door led out of the room, the voices I had heard were coming from there. I crawled back to the men.

"This is our way in. We'll take out the sleepers then see about the other Russians. Use knives, no shooting. If the Russians hear a shot down here, we're all dead. Clear?"

They all nodded.

"Müller, you can go in first. Take the beds on the left. Fassbinder, come with me, we'll take the middle. You men take the ones on the right. Remember, not a sound or we're all dead."

Müller slipped silently forward, the perfect killer. We followed him as he carefully climbed into the room, knife drawn. He glided forward, the knife plunging, each stroke slashing the throat of one of the sleeping Russians. I clamped my hand over the mouth of my first victim, saw his eyes fly open as my dagger pushed into his throat, up, up into the brain. Then his eyes glazed, within two seconds he was dead. I moved on, despatched the second man in the same way. My third victim was beginning to awake, perhaps alerted by some sixth sense that something was wrong. I saw him open his mouth to cry out. Then I desperately lunged forward and pushed my bloody dagger into his mouth to stop him shouting. He grabbed my knife hand, stopping me from pushing the blade any deeper. His eyes fixed on mine, there was no fear, just a rage, an insane rage that a fascist had invaded his space, was attacking him. He gripped my hand harder, pulling the knife away from his throat. His eyes widened as a shout formed on his lips. Then there was just a sigh of escaping air as Müller's knife reached around me and cut across the Russian's windpipe. I looked at him, nodded my thanks. He was trancelike, expressionless as ever when carrying out the serious business of killing. The others had done well, fifteen Russians lay dead without a sound being uttered.

I moved towards the door, it slammed into my face as a Soviet soldier, a lieutenant, pushed through it. His eyes were wide as he saw the Germans in the room, in an instant he shouted out.

"Alarm! Fascists!"

Before he could get away, I shot him with my Walther, three 9mm rounds slammed into his body in quick succession. He crashed back into the room, squirming in agony. We pushed forward, the men behind quickly finished him off. It was a communications centre, with cables strewn around the floor leading to four field telephones on the rough wooden table. That table was covered with documents, scattered randomly around. Two operators sat there, frozen with shock and fear. I shot them

both with my pistol. The man on the left toppled over dead, the other screamed with fear and pain, my shot had taken him in the shoulder. Before I could fire again, Müller pushed past me, the knife flashed and the screams ceased.

"Sergeant," I called to Fassbinder, "take Hoffman and watch the door. If anyone comes in, shoot them, they must have heard the shooting by now. Schultz, Wagner, watch the tunnel. Remember, if you see anything move, shoot. Got it?"

"Sir." They acknowledged the order, then crouched near the tunnel, watching. Fassbinder kept watch through a crack in the door.

"Nothing moving, Sir. I don't think they heard us."

I was pleasantly surprised, but it seemed we were in the middle of a major firefight going on right above our heads. We could hear the endless 'crump' of artillery shells landing, the chatter of machine gun fire, grenades exploding, hundreds of sharp reports from Soviet and German rifles, and through it all the screams echoing faintly down to this room. Screams of agony, of death, of despair.

Müller and I grabbed as many documents as we could carry, stuffing them into a Soviet knapsack. Corporal Schultz rummaged around and came up with two bottles of vodka, obviously the Russian unit's ration which at that time was a hundred grams per day per man. I let him take it, but gave him a grim look that said 'if I catch you drinking it before we get back, I'll shoot you myself'. He nodded his understanding, there was no need for words.

"We're still clear, Sir. Are we finished here?" Fassbinder called over to me.

"Sorry, Sergeant, but we need to find ourselves a nice, juicy senior officer to interrogate. Even better, try and get him back to our lines. Take a look in the passage, see what's the other side."

"Sir," he said, somewhat reluctantly. He went through the door then came back after a few minutes.

"There's no way out, the passage leads into a Soviet assault trench. They've got at least a company deployed there, I would guess. Too many."

"Right, back into the tunnel, we'll go further on and see if we can capture an ourselves that officer to take back."

The four soldiers looked at me apprehensively, we were well behind

45

Soviet lines. If it hadn't been for Müller they might have chanced shooting me and going back, blaming the Russians. Müller caught my eye, nodded slightly, he was watching for the first one of them to try it.

"Let's go."

Müller led the way back into the tunnel, taking us further into the Soviet positions. We rounded a corner, Müller almost bumped into a Soviet sentry standing half asleep and not paying attention. The Scharführer whipped his knife across the man's throat without even pausing, the man dropped with a clatter and we marched on.

Moving past the dead Russian soldier, the tunnel ended after another twenty metres and we found ourselves in a sewage pumping station. Was there any city in the world with more shit than this one, I wondered. I told the men to wait while I crept silently up a flight of concrete stairs. Peering over the top I could see a control room. A small single bed took up one corner of the room, on the bed was a man, a Soviet soldier. His bare arse moved up and down, up and down, pumping his organ into the woman who lay beneath him. I smiled briefly. It was, after all, a pumping station. I could see her eyes were shut and the Russian was too busy to see anything other than the woman beneath him. I turned and beckoned to Müller.

"Take him when he climaxes," I whispered. Müller grinned, nodded. He crouched just beneath the top of the concrete stairs, waiting. Then there was an ecstatic groaning, Müller leapt forward, knife flashing.

"Stop! Keep him quiet, don't kill him."

Müller managed to hold the knife under the Russian's throat, warning him into silence. He clamped his other hand over the woman, to stop her crying out.

"Scharführer, I think we have our captive, you see his shoulder boards?"

He looked, acknowledged what I had seen, the distinctive shoulder boards of a Soviet General officer.

"Can you keep quiet?" I asked the woman. She nodded.

"Let her go, Müller. Sergeant Fassbinder, find some wire and bind the Russian, gag him as well, we don't want him making a noise."

"Sir." The sergeant got Hoffman to help him secure the General. Schultz and Wagner took up positions guarding both the concrete stairs and the

door that led from the room. "Müller, take a look," I told him.

The Scharführer peered around the door into the main pumping station. A Soviet infantryman stood there, a bottle of vodka raised to his lips. Müller quietly closed the door without being seen.

"Who are you?" I asked the woman in German. "Do you live here?"

"Yes," she replied shakily, "my father was the chief engineer for the sewage works."

"So you are Russian?"

"Half Russian, my mother was Polish, Danzig."

"So that explains your good German."

She nodded. "Yes, we travelled around a lot, I learned Polish, German and of course Russian."

"Your boyfriend?" I pointed at the Russian general.

"Boyfriend?" She spat. "He raped me, the Russian pig."

Armies were not composed of nice people, I reflected, I doubted that our own army would have treated her any better. Perhaps even worse.

"Sir," she looked at me, "I can't stay here. They'll blame me for that pig." She nodded at the trussed Russian officer.

"What's your name?" I asked her.

"Tatiana Medvedev."

She was truly beautiful, in a way that seemed only to come to women who were the product of mixed races. She was quite short with an elfin face, her blonde hair cut short to frame her classic features. She pulled her coat over her, in fact a cloak that looked to be made of smooth, dark brown deerskin, embroidered at the edges. She pulled the hood over her head, she looked for all the world like some mythical Slavic princess, almost the creature from a fairy tale. I made a mental note to get this girl out of harm's way as soon as possible. With her looks, in the mainly male preserve of a battlefield, she would be a target for every man whose hormones had reached danger levels after months without a woman.

"Ok, Tatiana, you can come with us for the time being, you may even come in useful. There is a Russian soldier mounting guard next door, who else is here?"

"No-one, Sir," she replied. "The pig came here to rape me, that's all."

"Fair enough, we'll deal with the guard and then go back the way we came. Call him in." I ordered her.

She nodded agreement then called out in fluent Russian. "The General needs you, Private, would you come in."

We heard his shouted acknowledgment. Fassbinder and his men took the Russian general part way down the stairway and held him out of sight, Müller waited behind the door. I sheltered behind a tall cupboard. The door opened, in marched the private, "General, Sir...." He faltered as he saw only the girl then looked around for the general. Müller stepped neatly behind him, clamped one hand over his mouth and slashed once. I stepped out and watched in fascination as Müller lowered the man lifeless to the ground.

"That's it, let's get back." I ordered them. "We've got our prisoner."

I started towards the stairway. Müller called out.

"The woman, Obersturmführer."

I looked back, he hadn't moved. "Yes?"

"She's Russian, I don't think it's a good idea to take her with us. I can finish her off, leave her here."

Tatiana froze, looking between me and Müller. I stared at Müller.

"When the SS needs your opinion over that of a senior officer, Müller, you can share your ideas with me. In the meantime, the girl comes with us. Unharmed. Clear?"

He clicked his heels. "Clear, Sir." But the eyes were mocking me.

"She's a good looking woman, something to keep your bed warm, Obersturmführer?"

I pointed my pistol at him. "Carry on, Müller, and I'll shoot you for insubordination. What's it to be, my way or yours?"

"I was joking, Sir," he replied, but there was icy contempt in his voice. Did he think he could throw the knife he still held in his hand before I shot him? Perhaps he did, but he would be very wrong.

"Very well, let's go. Tatiana, you walk in the middle, keep quiet."

"Thank you, Obersturmführer." She smiled. "Will you tell me your name?"

"Wolf."

"That's your first name?"

"It's my name, it's enough." In truth, she made me feel uncomfortable, her beauty so at odds with this broken and stinking place.

She was quiet for a moment. Then I heard her whisper, "Thank you, Wolf."

We pushed along the tunnel back towards our lines, herding Tatiana, a beautiful trophy of our mission, together with the Soviet general. His hands were fastened with wire and his mouth gagged. But he was still resplendent in full uniform with red staff tabs, rows of medal ribbons and the overlarge cap that Russian senior officers tended to wear. He was on his way to a very uncomfortable talk with his captors, possibly Abwehr, although there may have been a Gestapo unit seconded to the 6th Army for just such an occasion. But what to do with Tatiana? Some decisions were not too unpleasant to mull over.

Our attack was reaching a crescendo, following repeated and urgent commands from the Führer, who had ordered that all German offensives were to be halted outside of Stalingrad, so as to concentrate resources on taking the city. On October 14th 1942 General von Paulus despatched five divisions to take the Tractor Factory and the Barrikady. This was to be 'the final offensive.' General von Richtofen's 4th Air Fleet flew three thousand sorties that day. Eight thousand Russian commandos, belonging to the Soviet 37th Guards Division together with thousands of armed factory workers fought the German attack.

In the next forty eight hours five thousand of them were killed or wounded. Large parts of the factory burned to the ground, rubble and debris lay strewn everywhere as the Stukas repeatedly dive-bombed. General Zholudev, commander of the Guards Division, was almost totally buried in debris following a direct hit from a shell on his command post. On the Volga, General Chuikov's command bunker came under intensive fire from artillery, and thirty men, including many of his staff, were killed. At the northwest corner of the Barrikady survivors of the 308th Division were pushed back inside the machine shops, leaving its commander cut off from his troops for many hours.

MARCH 1944

Another camp, the same response. Apparently the word had flown around the camps that this was how to humiliate the SS-British Freecorps recruiting officer. 'Stalingrad, Stalingrad, Stalingrad', the chanting went on, the PoWs shouting louder and louder as I came to the end of my recruitment speech. I turned to the sergeant in charge of the guards and spoke loudly in English. The man probably didn't speak English, but the prisoners would hear.

"Sergeant, I'll count to five. If you can still hear chanting on five, take the two prisoners nearest you and shoot them. Clear?" He looked at me blankly, so I translated. He looked worried, but acknowledged the order.

"Jawohl, Herr Obersturmführer."

One! Two! Three! Four! I paused for effect. The shouting began to die away. Then it stopped.

"Good. You are all dismissed. Those of you who wish to fight the communists report to me within the hour. I will be waiting at the guardroom. For those others, you may live to regret this day when the Soviet hordes are marching on London, raping and killing as they go. Frankly, I hope you never have to face a Soviet army on the march, but if you do, God help you."

They jeered loudly and began to walk away.

"Would you have given the order to fire, Obersturmführer?" the sergeant asked me.

"The SS do not take kindly to abuse, Sergeant," I replied, then smiled and left him. In truth I would never give the order to fire on unarmed Britishers. These were not the brutal, feral animals that Stalin had sent to fight us.

We had two recruits from that camp, Stalag VII-D, near Moosburg. When I left I reported back to Himmler's HQ in Berlin, the Prinz Albrecht Strasser, the Reich Ministry of the Interior, from where he ruled over his vast empire. The glorious building was situated near the Prinz Albrecht Palace. In its time it had been a glorious part of the Berlin architecture. Previously been the home of the Museum of Applied Art, it had become the headquarters of the Secret State Police, or Gestapo, and was conveniently housed near the home of Goebbel's newspaper, Der Angriff. I was shown into the office of an SD Intelligence Officer, SS-Standartenführer Neurath.

"This is not good, Obersturmführer.   Your puny efforts so far will not turn the war around."

"Sir, do we need to turn the war around?"

This was Berlin, in March 1944. Anyone but a fool would know that the British bombing raids were getting more and more numerous and the Luftwaffe seemed less and less able to stop them. The endless casualty trains from the Eastern Front bore witness to the charnel house that was turning the pride of the German nation into offal. Rumours abounded of a planned Allied landing in occupied France. He looked at me sharply, looking for any suggestion of sarcasm.

"I did not say that, Obersturmführer. The war is going exactly as the Führer planned."

"Of course, Sir," I replied, tonelessly.   But we both knew the truth. Germany was losing, the Soviets were gaining in strength and could soon threaten the very borders of the Reich itself.

"However," he continued, "these are difficult times.   Times when everyone needs to dedicate themselves to victory against the Bolshevik savages. That includes Britishers, of course. We have many foreign recruits to the SS, our volunteer battalions are doing brave work for the Reich. But he would like to see the British making a contribution against the Reds. As you yourself are doing."

"Yes, Sir."

"I am sending you next to Stalag III-D, a camp for British army NCOs and privates. When you are finished there you can continue directly to Stalag Luft I in Barth. It is a small town on the Baltic Sea twenty three kilometres northwest of Stralsund. The prisoners there are all British Air Force officers, so hopefully you will have better luck. Perhaps they will be more ready to listen to what you have to say. I am certain that the officer class more than any other, drawn from the British aristocracy, will have good reason to hate the Soviets."

I recalled that English officers were about as political as the average donkey. To them, Uncle Joe's Soviet hordes were taking the heat off of their family seats in the Home Counties and rural parts of England, thank you very much. Maybe they would change their minds if Russian troops landed at Dover, until then there were other more interesting things to be concerned with. Win this war then get back to a life of ease and privilege, cricket and hunting, chasing nubile, strong limbed, clear-eyed English girls around the county, foxhunting, drinking in the mess. And they expected these people to join the Germans, even worse, the SS. Were my bosses totally stupid? Maybe they were. Certainly my immediate boss, John Amery was stupid if not certifiably insane, a gibbering lunatic. It didn't look good for Germany or for me with his calibre of person in charge of an SS unit. But then, my fate had been written long ago. A cold grave on the Eastern Front, long before the English officers had a chance to restart their endless games of cricket. It certainly simplified things for me, there was no need to make long term plans. But first, to deal with the English officers. Were they much different from their Russian counterparts? Probably not, they hated you in the same way, just kept it hidden until the knife went into your back. Russians were more direct. They made no secret of their emotions before they killed you.

"Yes, Sir." I replied again, then I about turned and left the office. I made a note to prepare Müller for the forthcoming trip. There would be nothing better for the officer prisoners of Stalag Luft I than to take out their frustration on one of their own class in the uniform of the SS, symbol of the worst of Nazi brutality. I was a middle class Englishman, well aware of the deceitful, underhand tactics practiced by my peers, middle and upper class Englishmen. The product of a minor English public school, I had good experience on which to base my knowledge. The sirens suddenly sounded, the latest RAF raid was inbound. A warden shouted at me to take cover, so I dived into the nearest air raid shelter. It was dark and narrow with people pushing past me. The very smell of fear was all-pervasive in the fetid atmosphere, it reminded me of the sewer tunnel under the streets of Stalingrad. I spent half the night in the air raid shelter waiting for the bombers to pass. Afterwards I found out it was one of the new one thousand bomber raids. An endless night of bombs raining down on a hapless city as the bombers queued up like patrons of a theatre, waiting for their turn in the line, the chance to drop their bomb load on yet another Berlin apartment block or shopping centre. I got back to barracks in the early hours of the morning, collected Müller and we drove out to Stalag III-D.

"Herr Obersturmführer, the men are waiting."

I had been day dreaming, tired from the sleepless night of endless bombing.

Müller, the familiar faraway look in his eyes disguising what he was really thinking, was shaking my arm. Did he mistake my tiredness for fear?

"Thank you, Scharführer." I looked around, the PoWs of Stalag III-D were lined up and waiting The previous night two of these Englishmen had slipped away to sign up, not needing to wait for my coming recruitment pitch. They were immediately taken out of the main prisoner area and locked in the guardroom for their own safety. We would take them with us when we left, a poor result for Reichsführer Himmler's new British SS unit. But it was better than nothing. One of the British prisoners marched up to me, a formidable man, he looked tough, competent and experienced. Almost certainly he was a regimental sergeant major.

"Sir," he saluted, I returned the salute. "Two of my men are missing, taken in the night. I want an explanation."

"And you are?" I asked him icily.

"RSM Green, I am the senior British NCO in this camp."

"Very well," I replied to him, "it is no secret. The two men concerned have volunteered to join the SS-British Freecorps. They have both signed on to fight against the communists in Russia."

"I want to see them." he said to me.

The man was beginning to irritate me. I was not especially proud of having been coerced into becoming a member of the SS, nor of this demeaning assignment where it seemed that every man in the prison camps saw me as something more disgusting than a pile of dog shit. After everything I had been through, I still had some pride. Still, I was an officer in the SS, even if I had been transferred from the SS-Liebstandarte Adolf Hitler to the SS-British Freecorps. Despite everything, I had been fighting on the Russian Front while these men were picking their noses in this godforsaken prison camp. And I genuinely did not like communists. They were a bunch of loudmouthed thieves, even worse than the Nazis.

"I don't give a damn what you want, Sergeant Major. The only way you can see your men is if you have the guts to volunteer for the SS-British Freecorps and join your comrades on the Russian Front."

The soldier leaned forward. I could feel Müller tensing at the side of me. I didn't need to look to see his hand beginning to reach for the knife he kept hidden.

"Before I joined up, I was a union man, sonny," he hissed. "A lot of my friends are communists, good men, not like you, you piece of Nazi dog shit. A lot of us are waiting to meet you when we've won the war, my SS friend. There are plenty of us who will be very pleased to see you in the dock at the Old Bailey. You know you'll get a short rope and a long drop?"

I laughed. "Sergeant Major, not only have you not yet won the war, you're not even in it. You're just a prisoner. Unlike you, those two men are prepared to fight for what they believe in. Besides, before the war ends, we'll all be dead anyway, so I don't think any of us is going to get what we want. Dismissed!"

He gave me a piercing look of scorn, which caused me to smile, then he about turned and rejoined his men. They relished their barb about Stalingrad, the spectacular German defeat. A low chant began, 'Stalingrad, Stalingrad, Stalingrad.' Two or three of them started singing the Internationale, raising their hand into clenched fists. The Internationale, the de facto anthem of the communists, was the famous socialist, social-democratic and anarchist theme sung wherever communists met to spread their particular brand of poison. The camp guards were again beginning to get worried and I could see groups of them, Wehrmacht regulars, deploying around us, all of them with Kar98K rifles cocked and loaded.

We gained two further recruits that day, packed them off under escort to SS-Freecorps barracks in Berlin, then drove out to the town of Barth to locate Stalag Luft I, the air force camp for officers. Even this small village had not been spared the attentions of the Allied bombers. Whole streets lay in ruins, much like Stalingrad but in miniature. I was directed to Stalag Luft I, a short drive outside the town. Müller drove our vehicle through the gate, the sudden arrival of a Kübelwagen carrying two SS men causing a stir among both guards and prisoners alike. The Volkswagen Kübelwagen was a common enough sight throughout the Reich. It was an air-cooled military vehicle designed by Ferdinand Porsche and built by Volkswagen during the war for use exclusively by the German military. It was small, light and could be easily adapted to a multitude of different roles. It was certainly useful for negotiating the increasingly bomb damaged towns that littered wartime Germany, a testament to the effectiveness of the Allied day and night bombing, where a conventional car would have found it hard going.

The sentry saluted sloppily as we screeched to a halt.

"SS-Obersturmführer Wolf to see the Commandant, soldier. Where is his office?"

"Er, next to the guardroom, Sir. Erm, should I see your identification?"

I nodded to Müller, who smiled evilly at the man. "You'd better see our identification, Private, if you don't want to end up on the Russian Front. Here," he handed the man our papers. The man briefly checked them and handed them back.

"All in order, you may proceed." He stepped back. Müller laughed, slammed the Kübi in gear and drove forward, sliding the back wheels so that the sentry had to jump out of the way to avoid being knocked down. One hour later I was addressing the camp inmates, over three hundred officers, who stood at attention. Their eyes were viewing me with a mixture of hate, fear and fascination. I was thankful for Müller's presence next to me. I felt his particular brand of skills might be called into use here, the atmosphere was so charged with loathing. But we had survived Stalingrad, where the opposing armies hated each other with a depth that sometimes felt as if they wanted to charge into their enemy and tear them limb from limb, bare handed. Stalingrad, where war went beyond the very deepest pits of inhumanity.

CHAPTER THREE

OCTOBER 1942

When we had reported back to headquarters there was a mixture of jubilance and astonishment, jubilance that we had returned successfully with such a high ranking Russian who promised to provide us with good intelligence on the Russian order of battle and plans. Astonishment that we had returned at all, I realised that to some degree the 6th Army had interpreted the orders from Berlin fairly liberally. To put it bluntly, we had been sent on a virtual suicide mission, where failure could be blamed on Berlin and success claimed by Von Paulus' HQ. And then there was Tatiana. She was also received with both jubilance and astonishment. In the midst of that grim grey rubble, the unceasing crash of artillery shells and the perpetual butcher's shop stench of death that was pervasive, cloying, sticking in the nostrils for twenty four hours a day, suddenly I had produced this Slavic princess. A beautiful woman who every man lusted after, who reminded every man of his girl back home in Germany.

As Russian speakers we were given the task of interviewing the vast numbers of Russians who laboured for our army, some willingly, others, the prisoners, under duress. There was a huge investigation mounted when the engines of dozens of our Tiger tanks refused to start. The High Command suspected sabotage from the Russian labourers, the pressure only lifted when it was discovered that the damage had been caused by mice, of all things, gnawing at the electrical wiring. Yet despite all of the efforts, the tens, hundreds of thousands of troops, tanks, Luftwaffe strafing and bombing raids, there was already the smell of defeat in the air. We saw long lines of horses and draught animals, the motive power that pulled the 6th Army's guns and supplies across the vast Russian steppes, being sent to the rear to protect them from the battle. Yet what would the logistics geniuses use to pull the guns and wagons when the army needed to move on?

We were outside the canteen when infantry General Strecker walked past, apparently leaving a staff meeting with von Paulus. He caught sight of Tatiana.

"My God, what do we have here? She's a beauty, whose is she?" He stood there casually admiring her as he took out his cigarette case and put a gold tipped cigarette in his mouth. His aide rushed forward to light it for him. At that moment I was admiring his deerskin coat, one of the most prized articles of clothing in the chilly temperatures of Stalingrad.

I stepped forward. "Herr General, Miss Medvedev is an ally, she is assisting my unit as an interpreter."

"Interpreter? I imagine that's not all she is doing to assist you, Obersturmführer. I could use her, you know, I am looking for an interpreter at my HQ." He looked at Tatiana meaningfully, "how would you like to come and work for me, my dear? I can assure you that it would be well worth it, you'd be well looked after and well rewarded for your efforts. You will find a Wehrmacht General much more generous than an SS Obersturmführer."

"Herr General," I spoke before Tatiana could answer. "Miss Medvedev is already part of my unit and is under the authority of the SS-Liebstandarte Adolf Hitler. She is not available for other duties."

Strecker gave me a nasty look. "SS or not, Obersturmführer, don't you stand to attention before a senior officer?"

I snapped to attention, "Yes, Sir."

"If I decide this woman is to work for me, I only need to speak to General von Paulus. Perhaps I should do that now?" He looked at the door to von Paulus' office.

He was toying with me, enjoying the game, pushing me into doing something I might regret so that he could take the woman.

"Herr General, General von Paulus is not responsible for SS

administration."

Strecker raised his eyebrows, "Then who do you answer to?"

"Reichsführer-SS Heinrich Himmler, Herr General, in Berlin."

His eyes flared momentarily, but I had seen that look before when Himmler's name was mentioned. Not many took up the invitation to contact him. General Strecker stubbed out his cigarette angrily with his boot, turned on his heel and left without a word. I hoped that I wouldn't find myself looking for his co-operation in the near future. I was called into an office and introduced to Colonel Bernard Steinmetz, who was acting as a staff officer for von Paulus. I told my group to wait while I went to report to him. They immediately slumped down on the floor, totally exhausted. Fassbinder and his Wehrmacht men sat in a small group. Müller sat to one side and on the other side Tatiana sat wearily, trying and failing` to look inconspicuous in this strange world of men, rubble, filth, noise and death. I went in and saluted the Colonel, who returned the salute.

"Well done, Obersturmführer, the General was a valuable catch, I'm sure we'll get some very worthwhile intelligence from him. God knows we needed some luck. We shot off over twenty five million rounds of ammunition last month alone, some of our battalions have been reduced to less than fifty men. We need ammunition and we need men." He looked at me sharply. "That's information you need to keep to yourself, Wolf."

"Yes, sir," I replied.

"Now, some good news for you. I have your orders from Berlin. You are to report back to Prinz Albrecht Strasser for debriefing and further assignment. We have a transport aircraft, a Junkers 52, on the ground at the moment. They're getting her ready for takeoff in about two hours. I have made arrangements for you and your Scharführer to be on it, so you'd better not hang around, you need to get out to the airfield."

"Colonel," I told him. "I need a third seat on the aircraft. We have a woman who helped us on the last mission. I have given her the post of interpreter to my unit."

"Your unit?" He raised an eyebrow. "Isn't that just you and Scharführer Müller? Now that your mission here is over the Wehrmacht soldiers assigned to you will be returned to their companies."

"Sir," I replied, "Miss Medvedev has agreed to join us and is now under the authority of the SS-Liebstandarte Adolf Hitler. I appreciate the unusual circumstances, but she has been of tremendous help in the operation to capture the Soviet General. I believe both as a reward and in recognition of her future value she should stay with us." I realised that I was stretching the truth somewhat, but I was both fascinated and attracted by Tatiana Medvedev and I was determined to do my best to get her out of the rubble and hell of Stalingrad. As to the future, that could take care of itself, although I was doubtful of my own long-term prospects.

"It is the very least we can do for you, Obersturmführer. You have done well bringing us the Russian. I will ensure that you have a third seat on the aircraft. Now, I must wish you a safe journey, good luck."

He looked me in the eye as he spoke. He had no need to say anymore. There was something indefinable about the battle for Stalingrad that made men think that a return to Germany was not likely for many of them in the near future, if at all.

"Thank you, Sir." I saluted Colonel Steinmetz and left the office. Müller and Tatiana looked relieved when I informed them of the seats on the Junkers 52 bound for Berlin. We said our goodbyes to Fassbinder and the other Wehrmacht men.

"I'm sure it won't be long before you men are headed back to Germany," I said to them, not believing a word of it. Neither did they, Fassbinder shook my hand, smiling wearily.

"I hope you are right, Sir. Good luck, see you in Berlin."

By the time we got outside the Kübelwagen was waiting for us. Everything we needed to take we carried with us on our backs. Besides, even if we did have kit stored in a barracks room somewhere nearby, the urge to get out of Stalingrad as quickly as possible was overwhelming. We climbed into the vehicle and the driver, a Gefreiter, roared away to the airstrip. The journey was pretty hair-raising, with occasional shells landing around us. At one time we had to stop and take cover when a low-flying Sturmovik buzzed us, giving our driver a fright.

The Ilyushin Il-2, more commonly known as the Sturmovik, was a ground attack aircraft that carried out a very similar role to our Stuka dive

bomber. With excellent accuracy, bombs and deadly 37mm guns it could attack, damage or destroy almost any target it came across. To most it was nicknamed the Hunchback, Flying Tank or the Flying Infantryman. To us it was known simply as the Schlächter, the Slaughterer. This Gefreiter was perhaps right to be frightened of it, we had lost too many good men to the ground attacks.

We peered out from behind a broken wall, watching the attack aircraft swoop down on our Kübelwagen. Happily, the Russian pilot was not a good shot and his burst went ten metres wide. He pulled up and banked around, turning for a second pass. While he was still turning there was a roaring of engines and two of our Messerschmitt 109's swooped on him, machine guns chattering. The Russian didn't stand a chance against the faster moving fighters. We could see chunks of metal tearing off of the fuselage of the Sturmovik. The pilot was too low to bail out and his plane piled straight into the ground. More scrap metal to add to the growing pile that was Hitler and Stalin's creation. We climbed back into the Kübelwagen and drove off. The driver was clearly still nervous and put his foot down, going so fast that at one time we thought the vehicle would overturn. Thankfully we kept going, but still had to run the gauntlet of scattered Russian snipers taking pot shots at us. I felt the Kübelwagen take a hit to the bodywork but we managed to complete the journey otherwise unscathed.

The airfield at Gumrak was not a pretty sight. Pockmarked and scarred by the results of weeks of bombing and shelling, it seemed a miracle that aircraft were still operating from this desolate strip of ruined concrete. Nonetheless, the Junkers 52 was waiting for us on the tarmac. A group of frantic medics were loading the last of a group of casualties on the aircraft. It was a sickening sight. Men covered in mud, uniforms ripped, some with missing limbs, missing eyes, looking almost like Egyptian mummies with their bodies swathed in so many bandages. The Gefreiter drove us right up to the aircraft. We thanked him and got out. I handed my orders to the Luftwaffe captain who was supervising the loading. He looked at us questioningly, surprised to see two SS men and a strikingly beautiful civilian waiting to board the aircraft. He checked the orders twice, nodded to us to board. The cabin was like a scene from Hell

as if part of Stalingrad itself had been recreated in this aircraft. Which I suppose it had, after all, this was Stalingrad's debris. A brutal, bloody shambles populated by tortured and wounded men, both in body and mind. There were no seats in the aircraft, so we just squatted down on the floor amidst the wounded and waited. After what seemed like hours, but was probably no more than ten minutes, the Luftwaffe captain climbed into the aircraft, slammed the door shut and went forward to notify the pilot that we were ready to go. The engines had been idling ever since we had arrived, suddenly they picked up to a roar as the pilot throttled up for takeoff.

We bumped and bounced along the runway, then suddenly the bumping stopped and we were airborne. The engines stayed at maximum power as the pilot struggled to gain altitude in the heavily laden aircraft. We had taken off in an easterly direction, due to the prevailing winds. That meant that we had to literally head towards the city itself then turn 180° to take up a course for Germany. I got to my knees and peered out of the side window. I could see Stalingrad coming towards us, the ever present pall of smoke and dust cloaking the city with the residue of the battle raging beneath. I wondered briefly if we would have any fighter escort, in view of the occasional Russian fighter that ventured over the city. I was relieved to see three fighter aircraft heading towards us and thanked my lucky stars that we would have an escort over the disputed Russian airspace. My thanks quickly turned to shock as I recognised the Soviet marking on the wings of the incoming aircraft. They were not escorting us, they were attacking us. Even as I realised what was happening, I heard the hammering of machine guns and the banging of multiple bullet strikes on the corrugated fuselage of our aircraft. Almost immediately our Junkers 52 lurched and tilted towards the ground. I recognised the area we were flying over, it was the Stalingrad railway station, or at least one of them. Stalingrad had two railway stations, Number One and Number Two. We were flying at about twenty metres above the ruined roof of station Number Two, descending rapidly.

The pilot had literally worked a miracle. I found out afterwards that he had taken three hits from the fighters, injuring his leg and more catastrophically hitting his right lung and left kidney. He must have been agonised by the shock and pain of his wounds and the massive blood loss that resulted. Nonetheless, he had fought to keep control of the aircraft and bring it down in some semblance of a crash landing. When the aircraft hit the ground we were flung around the cabin, wounded and unwounded alike mingling together in a grotesque imitation of a hellish orgy. The screams of the wounded and dying were chilling, yet I had spent sufficient time in Stalingrad's killing fields to know that the downed aircraft would be a tempting target. Staying in this place would have only one inevitable result when the patrols, snipers, artillery or Sturmoviks found us. Müller was shaking his head, dazed by a blow he suffered when he was smashed against the bulkhead of the cockpit. Tatiana was lying unconscious, but I didn't have time to attend to her. The aircraft door had separated from the fuselage on impact and our exit was clear, provided we moved quickly.

"Müller, Müller!" I shouted. "We need to get moving, can you walk?"

He looked at me, his face a mask of blood where the metal had slashed into him. "I can move, Obersturmführer. They'll be here soon," he replied. I did not need to ask who he was referring to.

"Can you give me a hand with Tatiana?"

"Sir," he replied. Then before I could intervene he picked her up as if she was weightless and despite the obvious shock and pain of his injury climbed out of the aircraft. I followed him and we both ran for the shelter of a ruined block of workers' flats. We didn't stop to check for any enemy that may be lurking inside, we just ran through the door and into the shell of one of the ground floor flats. All the doors were missing, like most of the wooden fittings in Stalingrad that had long been chopped up and burned as firewood. The furniture had gone the same way as the doors and we ran through an empty, burnt out shell and took up a position where we could observe the downed aircraft. As we took cover, we heard the shouted 'Urrah', the Soviet battle cry as a company of troops stormed towards the 'plane, bayonets fixed. Several of the Russian soldiers entered the Junkers and began their brutal butcher's work. The moans and screams from within the fuselage rose to a high pitch as the bayonets rose and fell, inflicting a terrible coup de grace on men already suffering from severe wounds. We kept quiet. This was Stalingrad, never a place

to put your head up to be shot off. Eventually the bloody work ended, the soldiers having stripped out every usable item from the aircraft. I even noticed two of them ripping off the bandages from their victims, probably to be washed and reused for their own troops.

"Any ideas where we are?" I asked Müller.

"It looks like Number One Railway Station, Obersturmführer."

I agreed with him. To the southwest I could make out the destroyed roof of Number Two Railway Station, which as far as I knew was still in German hands. Our position in Number One was uncomfortably close to the Soviet central landing stage, which the Russians used to ferry supplies and troops to and from their tiny remaining strip of the city.

"Very well, Scharführer. We need to get across to Number Two, let's just hope that it's still occupied by our own people. Can you manage the girl?"

He nodded, then once again picked her up and followed me as I exited the rear of the building away from the site of the aircraft crash, which was almost certainly being kept under observation by the Russians. We made our way southwest, dodging from rubble pile to rubble pile, crouching low and making progress in short dashes. We were still in territory held by the Russians. Every time we broke cover I waited for the shock of a bullet in my back from one of the legions of snipers the Russians seem to have in inexhaustible supply. But no shot came near. Eventually we came to the edge of Number One Railway Station and peered across to the broken shell of Number Two Railway Station. I found a piece of old pipe and tied my white handkerchief to it, then crouched behind a wall held it up and waved it in the direction of where I knew our German troops were sheltering in the station building. I shouted out, once, twice, no reply, then a third time.

"We are German soldiers. We were in the Junkers 52 that just crashed in Number One Railway Station. We need to come across, don't shoot!"

Eventually there was a reply, the welcome sound of a German voice.

"How many of you are there?" I told him, he shouted back "You three can come across, move carefully, keep your hands up, or you'll be shot!"

I shouted my thanks and stood up very slowly, my hands raised, still clutching the pipe with the white handkerchief. Müller got up cautiously behind me. He hoisted Tatiana onto his shoulder and together we walked slowly and carefully across to our lines, very conscious of the MG 34 machine gun that covered us for every step of the way. We walked through a doorway and were grabbed by several Wehrmacht troopers who held us tightly. An officer came up and introduced himself as Major Schneider.

"What's the SS doing in Stalingrad?" he asked. "And what's this, a woman?" He went up to Tatiana and lifted her head cautiously, relaxing slightly when he could see that she was unconscious. He looked at Müller's bloody face and grimaced. "Well, what's your story?"

I explained to him about our liaison mission, about our flight intended to take us to the German capital to report to Himmler. He was singularly unimpressed by the dark influence of the SS supremo in Berlin, many thousands of kilometres and indeed many lifetimes away from this unworldly hell. Just then, Tatiana started moaning and began to recover consciousness. The major took a longer look at her and looked back at me.

"My God, she's a beauty! Yours?"

I shook my head, "Not at all, Major, she is our interpreter."

He smiled. "Interpreter? Is that what the SS call them these days? Well, whatever, how can I help you?"

"We need to get back to headquarters and arrange for a replacement flight back to Berlin, Himmler's orders."

"I couldn't give a shit about Heinrich, but in any case we just heard on the radio that the airport is closed, you must have been one of the last flights out before the artillery started. The Russians are throwing everything at us. It looks like a major attack. Artillery, tanks and a couple of infantry divisions, they're having a hell of a fight up there. We'll beat them off eventually, but I doubt that the airport will open for several days at least. It looks like you're in for a long wait. Come, I'll introduce you to the radio man, you can speak to HQ yourself and find out what they expect you to do."

I thanked the Major and followed him into what had once been a concrete store room, now with the roof missing it was just four walls giving the radio man and his equipment some protection from incoming fire. It turned out that these men were part of the 384th Infantry Division commanded by General von Gablenz. The soldier got me through to his divisional headquarters and they patched me through from there to Army Headquarters. Eventually, I heard the familiar voice of Colonel Steinmetz.

"We heard about the Junkers being shot down, Obersturmführer. Were there any other survivors?"

I told him that, apart from us three, the others had perished either in the crash or during the Soviet bayonet charge.

"We need to make our way back to you, Colonel, and wait for another flight. We've heard about the attack on the airfield, we'll just have to wait. Do you want us to come in now? There is a lot of Russian activity here. We could do with some support. Perhaps you could order Major Schneider to lend us a platoon to guide us back?"

There was a silence on the radio, after a short pause the Colonel instructed me to wait a few minutes for further instructions. I noted that the activity around the railway stations seemed to have died down. Obviously the Russians were concentrating their artillery and aircraft on the airfield. Through the open roof of the radio room I watched an air battle for a few moments. Once again the slow-moving Sturmovik's were no match for our fighters and I saw three shot down in as many minutes by a flight of Focke-Wulf FW 190's.

The Focke-Wulf FW 190 was an excellent general purpose workhorse aircraft designed for a wide variety of roles, including air superiority fighter, strike fighter, ground-attack aircraft and escort fighter. A great asset in the skies over Stalingrad, it was fast, powerful and commonly armed with two fuselage-mounted 7.92 mm MG 17s, two wingroot-mounted 7.92 mm MG 17s and two outboard wing-mounted 20 mm MG FF/Ms that made short work of its Russian opponents. A heavily armed fighter, we were very glad of its brutal firepower that day.

One of the Sturmoviks crashed in the rubble disconcertingly close to our position, sending up a spray of stone chips and dust when it hit. I realised that our fighters had not had it all their own way. Another Sturmovik, trailing smoke and flame, managed to put a long burst into an FW 190, causing it to catch fire and then explode in midair. It was clear that the Luftwaffe's dominance of the skies over Stalingrad was probably ending. Now it was the turn of the Red Air Force. The radio crackled and

I listened to Colonel Steinmetz.

"Apparently, Obersturmführer, Prinz Albrecht Strasser has been informed of your fate and has given von Paulus permission to use you until such time as the airfield is repaired. The Reichsführer feels that the services of the SS will be useful to us," he added sarcastically. "I want you to stay where you are. I'm sending a runner with your orders. I don't want to give any details over the radio."

I could hardly believe what I was hearing. My group had just survived a serious plane crash, I had assumed we would be helped out of the battlefield and given time to recover. We were all suffering from severe shock. Müller, it turned out, had broken his nose and taken a deep gash to the right leg during the crash. I had no cuts to my body, but my left ankle felt as if it had been sprained and my left arm was ripped and bloody where it had been gashed by broken metal. Tatiana had been knocked unconscious when the aircraft hit the ground and was obviously going to be feeling groggy until she recovered. I explained the situation to Colonel Steinmetz. By way of reply I heard a laugh through the headphones of the radio.

"Wolf, half the men in Stalingrad are in a worse situation than you are. We're an army of walking wounded, I doubt that the Russians are any different. We've got a simple job for you, just find somewhere to hide and observe. That's all. HQ out."

I handed the equipment back to the radio man. All we could do was make the best of it, I resolved to interpret my orders as liberally as possible and keep our heads down until the airfield was clear and we could get out of this nightmare.

We sat in a small group in the radio room, Müller, Tatiana and myself. The Russian girl had managed to keep her embroidered leather coat intact and undamaged in the crash. She clutched it around her with the hood pulled over her head, as if the garment would keep out the horrors of Stalingrad or ward off the perpetual incoming artillery and sniper rounds.

"Tell me about yourself Tatiana," I asked her, trying to get her to focus away from the crash.

She shrugged. "Well, my father was contracted to design and build a new pumping station in Danzig in 1920. He met my mother, married her and I was born in 1921." She smiled, "That's about it, so now you know my age."

So she was about twenty one years old, with an ancestry that was interesting to say the least. Danzig was the hotly contested northern corner of Poland, with a population that was both German and Polish speaking. That explained her languages. Yet, there was something more about her. She seemed to possess a poise that was more than just affected.

"So your father was an engineer, what about your mother?" There was something about this girl, something deep, something mysterious that made me want to know more.

"My mother was a Polish aristocrat, a countess," she laughed. "Sadly she was left virtually destitute after the Great War and was fortunate to meet my father. We returned to Russia in 1938 when he was offered the job here in Stalingrad. He had difficulties finding work in Danzig, my mother was Jewish and we suffered quite badly from both the Poles and the Germans. My mother and father thought things would be better here under communism. It didn't work out quite like that, but it wasn't too bad until the war started. Then you Germans came to Stalingrad and here we are." She held up her hands as if to say 'look at the mess you Germans created'.

"I'm sorry, it must have been terrible for you," I replied. "By the way, I'm not German, I'm British."

"British!" She exclaimed. "But I thought the British were fighting the Germans. Why are you fighting for the enemy?"

"It's a long story," I replied. "I'll tell you about it one day, I sometimes wonder myself how I got involved. But here I am, so here I stay."

She was looking at me with a puzzled expression. Then her eyes caught mine and we held the gaze for several moments, searching deeply into each other's souls. Oh no, for God's sake, not here in this shithole. She was very beautiful. In any other circumstances I would have pursued her to the ends of the earth. But here in Stalingrad there was one role that took precedence over everything. Survival.

Night fell, and the runner from headquarters had still not arrived with our orders. I found a stack of canvas mailbags in the corner of the room and made myself a makeshift bed to catch some sleep. Müller said something about preferring to sleep with a roof over his head and went off to sleep in a tunnel nearby that was being used as a makeshift store room. Tatiana had found herself a more or less intact office, with a working bolt on the inside door, and she used this as her bedroom. The Russians fired flares several times during the darkness but we ignored them, it was their standard tactic to wear us down, pretending that an attack was happening. Eventually I drifted off to sleep, noting that the radio man, like radio men the world over, had taken the opportunity when the signals equipment was quiet to slump forward on his desk and doze. I was almost asleep when a hand gently touched my face. I immediately became alert, grabbing my Walther.

"Schh," said a voice, quietly. It was Tatiana. "Be quiet, Wolf," she whispered.

"What's wrong?" I asked her.

"Nothing," she murmured gently, "I just wanted to be with you."

She pulled off her cloak. Underneath she was naked. I gasped as she climbed into my ragged pile of mail bags to get close to me. I began breathing hard as I felt her fingers probing my uniform, undoing the buttons and belts and gently pulling it off me. All the time she was touching me, kissing my body all over so that I felt the beginnings of the flames of passion that threatened to engulf me. She touched my penis that was already rock hard and I felt the gentle caress of her cool fingers. I held her to me feeling her soft and smooth skin, the gentle curves of her magnificent body and the two proud breasts that were brushing against me. Then, holding my penis in her hand she positioned herself over me and guided me inside her. I quivered with the electric sensations as I moved inside her moist warmth. We gently moved our bodies, alive to the incredible sensations of the moment. Then the urgency overwhelmed both of us. We moved faster and faster, our bodies desperate with the overwhelming lust that possessed us. We both climaxed in a massive explosion of emotions that shut out the whole world for what seemed like an eternity. It was bliss. Afterwards, I lit two cigarettes and we lay there, smoking peaceably.

"Tatiana, why did you come to me?" I murmured.

"Do you have any objections, Wolf?" I could hear the smile in her voice as she whispered to me.

"Tatiana, if I never have another experience like that for as long as I live I can still die a happy man. But why me? Why here?"

It was a reasonable question. I was an SS killer, even worse, a traitor to my own country. And we were in the middle of an epic battle that had turned her city into what must be as close as man could get to hell, without actually going there.

"I just wanted to," she said. "Isn't that reason enough?"

I nodded and felt myself drifting off to sleep, holding her wonderful body in my arms. In the morning I woke up and she was gone, almost as if that magnificent nocturnal visit hadn't occurred. The occasional shell passed over our position but none came near. We heard the odd 'ping' as a sniper round hit the masonry around us, but none threatened. Then a soldier came in to the radio room.

"Obersturmführer Wolf?"

I nodded. He handed me a packet of orders, then put a backpack radio carefully on the ground. As I opened them Müller came into the room, then Tatiana, who carefully avoided my eyes and sat casually on a pile of bricks nearby. The orders were simple. We were mounting an attack, due to start later that morning. 6th Army artillery needed spotters in the Number One Railway Station to direct their fire. Müller and I were to make our way into the railway station next door and make contact with HQ to direct the guns using the supplied grid maps. Were they mad?

"Get me HQ, now!" I shouted at the radio man.

"Immediately, Sir," he replied.

Five minutes later I was talking to Colonel Steinmetz.

"Sir, this order is insane. Railway Station Number One is occupied by the Russians. That's where we crash landed, they bayoneted the wounded survivors."

"Obersturmführer, intelligence reports that the Russians have pulled out of the station. We need you there to direct our fire, it overlooks the landing stage and we can stop the Russians ferrying reinforcements across the river. It's important."

"Colonel, I'm sure it is, but you must know it's a suicide mission."

There was silence for a moment, then the colonel's hoarse voice. "This is Stalingrad, Obersturmführer. Aren't they all suicide missions?"

I couldn't think of a reply. Then I heard his voice again.

"I have confirmed the order with Berlin. Reichsführer Himmler's office has every confidence in you and Müller."

"Fuck Berlin, Colonel, this is crazy and you know it."

"You have your orders, Obersturmführer. Crazy or not, I suggest you get on with carrying them out. You know the alternative. Out"

The radio went quiet. Yes, I did know the alternative. A firing squad here for disobedience, or a spell in the torture cellars of Prinz Albrecht Strasser followed by a firing squad.

"Müller," I called to the Scharführer. "You heard?"

He nodded. Tatiana came up to me. "Wolf, I'm coming with you."

I shook my head. "No, not in a million years. You know we're not likely to get back?"

"I can guide you," she said. I've lived here for nearly four years. I can get you there, find a hiding place, and get you back. I'm coming."

Maybe she was right. Besides, where was she likely to be safe in Stalingrad? I nodded.

"Müller, pick up the radio." I checked my watch. "It's eight o'clock. The artillery is due to start at eleven prior to the main attack at twelve. Let's move."

Our German forces attacked again on October 15th, "The Day of Decision." Russian losses were mounting massively. In two days two of our divisions had lost seventy five percent of their men. That night another Soviet regiment crossed the Volga and came into the fighting. But the real help came from the Russian artillery, the guns of the Volga flotilla of warcraft, and the Sturmovik planes of the air force, which were attacking German troops. Although they suffered very heavy losses. Stalingrad still refused to be beaten, much to von Paulus' discomfort, and Hitler's increasing rage. We afterwards found out that General Chuikov had a visit from General Yeremenko on the 17th of October when Yeremenko promised him one day's supply of ammunition. Chuikov complained bitterly and more was promised. The Russians were conserving ammunition. The question for German intelligence was why? With the Germans so near Chuikov had to move his headquarters south. They set up in a ravine close to Mamayev Hill, their HQ actually inside the Volga cliffs. This tiny strip of the west bank of the Volga was all that remained of central Stalingrad in Russian hands.

MARCH 1944

The British officer marched forward and saluted.

"Colonel James, I am the senior British officer in Stalag Luft I," he shouted at me. I wondered was he trying to intimidate me in some way with this soldierly display of precision. I returned the salute lazily, "Obersturmführer Wolf, Colonel, SS-British Freecorps, you know why I'm here?"

He didn't answer at first, just inspected me minutely, pausing for a long moment on the Union Jack badge sewn to my sleeve. Then he looked me in the eye.

"Yes, Obersturmführer, I know why you're here. I know that you are a traitor and you are trying to recruit more traitors to get themselves hanged when the war is over. It won't work you know, there isn't a single officer in this camp prepared to join your filthy cause, so carry on."

"Oh, I intend to carry on, Colonel. And you can take it from me that a good number of British soldiers, both officers and men, have already joined the SS-British Freecorps."

"Not here, Obersturmführer, not here. I can smell the stench of a traitor, it's all over you, but you'll not find a single traitor in this camp." The volume of his voice dropped, and he spoke to me in what he obviously thought was a confidential and persuasive manner. "Look, you're obviously British. Whatever you've done, it's never too late. If you came back to the British side now, I could put in a good word for you when it's all over. Chances are you'll defeat the hangman. Think about it, man."

I laughed in his face. "End of the war, Colonel? You must be joking, I've had more than my share of luck to survive this far. By the end of the war I'll be long dead and forgotten."

He laughed at me, then stepped back, about turned and rejoined his men. I wondered had he or his fellow RAF officers any idea of the carnage they had inflicted on Berlin and scores of similar towns and cities all over Germany. Civilian carnage, not military. Women, children, the sick, the elderly. But would they care? Probably not, but would I be any better than them? I thought about the countless numbers of men, some women, that I had seen die over the last four years. Hundreds, thousands, tens of thousands. And then there was Stalingrad, where the numbers just defied belief, where the human brain stopped calculating and switched off, numb to the carnage and death that carpeted the whole of Stalingrad during that long and bitter battle.

"Sir, Sir," I snapped back to the present. I had not had much sleep, I had to be careful, I was daydreaming again. Müller was tapping me on the shoulder, looking anxious. "Sir, are you alright?"

"Thank you, Müller, I'm fine. Now where was I?"

"You were going to talk about the rules of engagement for the SS-British Freecorps, Sir," he replied.

"Yes, of course. Men, if you join the SS-British Freecorps, you officers will become part of the global fight against the communist threat. You may think that Germany is your enemy, but that is just not true."

I was just going through the motions, it was absurd for me to stand here and tell German held prisoners of war that Germany was not their enemy.

"The Soviet Union is the enemy of the entire free world. You are being offered a unique chance to join the crusade to stop the Red hordes from destroying the entire system of western civilisation."

The rhetoric, carefully scripted by Himmler's staff, was going from absurd to utterly surreal. Russia, the Soviet Union, was of course an ally of Great Britain. Telling these prisoners that their ally was in fact their enemy, and their enemy was their ally, seems like some kind of a music hall joke. Still, that was the job I was being paid to do. I had only one alternative to this work, Himmler had made that perfectly clear. That alternative was to go back to the Eastern Front. So I continued with this charade.

"Pay and conditions will be the same as for every other member of the Waffen SS. Now men, are there any questions?" I asked them. A hand came up at the back.

"Yes?" I asked him.

"Obersturmführer, after the war, do you prefer to be hanged or shot?"

There was a chorus of hoots and yells as the officers gave their best public school cheer catcalls and insults. I ignored them. A voice called out.

"What gives you the right to condemn Russian civilisation? It's been around a lot longer than your German friends so-called civilisation?"

I looked at the group of officers but couldn't make out who had asked the question, but it was a fair point. What did give me the right to condemn Russian civilisation? I had an answer. It was one word, a name. Stalingrad! I remembered the Russians scrambling towards our stricken aircraft as it lay broken on the ground, like a pack of wolves racing to rip the wounded animal to shreds. No, my British officer friend, fight the Russian and you will find he is anything but civilised.

I was drifting again. Memories of Stalingrad had that effect on the tired mind, the nightmare returning. The faces of the two hundred and thirty eight British officer prisoners floated back into focus.

"So, if any of you have any sensible questions to ask, Scharführer Müller and myself will be here for another two hours to answer them. You can come to the guardroom and you will be shown to our quarters. Remember, whatever you think about the Germans, it is the communists that are your enemy and mine." I nodded to Müller. "You can dismiss them, Müller."

"Yes, Obersturmführer." He faced the officer prisoners and stood at attention. "Parade, dismiss!" he shouted.

They totally ignored him. Then Colonel James stepped forward, turned to face the men and called, in what was obviously a mocking parody of Müller, "Parade, dismiss!"

Müller's expression darkened, I didn't blame him. The Colonel had tried to make a deliberate fool of him. Who the hell did he think was the prisoner here? I thought it just as well we would be leaving the camp shortly. Müller had a very painful way of dealing with people who made a fool of him. We walked off towards the guardroom and found the office that had been put at our disposal. I sat down behind the desk and Müller slumped in an old armchair. We had a couple of hours to wait so we both close their eyes and just dozed for a while. We knew we were unlikely to get any recruits from amongst these prisoners, so this was one of those rare moments during the war when there was a little peace and quiet, a time for reflection and catching up on some sleep. I snapped awake when I heard the crash of broken glass. It sounded as if it had come from the office next door. Müller was already on his feet, his right hand pulling his Walther out of the holster. We dashed out of the door and into the office next to us. The scene that greeted us was one of a fiery hell, the whole room seemed to be ablaze. The clerk, a Wehrmacht Feldwebel, was also ablaze, screaming in agonised shock. There was a coat on a peg behind the door, I grabbed it, threw it around him to extinguish the flames and dragged him out through the door. Müller had taken a fire extinguisher off of the wall and was squirting it at the flames.

"Guard, guard!" I shouted, "Fire, we are on fire, hurry, get help, we need more extinguishers and fire buckets to get the flames out."

A squad of Wehrmacht troopers clattered along the corridor towards me, I grabbed one of them. "Take this soldier to the sick bay, be very careful, he's been badly burned." The man nodded and took the injured Feldwebel out of my hands. The other soldiers grabbed buckets from the wall filled with sand, and began throwing them over the flames. Within a few minutes we managed to put out the fire. The camp commandant had arrived and Müller and I accompanied him to inspect the wrecked office. Amidst the shards of glass from the broken window we could see the remains of a smashed bottle. The smell of petrol was strong, "Molotov Cocktail, no question," I said. The other men nodded.

"I think you are right," the commandant said to me, "I suspect it was an attempt on you and your sergeant by the prisoners. It seems the SS did not win any converts today," he smiled.

"Maybe not, Sir," I replied, "but your security is less than impressive, and you now have a seriously injured corporal as a result. Perhaps I should suggest that Prinz Albrecht Strasser send some Gestapo men here to investigate the incident, they could check your security operation as well?"

"That won't be necessary, Obersturmführer," the commandant replied hastily, "I will deal with this internally. Perhaps it is time you were on your way."

"Yes, Sir." I saluted, "Thank you for your assistance. Good day, Sir." He acknowledged the salute and stalked off, glad to see the back of us and shaken by the incident and my threat to involve the Gestapo. I doubted very much that we would be welcomed here again.

As Müller drove us away in the Kübelwagen I tipped my cap forward, reclined back in the seat and began to doze, drifting slowly and gently back to Stalingrad.

CHAPTER FOUR

OCTOBER 1942

It was as if Stalingrad held its breath, waiting for the attack that was due to start at midday. Even the snipers seemed to be having a rest, and the artillery contented themselves with just the occasional ranging shot. For one moment I fancied that I heard the sound of birdsong, but I was mistaken, it was just the distant echo of a tank as it trundled across the broken landscape. Even with the supposed intelligence that Number One Railway Station was no longer occupied by the Russians, we crawled carefully, scrambling from one rubble pile to another. Despite my misgivings, Tatiana took the lead. She was adamant she knew the way and it certainly seemed that the route she took us kept us sensibly out of sight of the Russian lines. Of no less threat were the German lines, where the site of a tempting target would likely prove too much to resist to a nervous sentry. Once, as we crawled past some steps that led down into a basement, I thought I heard the sound of voices coming from below. But I couldn't distinguish which language they were speaking so I ignored them and we pressed on. Eventually, we crawled through a jagged hole in the side of the station building and worked our way along the Number Five platform towards the twisted and wrecked tracks. Tatiana was leading us towards the station signal box, which she had identified as the best vantage point to view the Russian lines. We got to the end of the platform without incident and there stood the signal box, but only just. The building, which was sufficiently prominent to have attracted the attentions of the Luftwaffe as well as the artillery of both sides, was badly damaged. It had consisted of what looked to be four floors, now the top floor had virtually disappeared, leaving only three floors still standing. We crawled across the tracks and I looked around and saw no obvious signs of the enemy. I stood up and called to the others.

"It looks all clear. Let's make a run for it. Go!" I shouted.

We rushed across the short open space between the tracks and the signal box, through the open door and into the ground floor. Müller broke left, covering the interior with his MP38. I was carrying a Soviet PPSh, which I had scrounged just before we departed. I preferred the Soviet weapon to our own automatic pistols for its high rate of fire and better drum capacity. I broke to the right and could immediately see we were on our own, the Soviets appeared to have departed. I pointed to the stairs, and Müller dashed up to check the first floor. He burst in, again broke left, while I went to the right. It was eerie, so strange that such a desirable strategic observation point should be left alone by the Russians.

There were documents on the table, I slung my PPSh on my back and went forward to check them. Sadly, they were only pre-war train schedules, of no use to us. Müller headed for the third floor and I was about to follow him when I heard the sound of a door opening in the room. I snatched up my Walther and aimed, just as a startled Russian sentry walked through the door carrying a kettle of boiling water. He was whistling, happy to be preparing tea in time for his breakfast. I shot him, just once, between the eyes. A red spot burst open on his forehead and he went spinning to the ground, dropping the kettle with a crash. I rushed through the door, only to find that it was a small mess room that had been used by the railway workers. The soldier had brewed his kettle on a small kerosene pressure stove that stood on a pile of wooden crates. The room was empty, as evidently the soldier had been left behind as a lone sentry.

Müller came down the stairs, "Top floor is clear, looks as if we have the place to ourselves." He looked coldly at the dead Russian. "Nice shot, Obersturmführer," he said dispassionately. I nodded at him, "Get the radio set up and report in, they'll be waiting to hear from us. I checked my watch, it was almost ten o'clock.

"Tatiana, are you okay?" I said.

"I'm fine, thank you."

I could see that she was anything but fine. My casual killing of the Russian soldier had come as a shock to her, the almost casual way in which I swatted him like a fly. Well, she would certainly see a few more killings like that before we were able to catch a flight out of the city.

"Right, let's go upstairs and see how the land lies," I said to her.

She followed me up the steps and we walked out on to the third floor, which following the loss of the fourth floor was now an open roof terrace. As she had said, it was a good vantage point. Müller was crouched in a corner, out of sight of any snipers in the vicinity. I told her to do the same, warning her about the danger from snipers. Russian snipers, German snipers, it made no difference. A sniper was a sniper and if you appeared in their sights you would almost certainly die. I could hear Müller talking to HQ, he finished and filled me in.

"I've reported in, told them we are in position and there's no sign of the Russians. Our orders are to wait until the barrage starts then direct fire onto the Russian positions over by the landing stage."

I looked across to the central landing stage. In the distance, and through the smoke, I could just make out Russian boats crossing backwards and forwards. There were hordes of Russian soldiers queued up on the opposite bank waiting for the crossing. I shuddered to think how many had crossed already and how many of them would be joining the Russian forces that we were about to engage. Hopefully I could bring down some artillery fire on them and thin them out a bit. Then my blood ran cold, I heard shouted orders and looked across to the north where a large group of Russian soldiers were crossing the open ground. I crouched down and warned Müller and Tatiana to keep quiet.

I crawled forward so that I could observe the newcomers. There were about forty Russians. In the lead was the familiar black leather jacketed figure of a Soviet commissar. I had to look twice before I recognised the bound man being dragged forward by four of the troops. It was Vasyl, the giant Ukrainian who had saved us from the Russian ambush. Evidently he'd been caught and I assumed the Russians would take him to a wall and shoot him. Then things got worse, they started to pick their way towards our signal box. I crawled across to Müller and Tatiana, "Quick, find something to shelter behind. If they come in here for a look around we may be lucky and stay out of sight."

I didn't like to think what would happen if we weren't lucky. For most people in Stalingrad there was only one exit. We dragged some wooden crates into a corner and covered them with an old ragged tarpaulin. We crouched behind the boxes, our guns ready for the worst. I gave my Walther to Tatiana.

"You know how to use this? You just take off the safety," I showed her how to push the safety catch to fire, "then point it and pull the trigger."

She looked doubtful. "I'll try, but I don't know if I'll hit anything."

"Just do what you can, and if the worst comes to the worst, you know you always have a bullet for...well, you know." I looked at her meaningfully. She nodded her understanding. A quick bullet would be infinitely preferable to mass rape, torture and execution. I smiled at her. "The Russians call Stalingrad 'The Street Fighting Academy'. It's where we all learn the trade of close quarters fighting, including firing an automatic pistol."

We heard the Russians enter the signal box and climb to the second floor, where they threw themselves down to rest. The commissar shouted, "Take the bloody traitor upstairs and put a bullet in his head. When you're done, throw his body over the side and stay up there to keep watch. Understood?"

I heard their reply and then the sounds of their boots coming up the stairs. They emerged on our third floor with Vasyl, dragged him into the middle and flung him to the floor. Peering through a crack in the wooden boxes I could see his face, he was in a terrible state. It looked as if his face had been burned with cigarette butts. Several teeth were missing, his face was black and blue with bruises and it seemed they had even dragged out clumps of his hair. If he hadn't been tortured, the clown like effect would have been comical.

"Stay down there, you fascist traitor scum," one of the soldiers snarled. Vasyl didn't look as if he had much fight left in him. He just lay there with one elbow propping him on his side, his wrists tied tightly with strong twine.

"Right, let's finish this bastard off, then we can relax and have a break.

Of course," he added hurriedly, "we'll keep a sharp eye out for the enemy." His comrade nodded agreement, this was the Soviet Union, you always had to be careful about what you said. Comrade Stalin could be listening. Some soldiers were even reporting a miraculous apparition of Stalin that had appeared in the midst of the fighting. Was it possible? He shrugged, best to take no chances. He was carrying a PPSh submachine gun, he cocked it and walked towards Vasyl. His companion carried a bolt action Mosin Nagant which he kept trained on the Ukrainian, the action obviously already loaded with a bullet.

I looked around, Müller was waiting for the order. I turned my PPSh around, holding it like a club. This was no time for an unwanted burst of fire. Müller whipped out his knife and we crept behind the two soldiers. I stumbled on a small piece of rubble which made the man in front of me start to turn. I leapt forward and smashed him on the head with my PPSh. Simultaneously I could see Müller out of the corner of my eye slash forward with his knife, hitting his victim in the carotid artery and causing blood to spurt out as the knife travelled round to the man's throat and cut through his windpipe. We grabbed both victims and lowered them gently to the ground. Müller bent over the soldier I had clubbed and with a quick slash finished him off. Then he untied the Ukrainian and helped him to his feet. I went to listen at the stairwell, but there was no indication that the Russians had heard anything untoward on the roof.

I went back to Vasyl. His dark eyes looked at me and then Müller. "I thank you," he said. "You have saved my life."

"A favour returned, Vasyl," I replied. "I think we owed you that one."

He managed to smile although I could see his injuries were causing him terrible pain.

"We need to deal with the men downstairs, two of us won't be enough. Are you up to it?" I asked Vasyl.

He nodded. "I don't think I have a choice, let's do it." He picked up the PPSh, and thus armed with three submachine guns we crept quietly to the stairwell. I listened, but there was only the normal murmur and chatter of conversation. I looked at the men, they both nodded. They were ready. I could see Tatiana standing partly hidden behind the boxes. She had drawn the Walther and stood ready too. Her lips moved as she

mouthed the phrase 'good luck'.

"Start shooting when I do, not before," I whispered. Then I walked quietly down the staircase. The room was already full of smoke. The Russians had lit up their foul smelling cigarettes and were making the most of a temporary break. The commissar was talking urgently to three of his men, probably some communist nonsense that they had heard a thousand times before. I checked my weapon, made sure the safety was off and rushed down the last few steps and into the room, pulling the trigger on full automatic. Müller and Vasyl followed behind me and opened up. There was total and utter chaos as the burst of fire smashed into the Russians. Not one of them managed to reach for their weapon, and by the time I came to change the drum on my PPSh most were already dead or severely wounded, and a small group held their hands up in surrender. I snapped in the new drum and looked around carefully. Müller rushed forward with the knife and began silencing the wounded. Amongst the group that had surrendered I noticed with some satisfaction the commissar, looking a little less arrogant than he had a few minutes before. I made the captives get down on their knees with their hands held over their heads and checked all of them for weapons, there were only seven men left alive from the Russian squad.

I joined Müller and Vasyl.

"We need to finish off the prisoners. Obviously we can't take any with us or leave them behind. I only want the commissar, he could be useful to us, although I doubt we'll manage to get him back. I'll see what headquarters has to say, they may want to speak to him."

We walked behind the shaking prisoners and finished off the six men with a quick, merciful shot in the back of the head. The commissar seemed less than grateful to be left alive, "You fascist scum. You will never leave this place, you know, the bones of you and your Nazi filth will fertilise this ground for evermore."

I remembered that Stalin took a very hard line on Russians taken prisoner by the Germans who then managed to get back to their own lines. They usually wound up in prison camps, suspected of being traitors. It was quite probable that a commissar would receive a much harder and nastier fate. No doubt he was regretting that we hadn't killed him at the same time as his men. Well, perhaps we would satisfy him later. A sound on the stairs made us turn, it was Tatiana coming down from the roof. She still carried my Walther automatic.

"It's all clear, there's no sign of any other Russians."

"Excellent," I said, "we need to tie up the commissar here and make sure he doesn't cause any trouble. Müller, you can have a word with him later."

But Tatiana was walking towards the commissar, her expression full of the most vicious hate I had ever seen on a woman's face. She walked up to him.

"You!" She snarled. "You dirty, filthy, stinking piece of dirt. Do you remember me?"

The Russian looked at her puzzled. "No, I have never seen you before in my life, why would I, you are one of the fascists."

"So you do not remember coming into my father's house with your soldiers, killing my mother and father only because they had lived in Danzig and spoke German, then raping me and giving me to the rest of your soldiers for their entertainment? You tell me you don't remember?"

The commissar looked at her then realisation dawned. "The engineer's girl. You were all traitors, Jews, I remember."

"Good!" Tatiana spat out then she lowered the pistol and shot the man in the groin, hitting him squarely in his manhood. He reeled backwards, squealing and shouting like a stuffed pig.

"Müller," I nodded, "shut him up."

Müller moved forward, the knife flashed once again and the screams stopped.

"I'm sorry Wolf," she said, "you heard what he did. It was too much for me to bear, seeing his pig face again."

"It's okay," I nodded. "Let's get back on the roof. We have to man the radio. The barrage will be starting soon, besides we need to make sure the shooting hasn't attracted any more Russians."

A swarm of aircraft roared across our position, Luftwaffe Stukas on a mission to bomb the Soviet defences, escorted by a trio of Messerschmidt 109s which swooped down low, heading to the central landing stage for a strafing run. The Junkers Ju 87 or Stuka was our ground attack aircraft and the hero of the victories over Poland and France two years previously.

The plane was a two-seater, pilot and rear gunner, and optimised for gun and bomb attacks of ground targets. It had inverted gull wings, fixed undercarriage and its infamous Jericho Trumpet wailing siren. The siren was in many ways as important as the bombs it dropped. It was wailing now as it came in to bomb the landing stage. Then, at exactly eleven o'clock the barrage started, Germans were nothing if not punctual. Hundreds of shells whistled overhead and to the east of our position, aimed at the small Russian enclave that was the only part of the city that they still held. I could see more Russian boats shuttling to and fro on the river.

"Müller, warm up the radio, we need to advise our people about those Russian boats."

He switched on and quickly made contact with our HQ. Before long we were in direct communication with the gunners and able to give accurate reports on their fall of shot so that they could shift their aim onto the Russian reinforcements. Very soon the Volga was shrouded in a pall of smoke as boat after boat was hit by shells, sending their cargo of screaming soldiers into the icy waters to drown. The barrage built up in intensity until the very air seemed to be covered by a blanket of hot, spinning and exploding metal. The firing continued, on and on. Then we heard the squeal of our tanks and the burst of small arms fire that announced the arrival of our troops. Soon the Russian counterfire began and the enemy artillery shells started bursting all around the oncoming German tanks and troops.

"Obersturmführer," Vasyl said to me, "do you know what that party of Russians downstairs was coming here to do?"

"No," I shouted, the noise was so intense that it was difficult to make out a conversation.

"They were here to do exactly the same as you are doing. After they had executed me they were setting up their radio to spot for the Russian artillery. They knew you were attacking and wanted to direct their artillery fire onto your leading troops to blunt the edge of your attack, then launch their counter-attack."

I was puzzled. "Fair enough," I replied, "why are you telling me this?"

"Because if they do not hear from their men, they may wonder why and

91

send someone to see what happened to them."

"Are you suggesting we should pull out of here then?" I said to him.

"What I am suggesting is that we carry out the mission for them, use their radio equipment and direct their artillery fire."

"Won't they suspect anything?"

"Why should they?" He asked. "I am an officer in the Red Army. If I give them fire control orders they will just carry them out."

"Get the radio equipment, quick!" I shouted.

Within minutes we had carried the backpack with the heavy Soviet radio up to the top floor. Vasyl fiddled with the set and soon he was talking to the Russian artillery position. The reinforcements that were advancing on our bank of the Volga were clearly visible to us. Vasyl gave directions to the Soviet gunners and soon their shells were falling on top of their own men. There were very few moments during the Battle of Stalingrad that I felt any real pleasure or satisfaction in what we had achieved, but this was one of them.

"Vasyl," I said to the Ukrainian, "that was brilliant. But why do you hate the Russians so much?"

He paused for a moment. "Obersturmführer Wolf, I do not hate the Russians at all. It is the Soviets I hate. My family lived quite happily in the Ukraine until the revolution came. Soon the Soviets were all over us, and before long my family were declared to be Kulaks."

The Kulaks were former peasants in Russia who owned medium-sized farms as a result of the reforms at the start of the century. These people were generally the more affluent of the poorer class and were therefore often targeted for deportation, punishment or simply executed. Of course there was the old joke that anybody who has enough to eat is a Kulak!

"They were sent to a camp in Siberia through the snow, over two thousand miles away. They were forced to walk, every step of the way. My mother died, my sisters died, my two brothers died, only my father and I survived. The camp was sheer hell, we were worked like slaves and given the barest minimum of food to survive. Eventually, my father died. The official reason was heart failure, the real reason was starvation and despair. I was a little stronger, I realised afterwards that he'd been giving me some of his food rations. I always wondered would he have lived if he hadn't done that. I managed to escape and made my way back to Kiev, where I was able to steal identity papers and start to build some sort of a life. When Germany invaded the Soviet Union I was immediately conscripted into the Red army. I fought in the Battle of Moscow and came out as a captain. But all I lived for was the hope that one day I would be able to get some sort of revenge on the communists. That is why I am here, Obersturmführer, for revenge, nothing more." I understood all too well, we were fellow travellers. Both fought for different reasons, neither expected nor wanted to survive the war. It was enough.

Müller was doing sterling work on the radio. He was giving fire control directions to the German guns then moving to the Russian radio and bringing their fire on their own troops in fluent Russian. Meanwhile, Tatiana roamed the roof spotting for targets and pointing them out for Müller to call in. It was a strange situation, quite surreal. Vasyl asked me about my reasons for being here and I told him of my conviction for murder in Berlin after I accidentally killed the man in a fight over a girl. Then my SS commission, following Heydrich's intervention. We both knew that the Allies would almost certainly win the war. It was impossible that Germany could in the long term survive the terrible slaughter and attrition of the fighting on the Eastern Front that was at its height here in Stalingrad. So here we both were, both fighting on the side of Germany, yet knowing that when the war was lost neither of us could go back to our own countries without being hunted like dogs and executed as traitors.

"Sir," Müller shouted, "Colonel Steinmetz is on the radio, he's asking for you."

"Yes, Sir?" I said to him.

"Wolf, a good job, we are all very grateful to you."

"Yes, Sir," I replied. "What did you want me for?"

"Ah, yes, well, we have a change of orders for you. Your Scharführer has told me about the Russian captain who has come over to our side, will you ask him if he has any information about Russian plans for a big attack. Intelligence has suggested that there are large troop movements in the rear and we cannot work out exactly where they are headed. Ask him if he knows anything, I'll wait."

I spoke to Vasyl. He had indeed seen elements of several Russian divisions building in the rear, both to the south and the north. If the Soviets managed to put together sufficient troops to both sides of Stalingrad this could only mean one thing. Encirclement. I told Colonel Steinmetz what he had said.

"Does this Ukrainian have any idea where the southern troop movements have been building?"

I asked Vasyl, "Yes, I have a good idea of where they have been assembling."

I passed the information to the Colonel. "Very good, hold your position. I'll get back to you in a few moments."

Once again the radio went silent. We sat watching the developing battle around us, feeling like Roman citizens watching teams of gladiators slaughtering each other in the Colosseum to slake our thirst for entertainment. Then Steinmetz came back on the radio.

"Right, listen carefully Obersturmführer Wolf. If Captain Vasyl agrees, we want you all to head south down the Volga until you are outside of the battle area. Then cross over the Volga, find a bridge or a boat. Head inland and find those Russian divisions. We need to know where they are, how strong they are, how well-equipped and the numbers of tanks. We have sent over a number of aerial reconnaissance missions but they must be very well hidden. The pilots haven't been able to find them so far. Is that clear? Ask Captain Vasyl."

Our ill-fated ride out of Stalingrad had taken yet another turn for the worse. How on earth could we make our way through territory that was infested with tens of thousands of Russian soldiers? I must have asked the question out loud, for I heard Vasyl supplying the answer.

"If we are hiding in a wood, surely we would surely disguise ourselves as trees. If we are hiding amidst an army of Russian soldiers," he paused.

Of course, the uniforms, the dead Russians in the room below.

"You realise of course that if the Russians catch us in their uniforms we would be tortured and shot as spies?" I told them.

"Do you think that if they caught you in German uniform it would be any different?" Vasyl replied.

None of us needed reminding of the atrocities that the Russians carried out on captured German soldiers. They were not noted for the niceties of war. Then again, our own troops were just as bestial to captured Russians. The technical difference of uniform was not even worthy of consideration. Capture would mean a painful and horrific death.

"We'd better make sure we are not captured," Tatiana said suddenly.

"We?" I said. "There is no we. If they catch us wearing their uniforms you would suffer much worse than us. We need to get you back to our lines."

"Wolf," she said to me, "I'm coming with you, do you honestly think that I would be safe in the midst of your troops?"

It was true. Both armies had been bestialised by the terrible slaughter of Stalingrad. The battle had turned ordinary men into vicious animals, clawing tooth and nail to survive in the tortured hell that was once a major industrial city. Her best chance for survival could be to come with us. If we were caught she would at least have the opportunity of a quick bullet in the head from her comrades, rather than the lingering torture of mass rape from sex starved Russian soldiers.

"Very well, it's agreed. Vasyl, would you go downstairs with Tatiana and sort out uniforms for the three of us."

The Ukrainian took Tatiana downstairs and began the gruesome task of sorting through the bodies to find the most usable of their uniforms and equipment. Within twenty minutes we were fitted out as a unit of the Soviet Political Commissar's Department. I wore the black leather jacket that was the mark of the commissar, with a pistol holster belted over the top carrying a Tokarev.

The Tokarev was the standard automatic service pistol for the Soviet military. The pistol was chambered for the 7.62x25mm Tokarev cartridge, luckily for us the cartridges were nearly identical to the German 7.63x25mm Mauser cartridge. We could use our own ammunition in these guns. Not that this was really a problem as we would find plenty of Soviet ammunition, usually on the large numbers of dead Soviet soldiers lying around the city. Very handy.

I tucked my Walther in the side pocket. In this conflict you could never have too many weapons. I had a Soviet standard issue helmet and carried my PPSh which was standard equipment in any case for the Soviets.

Müller was dressed as an NKVD sergeant, with Tatiana as his private soldier. She had managed to tuck her long hair up inside the helmet and had disguised her female face with streaks of black soot. Vasyl had kept his rank as a captain, but was now wearing the unit badges of the NKVD.

The NKVD, or correctly the People's Commissariat for Internal Affairs was the public and secret police organisation of the Soviet Union. This organisation directly executed the rule of power of the Soviets, including political repression, during the era of Stalin. The NKVD was large, even by Soviet or German standards, and contained the public police force of the USSR but is better known for the activities of the Gulag and the Main Directorate for State Security (GUGB).

Müller quickly transferred our radio equipment into a Soviet issue radio pack then smashed his MP38 so the Russians wouldn't be able to use it. He picked a PPSh for himself and gave Tatiana a Mosin Nagant. Although this was the standard issue of the Soviet infantryman he had managed to find her a sniper version of the rifle, a weapon I was well acquainted with and may well find a use for in the near future. Müller tucked his own Walther in his pocket, like me, and a Tokarev in another pocket. Vasyl came up to Tatiana and gave her another Tokarev pistol which she fastened in her belt under her jacket. You never knew when a concealed weapon would come in useful. He also had a PPSh and so we were able to feel reasonably confident that we could survive a very casual brush with the enemy. If the power of the NKVD and the fear they inspired did not do the job, our three submachine guns and the sniper rifle would stand us in good stead. We hoped.

"I understand that a Russian counter-attack is due at five o'clock," Vasyl told me. "It's almost certain that they will precede it with an artillery barrage, probably about an hour or so before the attack goes in. Might I suggest that we wait for the noise and chaos of the barrage to move off?"

That sounded like a good idea, I agreed with him, we would have about two hours to wait but it would be worthwhile. "Always assuming that the barrage doesn't target us," I replied to him.

He shrugged, if that happened the mission would be the least of our problems. We settled down to wait, keeping a wary eye on the ground around the signal box. Tatiana, surprisingly, went over to speak to Müller.

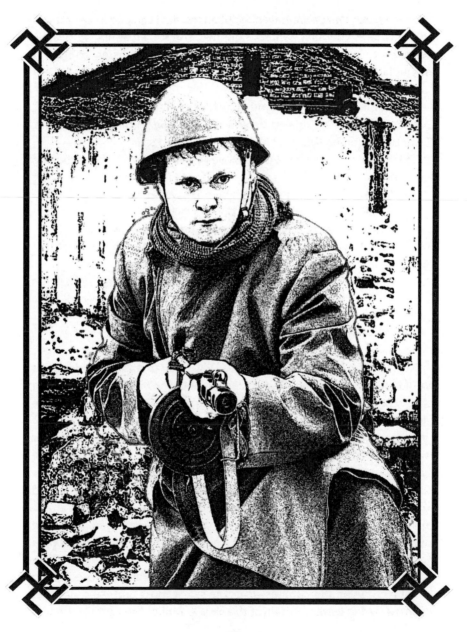

"Scharführer Müller, we haven't spoken much. I can't keep calling you Müller, what is your first name?" I grinned, she smiled at him so sweetly that the normal psychopathic grunt that came immediately to his lips was replaced by a mumbled and polite reply.

"It's Albert," he replied.

"Well, Albert, you never say much. Tell me something about yourself."

"Nothing to tell," he replied defensively, casually lighting his cigarette. "I was born, I joined the SS, I kill people. What's to tell?"

"Tell me about your father, did he love you very much?" She asked him earnestly.

"Stepfather! He hated me," he told her. "He was an absolute bastard."

"I'm sorry," she said. "What did he do for a living?"

"He worked on ships, running between Germany and Russia."

"So that's how you learned your fluent Russian? Haven't you got him to thank for that?"

"He beat it into me with a strap. No I didn't thank him for it, I killed him for it."

"You killed him? Your own father?" She asked, aghast.

"Yes, I killed him."

"You killed him because he beat you with a strap?" She asked.

"No, I killed him because he beat me with a strap and kept asking me stupid questions." Müller's eyes blazed at her. She flinched at the depth of hard bitter cruelty that she saw in the depths of his dark soul. Then she got up and moved away. Müller just closed his eyes and began to doze.

We were jolted by the start of the Russian artillery which started at twenty past four. We watched the shells landing to stir up even more rubble and dust, thankfully they were landing some distance from us. The quiet of the afternoon, so unexpected in this benighted city, had ended. Now the familiar crash of the guns firing, the explosion of shells, the whiplash crack of the sniper and small arms fire returned. Soon the city was once again hidden under a pall of smoke and dust, the senses assaulted by the endless barrage. It was time to move.

Müller picked up the radio pack. Vasyl led with Tatiana close behind him, then myself, the commissar, in the safest most protected position guarded by the lesser mortals of the NKVD. Müller brought up the rear carrying the radio pack. We left the station and trudged south, avoiding the bank of the Volga next to the central landing stage, until we were clear. At one time shots were near us, but a voice shouted in Russian and the firing stopped. After almost an hour we took a break. We were outside of the worst of the fighting area. It was time to move down to the river and find a crossing.

"Are you aware of any bridges, Vasyl?" I asked.

He shook his head. "No, none. They were all destroyed on Stalin's orders to stop the German advance."

So it would have to be a boat. We sipped water from our canteens then carried on. Soon the river came into view. A Russian soldier on the opposite bank waved to us. We waved back. Did he wonder if we were deserters from the fighting around the city? Even if he did, he would not dare to approach a commissar accompanied by an NKVD escort. We rounded a bend in the river and suddenly came across a boat tied to the bank, a rowing boat sufficient to carry us to the opposite bank. It was guarded by two soldiers. We approached them and they saluted nervously. I ignored the salute, I was a commissar.

"Whose boat is this?" I shouted at them.

"Captain Kerensky ordered us to guard it, Commissar, it is to be used to ferry our snipers across the river."

"I see. I am commandeering this boat for the People's Commissariat. We are on a special mission, stand aside."

"Yes, Commissar, but Captain Kerensky ordered us to guard it with our lives. We were not to give it to anyone, regardless of rank." The soldier, a corporal, squirmed as he spoke but bravely stood his ground.

"With your lives, eh?" I asked him.

"Yes, Commissar."

"Very well, so be it. Sergeant!" I called to Müller.

He was already behind them, the knife flashed twice and the two soldiers fell dying to the ground. I could feel Tatiana shudder. She was finding the killing overwhelming. An assault on the senses, a descent from the life she had known into a quagmire of brutality.

"Müller, Tatiana, get in the boat! Vasyl, give me a hand to throw these two in the river. There are enough bodies floating down the Volga, two more won't be noticed."

We threw the Russians into the river and Vasyl got into the boat. I untied her and pushed off, jumping in at the last minute. Vasyl got out the oars and began rowing. We crossed unnoticed, then scrambled out of the boat and up the bank. We stepped out into the Russian held sector and began hiking into the rear. After only ten minutes we were walking along a narrow lane between two hedgerows when a voice shouted out "Halt!"

A Soviet soldier stepped out, wearing the green flashes of an NKVD lieutenant. Camouflaged behind a bush I could make out the snout of a heavy machine gun pointed at us, with two more soldiers just visible behind the shield of the gun, manning it and ready to fire. This was not going well.

Neither were things going well back in the city, we afterwards learned. German tanks and infantry had completely surrounded the tractor factory and Spartakovka. They had cut the Soviet 62nd Army in two and almost captured its headquarters, but the Russians survived. By the night of October 16th our exhausted German divisions saw their attack halted. General von Paulus called Army Group B for all the reinforcements they could give him. Hitler had already sent reinforcements from the Replacement Army in Germany, there were no more fresh troops available to the 6th Army. The only option left open to him was to move troops from the quiet parts of the front, weakening their defences. The 6th Army was almost at a standstill.

APRIL 1944

I stood before the commandant of Stalag Luft III, a former Stuka pilot, Major Hans Buchmeister, now seconded to guard allied airmen prisoners after a Stuka mission in Stalingrad that had resulted in his injuries. Buchmeister had left Stalingrad on a Ju52 medical flight, his right arm torn off at the elbow, his lung punctured and his left leg shattered beyond repair. He now walked with a limp, obviously in constant pain. He looked at me incredulously.

"You come here to recruit for your SS-British Freecorps? Are you mad?

Squadron Leader Bader, although not the senior officer, virtually runs this camp. The other prisoners see him as a hero, as an inspiration. If you try and spout your Nazi nonsense here, they'll attack you."

"Then you'd better make sure your guards are alert, Major," I replied acidly. "Nazi nonsense? Are you referring to the Führer's policy of recruiting foreign prisoner volunteers for the SS? I wonder if Reichsführer Himmler is aware of your ideas?"

"You can't intimidate me, Obersturmführer," he smiled. "These wounds I took at Stalingrad, they give me nine months at most to live. So what can the SS or Gestapo do to me?"

"To you, perhaps nothing. To your family?" I replied softly.

"You SS bastard, now you threaten women and children?" he shouted.

"No, Major," I told him quietly, "I was at Stalingrad too. I'm just trying to stay alive. Why don't we both just do our jobs? Eh?"

He nodded and turned to the armed soldiers drawn up at the side of the guardhouse.

"Make sure you protect the Obersturmführer and his Scharführer at all times. Weapons loaded, any trouble or threats, open fire!"

"Sir," an anxious Luftwaffe corporal asked, "what if it is Bader?"

The major thought for a moment. "No, not him. If he causes trouble, and he will, just bring him to me."

The camp was based in Sagan, in Poland. It possessed a celebrity status, as the current home of the prisoner Squadron Leader Douglas Bader. The Royal Air Force officers stood at attention in front of me. Prominent in the front row was Bader. I thought of him flying a Hurricane fighter aircraft with artificial legs. I was unaware of any of our Luftwaffe pilots who flew with both legs missing. Quite a feat, how did he do it? During the summer of 1941 alone Bader obtained twelve kills. His overall total of twenty three victories made him the fifth highest ace in the RAF. However, on August 9th 1941 he suffered a mid-air collision near Le Touquet, France. He parachuted to the ground with both his artificial legs badly damaged. An impressive man, and one to be wary of. A man had to possess the most incredible amounts of guts, bravery and determination to have done what he did.

I mentally compared this neat, well run prison camp with those I had seen in Stalingrad. Of course, there was very little food in the Cauldron. I had visited the camp at Karpovka, the very name a byword for the cruelty of the guards, mainly Russian Tartars and Ukrainians. The inmates were literally starving to death. The tiny amount of food that was flown in by the Luftwaffe after the Russian encirclement was immediately seized on by the Werhmacht to feed the starving troops, although there was never enough even for them. Many of our German troops literally starved to death towards the end, thousands in one day. A Russian pilot shot down over Stalingrad or soldier taken prisoner, had only the prospect of slow starvation and freezing temperatures that would quickly kill him, or her. There were women pilots in the battle, women soldiers too. If starvation or typhus didn't get them, cannibalism was an option by no means uncommon. I realised that the nightmare was returning and I made a conscious effort to snap back to the present. Was it this prison camp that had made me think of capture? However, the Russian treatment of German prisoners would certainly have been very different to our own treatment of these captives. I shuddered at the cruel prospect of a Russian prison camp.

They stared at me in a hostile manner, middle and upper class Englishmen, the remnants of the once great but now crumbling British Empire. Fifty years ago their class would have been shooting tigers, or poling a punt at the Henley Regatta. They clearly wished that I was one tiger they could hunt and shoot. Thankfully they were not armed with hunting rifles. I gave them the standard speech. There was a brief silence then Bader stepped forward.

"What are you then, Hitler's bum boy?"

There was a roar of laughter. I had expected this. I nodded to the guards and they cocked their weapons. They were all armed with either MP38s or Kar98kinfantry rifles.

"No, Squadron Leader, I am an officer in the Waffen SS. Unlike you, I was not captured by my enemy," I replied acidly, managing to keep civil. It was a good return. The officers booed.

"Maybe you weren't captured by them, but you're fighting for them, old boy. How does it feel being a traitor?" Bader asked with a scowl.

"Not at all, Squadron Leader, I'm fighting the Russians, not the English.

Russians are your enemy, not the Germans. I do not fight you Britishers. My unit was formed exclusively to fight against the communists."

"That's a load of bollocks, and you know it," Bader said. "Whatever your story is, friend, you'll hang for it when the war ends, and that won't be too far away."

He was probably right. The Soviet counter-attacks were beginning to wear down our forces. The Russians were hitting us hard. I finished with my standard speech, invited any volunteers to come to the guardroom, knowing that none would come forward in this camp.

I turned away and began walking back to the guardroom. We would wait for a short time in case anyone did come forward to volunteer, then we could move on to the next and hopefully more productive camp. I felt something brush past my neck and fly past me, landing in the ground a short distance away. I walked over and picked it up. It was a sliver of glass, shaped like a knife. Bader stood there, he had obviously thrown it, he was challenging me to retaliate. I looked at him for a few seconds.

"With shooting like that, it's no wonder you were shot down by our Luftwaffe, Squadron Leader."

His face darkened as I turned away. I had taken a dislike to the Englishman, not for his politics, but there was something of the bully about him. I thought back to the genuinely good people I had fought with in Stalingrad.

Of Vasyl, the Ukrainian. And of course, Tatiana.

SS ENGLANDER

CHAPTER FIVE

OCTOBER 1942

For a moment, we froze at this unexpected obstacle. The NKVD lieutenant looked at us suspiciously, although I suspected that looking at people suspiciously was part of his training.

"Commissar, we did not expect a political unit to be coming this way. Could I see your orders?"

It was an awkward situation. I could see that he was confused about how much power he could exercise in this encounter. It was not that he suspected we may have been anything other than what we appeared to be, a political commissar with a small NKVD escort. No, this unit was here for one reason and one reason only. Comrade Stalin and his order "not a step back".

Order No. 227, as it was known, had been issued in July and it was the order that gave the entire Soviet war machine its overall war strategy. The basic principal was that each Soviet army had to create blocking detachments and penal battalions to stop the continued retreat of Soviet forces. The most important line though, was that no commander had the right to retreat without an express order. Anyone who did so was subject to a military tribunal, usually the kind of tribunal that involved a 7.62mm bullet to the head. The NKVD had been tasked to implement the order in the most basic way. Soldiers had a simple choice of going forward to fight the Germans in Stalingrad, or back to be shot by the NKVD.

I began fumbling in the pocket of my leather jacket as if looking for my orders. It was a situation that seemed to be doomed to failure no matter what we did. Quite simply, without being able to offer the proof of a written order, even a commissar could be arrested and shot on suspicion of deserting the battle. That was Stalin's order, and they were carrying it out enthusiastically. Very enthusiastically. It was not just soldiers who were subject to this draconian treatment. Unarmed and innocent civilians seen moving in the direction of the German lines were frequently fired on by the Russians, who regarded them as nothing more than traitors. Men, women, children, it made no difference.

"One moment, lieutenant, I have it here. May I compliment you on your conscientious performance, you are perfectly correct to ask to see our orders." I could feel the butt of the Tokarev in my hand. I was trying to work out how to shoot the officer through the pocket of my leather jacket without alerting the soldiers manning the machine gun. If any of us had tried to openly raise a weapon, the gunners would surely open fire immediately. The only way was to finish this lieutenant quickly and surreptitiously. I fumbled a bit more, seeing his eyes harden with suspicion at the delay. I managed to release the safety catch of the Tokarev and began to take up the pressure on the trigger. In the instant before I was about to fire, a roaring noise filled the sky as a pair of Luftwaffe ME 109's hurtled down towards us.

"Attack!" The lieutenant shouted, diving for the shelter of a ditch next to the track. The four of us tumbled after him, just in time to escape the hammer blows of machine gun bullets that sprayed the ground around us, sending up spurts of dust and foliage to obscure the position like a cloud. I could hear the raucous clatter of the Soviet heavy machine gun as the gunners tried to range in on the Messerschmidts. With a powerful and improved Daimler-Benz DB 601 engine and heavy cannon and machine gun armament the Bf 109E was deadly to both ground forces and anything the Soviet air force could throw at it. And so it proved today.

The machine gun nest disappeared in a hail of machine gun fire and the slamming, heavy punch of cannon rounds as they carried out their deadly work of destruction. The guns ceased firing. I could see the machine gun crew flung into awkward positions on the ground, their uniforms and bodies covered in blood where they had been literally shredded by the incoming fire.

I heard a gurgling noise, fearing one of us had been hit. I looked around and saw Vasyl with his hands around the throat of the lieutenant. The man's face had gone purple as he struggled to drag air into his lungs. Then his eyes bulged and his struggles stopped, his body going limp. I looked at Vasyl, he nodded, the man was dead.

"The machine gun," he said, "we need to deal with it."

I shook my head and pointed towards the destroyed weapon and crew.

"We need to move on," I ordered, "let's go."

We pushed on into the countryside. In the distance we could faintly hear the sound of gunfire coming from the direction of Stalingrad as the opposing armies continued slugging it out with each other. As we moved on the battle seemed to diminish and almost disappear. There were no aircraft in the sky near us, the artillery fire was quite faint to the ears and for the first time in Stalingrad I actually heard the sound of birdsong. The only thing that flew over us was a flight of ducks, sensibly heading away from the city. They honked occasionally, a cheery reminder that there was more to life than the mechanical destruction of property and human beings. A group of trees stood near the track we were following, an amazing sight in itself after the fighting in Stalingrad where every single tree had either been destroyed by gunfire and high explosives or chopped down for firewood. Roosting in the trees was a group of wood pigeons. Müller seemed fascinated by them. Then he astonished us by identifying and describing them.

"They're Turmani pigeons," he said. "They're native in this part of Russia as well as quite a few other areas in this part of Europe. They're one of the oldest established groups of Russian pigeons and by far the most unique family of breeds in Russia. You can see their defining features, long sweeping backs with their wings carried below or on the sides of the tail and a boney, squarish head with rounding edges."

The three of us were open mouthed with astonishment. "Scharführer, did I hear correctly? How do you know so much about pigeons?" I asked him.

"It was my hobby when I was a boy. My father spent much of his free time bird watching. Occasionally he took me."

"Yet you killed him," said Tatiana, aghast.

"He was good with birds, but not with me," he replied significantly.

We all wondered what on earth his father could have done to him to deserve being killed by his own son. What horrors had Albert Müller suffered to drive him to do such a terrible thing? And what kind of man was the father? One moment the passionate birdwatcher, the next the cause of infinite suffering to his own son.

We walked further along the track, enjoying the late afternoon sunshine. We cautiously entered a village, perhaps it would more accurately be called a hamlet. It was just a collection of eight roughly made huts, squalid and in disrepair with no glass in the windows and just old sacking hanging in the gaps to keep the elements out. There were several peasant women working around the huts, cutting wood and preparing vegetables in the open. Two old men sat outside a doorway staring at us. They were toothless and bald and looked to be a hundred years old, although in this desolate place they were probably no more than fifty. There were no children. The men and women eyed us cautiously. No doubt they had seen NKVD and political commissars before, living this close to Stalingrad. I greeted the women in fluent Russian.

"Good afternoon, grandmothers. It's a beautiful day."

None of them replied, they just stared at us. Then a man came out of one of the houses. He was a pitiful sight with one arm missing and one leg obviously amputated from the knee down. He walked awkwardly on a wooden stump, but he greeted us cheerfully enough.

"Comrades," he called. "May I welcome you to our village. We are always happy to see our comrades of the Red Army. Will you take some food with us?"

We looked at each other, Müller shrugged. Vasyl raised his eyes, why not? I accepted the invitation and we went into the man's house. It was rank and stinking, I doubted that hygiene was one of his priorities. But he was friendly enough and it turned out he was an old soldier who had been wounded last year during Barbarossa, the massive German invasion of Russia in July 1941. Our incredible invasion of the Soviet Union had involved over four and a half million troops. It was the largest military offensive in history. Over half a million motor vehicles were used and it was the showcase of our armed forces. We conquered vast areas of the Soviet Union and inflicted heavy losses on the Red Army, but they were still fighting.

We chatted about the Battle of Stalingrad, it was not difficult. We were able to describe in accurate detail the course of the battle, from the Russian point of view of course.

"And when the new armies attack the fascists, we will drive them out of mother Russia forever," he said.

I looked at Müller and Vasyl. 'New armies' sounded ominous, it was the kind of information we had come to get. Something about the man's voice suggested that these new armies were a 'fait accompli' rather than Russian future planning. He described them as if they were existing armies. If we were hit in Stalingrad with a major offensive by substantial new Russian forces, it would be devastating. Vasyl tried to draw him out.

"Yes, we are on our way to headquarters at the moment, I think we may be lost. Are we going in the right direction?"

The man laughed. "Of course, of course. There is only one way, we are not living in the city of Moscow with many streets. The lane outside is the only route to 8th Shock Army HQ. It's about ten kilometres further along."

Vasyl thanked him and a woman, presumably his wife, brought us food. The bowls were roughly hewn out of pieces of wood. The stew in them was thin and stringy, it tasted awful. But it was hot food, probably the last we would eat for some time. We ate the meal in its entirety, then the woman brought us second helpings, which we also wolfed down. I handed out cigarettes and we all lit up, smoking contentedly. The old soldier brought out a stone jar of vodka from under the table. It tasted like cleaning fluid and was certainly home-made but strangely we enjoyed it, this humble food and drink from these poor peasants in the decrepit hut. It was like the widow's mite, they gave us everything they had to offer. Afterwards I pressed some roubles into his hand. He shouted that he would not take money from comrades, so I gave it to his wife and told her to use it to buy some meat. She smiled in appreciation and tucked the money in a drawer. Then we picked up our weapons, shouted our goodbyes and carried on along the track. I felt guilty about deceiving the crippled old soldier whilst receiving his hospitality, but I mentally shrugged, it was war.

Soon the track widened, then widened still more, it appeared to have recently been enlarged. A platoon of Russian infantry came towards us, the officer giving me a salute which I returned gravely. We came upon a wood just off of the track, through the trees we could see the dark steel outlines of T34 tanks. We kept walking and there were more tanks, then still more. There must have been dozens of them, possibly a hundred. We got to an intersection where a Willys jeep was stopped right on the crossroads.

The Willys MB US Army Jeep was a small four-wheel drive utility vehicle that performed a similar role as our own Volkswagen Kübelwagen, though the VW used an air-cooled engine and lacked four-wheel drive. Large numbers of these vehicles had been sent by the Americans to help the Soviets in their fight against our forces.

A Soviet Lieutenant-General was standing to the side of the jeep, red faced and shouting at the men around him. Then he saw my unit and called over to us.

"Comrade Commissar, you, I want you over here, quickly!"

We went over to find out what he wanted. "Yes, General?" I replied, slightly coldly. He may have been a full general but I was a political commissar and even generals had to treat us with a little respect.

"Commissar, what mission are you on?" he asked me.

"General, we have just completed an operation in the city, we are reporting back to our unit."

"Excellent," he said. "I need to borrow you for just a couple of hours. I have two divisions of tanks, T34's, coming along this road in the next twenty minutes or so. I need somebody capable and efficient to point them in the right direction, these fools haven't got a clue," he gesticulated at the hapless Russian soldiers that surrounded him. "I need somebody with some authority and intelligence to point my tanks in the right direction. Otherwise we'll have them driving all over Russia. Will you do that for me, Commissar? I just want you and your men to direct my tank divisions for an hour or so, maybe two hours until they have passed, send them in the right direction."

I had little choice. To refuse may well have invited suspicion.

"Of course, General," I replied. "May I have your name, Sir?"

"I am General Shumilov of the 64th. Make certain that my tanks take the road to the west," he pointed in the direction of Stalingrad. It was another track that had also been substantially widened recently. "If you send them down that road," he pointed to the track we had just emerged from, "they'll get totally bogged down and stuck, it will be chaos. Any questions?"

"That's perfectly clear, General. I will make certain it is done exactly as you say."

"Excellent, man, excellent. Driver!" he shouted. "We need to get going. You men," he pointed towards the soldiers, "you can rejoin your unit. Hurry up men, double time." He climbed aboard the Willys jeep and roared off.

I looked at my people, Vasyl, Müller and Tatiana. Slowly we started to smile, then simultaneously burst out laughing.

"My God, Wolf," said Vasyl, "what an opportunity. We'll direct his tanks, no problem."

"Straight into the Volga, I presume?" said Müller.

"Definitely," I said. "We'll see how many of them come through, send them down through the village and then we can make a report to headquarters. I imagine that Colonel Steinmetz will be interested to hear what we have seen and heard this afternoon."

"Your colonel may be interested," said Vasyl, "but I don't think he will be pleased. Neither, I think, will the 6th Army High Command."

None of us were in any doubt it was the worst possible news we could be giving them.

For the next two hours we happily carried out the orders of General Shumilov. Tank after tank rolled past, every single one a brand new, gleaming T34. Without doubt the Soviets had been putting massive resources into building up their stocks of tanks and we were now observing the results at first hand. When the last tank had rolled by we compared notes. We estimated two hundred and ten tanks had rolled past us, together with their supply vehicles and fuel bowsers. I estimated that this quantity of Soviet tanks in the right hands could punch a hole right through our lines in the city. Assuming, of course, that Stalingrad was their destination. Was this the only element of tank reinforcements or were there others? With a few tank divisions both to the north and the south of Stalingrad, together with enough divisions of motorised infantry, the Russians would be able to turn the tables on our German forces. In effect they would be in a position to use the German tactic of encirclement against ourselves. Did they have the generals clever enough to plan and implement this kind of grand strategy, I wondered? It was common knowledge that Stalin had all but annihilated the senior officer corps of the Red Army in the late thirties.

Between 1937 and 1938 a series of massive repressions against kulaks, ethnic minorities and family members of the political opposition were undertaken throughout the Soviet Union as part of Stalin's Great Purge that lasted until the end of 1938. The purge was also responsible for the deaths of the majority of the senior Red Army officers, leaving only new and inexperienced commanders to face the German onslaught. At least a million Soviets, civilian and military, were executed and millions more sent to labour camps.

Now, however, we were faced with an enemy who was learning fast. The commander of the Stalingrad defences, General Chuikov, was proving himself to be no fool. After the collapse of the Soviet army and air force during the invasion of Barbarossa last year, it had become much too easy for the German forces to severely underestimate the Russians, often with fatal consequences. Who would have believed after the massive German attack on Stalingrad that the city would still be holding out? Yet it was, not only holding out, we had seen the evidence of Russian preparations for a probable counter-attack. One thing was certain. We had drastically underrated the ability of the Russians to fight, and to fight back.

"Ok, we'd better get moving," I said to the others. "The Russians we sent down to that little village will have realised by now that we misled them. Once they have untangled themselves and turned around they'll be back in force, and I don't want to be around when two hundred T34s start shooting at us."

We picked up our packs and headed across country, moving further south away from the city and also further away from the massive Russian build up. Without looking further, it was clear that Russian intentions were to mount a major counter-attack in the near future, using overwhelming

force. Russian tactics with tank divisions always meant the inevitable accompaniment of several divisions of motor-rifle troops, together with the Red air force flying Sturmovik fighter-bombers. It was time to report to Steinmetz. We walked south for an hour, the light was fading and we found a convenient clump of trees in which to camp overnight. Müller set up the radio and almost immediately got in touch with HQ. I gave my report to Colonel Steinmetz.

"There cannot be any doubt about this? He asked. "Over two hundred T34s, all brand new, all taking up positions near the city?"

"Sir, I have no doubt about the numbers, but where they will be deploying is impossible to estimate."

I told him about my suspicions of a Russian encirclement of our position in the city.

"My God," he said, "it hardly seems possible. Intelligence has been reporting that the Russians are all but beaten. Now you're telling us that they have fresh divisions of tanks ready to mount a new attack, with heaven only knows how many divisions of troops in support. It defies belief. All we have on the flanks are the Romanians and the Italians." He didn't need to add that these 'allies' were not expected to put up an effective resistance to a mass Russian attack, ill equipped and badly led, they were, with a few notable exceptions, little more than useless.

"That may be, Sir," I replied. "But we have seen it with our own eyes. If the Soviets do go for an encirclement they could trap us completely in the city and pick us off like dogs. Perhaps it's time for von Paulus to consider withdrawing to the west."

"Impossible," he replied. "The Führer has made it quite clear. The 6th Army has been ordered to take Stalingrad at any cost. Any kind of retreat is out of the question."

"I understand, Colonel," I said. "But if the Russians do attack to the north and south using huge numbers of new tanks and troops, I can only hope that our next flight out of Stalingrad doesn't crash like the last one. I have a very bad feeling about this."

He told us to wait and went away to talk to his superiors. In view of the information we had just given him I imagined that he may well be talking to von Paulus himself. I afterwards found out that Paulus was struck

114

down with dysentry and wasn't available to discuss anything, other than when the next supplies of toilet paper would arrive. In any case, he came back on the radio after forty minutes to give me his orders.

"Obersturmführer, you are to bring your party back to the city. I know you are anxious to get a flight back to Berlin and we have had enquiries from Prince Albrecht Strasser requesting your return to Berlin. Despite the obvious difficulties that your information has given us, currently we hold most of the city. It is almost ours, perhaps one more push and it will be ours. I want you to make your way back through the Russian lines to an area just north of the central landing stage. You will see the Red October Factory in front of you when you know you are in the correct place."

He passed on information about times, recognition signals and the means of getting us across. Apparently German sappers would be coming over in an inflatable boat to ferry us over the Volga.

"When you can see the hill of Mamayev Kurgan in front of you and the tractor factory to the right, you will be in the right place. One more thing, Obersturmführer, you remember the Russian general you brought in for us?"

"Of course, Sir," I replied. "I trust that he has been singing to your intelligence people."

"That's just the point. They have managed to squeeze some information out of him." I wondered as he said it quite what form the squeezing took. I didn't need to wonder about whether it was painful not, neither our army nor the Russians were known to use soft tactics when questioning prisoners.

"The problem is," he continued, "I've gone over the report of his interrogation and there's nothing there to substantiate your report about the new tanks. It could be he's holding out on us, or he may not know anything about it. Either way, people are going to have another bash at him and see what they can find out. In the meantime, Obersturmführer, headquarters wants you to do your best to bring in another high ranking officer on your way through their lines. We must have more intelligence. I doubt you'll be lucky enough to pick up another general, but a major or other senior officer would be sufficient. We'll be expecting you at about ten tomorrow night, make sure you give the correct recognition signal, I don't want our machine gunners opening fire on your group."

I heartily agreed with him, neither did I want our machine gunners shooting up my unit. As for another prisoner, a senior officer, we would be making our way through Russian lines masquerading as a Political Commissar and NKVD escort, so we would be in a good position to take the opportunity to grab a suitable officer if it arose. I smiled to myself, with my credentials, if I found someone useful I could just arrest them. That was the kind of power that the Commissars Department and the NKVD possessed.

"We'll do our best, Sir, we'll see you tomorrow night. Wolf out."

The others had overheard our orders. Nobody was happy about making the crossing directly back into the Cauldron of Stalingrad. We had been planning to cross further south, several kilometres down river, well away from the main fighting. But orders were orders.

"Scharführer Müller," I ordered, "we'll be pushing off at two thirty in the morning. We'll get some rest here, I want you to take the first watch. Wake me in an hour. Vasyl, you can take the watch after me."

The Ukrainian nodded. "What about me?" Tatiana asked. I smiled, "You get your beauty sleep, you'll need it for tomorrow. Who knows, you might be able to charm us through the Russian lines with your smile."

Vasyl and Müller laughed, Tatiana just looked tight-lipped.

"Wolf, in the Red Army women fight alongside men and are given the same duties."

"Tatiana," I smiled at her. "You are not a trained soldier, not like the ugly women that I've seen fighting in the Russian lines. Besides, we are only trying to look like Russian troops, we don't want to copy their chain of command. Or would you like me to send you to the Gulag for disobeying an order?"

The others chuckled, but Tatiana just did not see the joke. She sat down and made herself comfortable, getting ready to get some sleep. Vasyl and I lay down too and before long I started to doze, leaving Müller on watch. We took our turns on sentry duty and while the sky was still dark, we picked up our packs and weapons and began to trek northwest, heading back to the city of Stalingrad through the lines of the Red Army.

I estimated that we had fifteen kilometres to travel, the timing would be critical. We needed to arrive opposite the Red October Tractor Factory just before ten o'clock, without arousing any suspicions in the inevitable ranks of Soviet troops we would encounter on the way.

Progress meant endless detours to avoid Soviet checkpoints, the real NKVD were on alert and obviously suspicious of everyone that passed. In fact, apart from the NKVD checkpoints, the first twelve kilometres were impossibly easy. We were amazed at the scarcity of Russian troops on the ground and the ease with which we got past them. Our disguise was our biggest weapon, taking advantage of the terror that the average Soviet soldier had of Stalin's political police. We took a break when we were only three kilometres away from our destination, the Russian held east bank of the Volga. It was lunchtime, so we ate some of our rations and sipped water, totally exhausted by our journey so far. We had time to spare as we had several hours in which to cover the last three kilometres. Finally I ordered the group to get moving. Wearily we got up, shouldered our packs and weapons and moved off. Within half a kilometre we were in trouble.

We had reached the edge of a small thicket and were about to emerge into the open when we saw a camouflaged position consisting of several tents in front of us. There were at least twenty NKVD guards around it and aerials mounted on poles close to the main command tent. We had bumped into somebody very senior indeed, it was certain that only a senior officer or commissar would have such a large NKVD contingent guarding them. Vasyl slipped away to find out more. We took off our packs and sat down to wait for his return.

"Who are you? Identify yourselves, which unit are you from?"

We all jumped and I whipped round to see that an NKVD officer had come up stealthily behind us. I assumed he had been relieving himself in the bushes and had found us unexpectedly.

"The question is, who are you, Captain? Or do you normally address Comrade Stalin's political commissars so rudely? Identify yourself, man."

His belligerent expression softened a little, but he was still clearly suspicious. He was holding a Tokarev pistol in his right hand and although he lowered it a little, he didn't put it away.

117

"I am Captain Poliarkov, Comrade Commissar, attached to Comrade Khruschev's NKVD escort. And you, Comrade Commissar?"

Stalin had appointed Khruschev as a senior political commissar. He had served on a number of fronts as an intermediary between the local military commanders and the political rulers in Moscow. Stalin used him to keep his commanders on a tight leash, while the commanders themselves sought to have Khruschev influence the communist dictator. It was well known that he was working with the military here in Stalingrad to stiffen the defences to help save the city. It was also well known that he was one of the chief butchers.

"I am Commissar Ivanov, Captain, on attachment to General Shulimov's staff."

His eyes narrowed with suspicion. To all outward appearances we were exactly who we pretended to be, a political commissar with his NKVD escort. I was however unlikely to carry the authority of his own boss, Stalin's personal political representative on the Stalingrad front, Nikita Khruschev. My best guess was the NKVD Captain was fairly certain that we were deserters, and his next words seemed to confirm this.

"But General Shulimov is nowhere near here. I need to see your papers, Comrade. Now!" He held out his left hand for my papers.

"Certainly, Captain," I replied. "I have my orders in a pouch inside my pack."

I took off the pack playing for time, trying to gain some advantage so we could somehow get past the Tokarev that was pointing at me once more.

"Be careful, Comrade Commissar," the captain said. "I have no doubt that you are who you say you are, but we have direct orders from Comrade Stalin to check everyone who doesn't seem to be at their proper post."

"That's no problem," I replied, smiling at him, "I have my orders here."

I rummaged through my pack, wishing I'd had the foresight to have hidden a pistol there for just this kind of occasion.

"Captain," I said, standing up, "I cannot find them. I'm sorry, we have seen some action, they must have been lost."

"Perhaps so, Comrade Commissar," he said. Now the menace in his voice was unmistakable, he was absolutely certain that he'd come across

119

a group of high ranking deserters. "You must come with me to Comrade Khruschev's headquarters, you can speak to him. He is the senior ranking commissar on the Stalingrad Front and he has complete authority to decide if you are to be believed. I must insist that you put your hands up and....."

He collapsed on the ground with a sigh. Vasyl had returned and worked his way behind the man. Now his hunting knife stuck in the captain's back as he lay lifeless on the ground.

I considered briefly making a try at Khruschev, but then dismissed it. He was surrounded by at least twenty guards that we could see, almost certainly there were many more in the immediate vicinity. This was a very powerful man indeed, Stalin's own protégé. Vasyl pulled his victim into the undergrowth and Tatiana helped to cover the body with foliage. Already she seemed to becoming hardened to the blood and death that was Stalingrad. We retraced our steps for two kilometres until we were well away from Khruschev's headquarters. Then we took a detour, heading northeast to go past our intended destination and then cut back along the riverbank. My memory of that incident stayed with me for a long time, I had come so close to Nikita Khruschev, Comrade Stalin's right-hand man and personal butcher. Would it have altered the course of the war to kill him? Probably not. History would have to be the judge of that.

We had been weaving in and out of the Russian lines, carefully avoiding any obvious concentrations of troops. So far our cover had held and the Russian soldiers tended to avoid us. Darkness began to fall and we could see the river looming about half a kilometre ahead of us, backlit by the flames of Stalingrad. So far, we had not managed to find a single senior officer we could have taken prisoner without starting a firefight we couldn't win. Then fortune favoured us in the shape of a Soviet jeep, apparently broken down at the side of the track we were walking down.

The vehicle was a GAZ 64, the Soviet equivalent of the American Jeep and our own Kübelwagen. It was lightweight, equipped with a 3.3 litre petrol engine and intended to be used as a command vehicle. It was very rugged, versatile and excellent off-road, though of inferior build and reliability to its German and American equivalents.

A colonel of the Red Army sat in the jeep, with a lieutenant next to

him. The colonel was haranguing a hapless Russian corporal who was trying to restart the engine, his head under the bonnet as he worked. I looked around. We seemed to be in the clear. I nodded to the others to be prepared and walked forward to the jeep.

"Comrade Colonel," I said. "You seem to have some sort of a problem."

The colonel looked startled. It was difficult to tell in the fading light but was that fear I could see in his face? And the jeep was obviously heading away from Stalingrad, not towards it. A deserter?

"Yes, Comrade Commissar, this fool of a corporal stalled the engine and now he can't get it started."

I tried to put my nastiest, most suspicious face on. I needed to totally subdue this man by the sheer force of the political department that I represented with commissar's credentials and NKVD escort.

"Your papers, Comrade Colonel!" I asked, my hand held out.

"Err, yes, Comrade Commissar. We are going to collect supplies from the quartermaster. I do not have a written order."

I smiled. "Colonel, I must place you under arrest, you will come with us. You two," I said pointing at the lieutenant and the corporal, "you may leave the GAZ where it is and report back to your unit. You can tell them that your colonel will be answering some serious questions for the Political Department. Now go, I suggest you hurry, before anyone thinks you may be trying to leave the battlefront."

The two men saluted, mumbled their thanks and headed towards the river. I imagine they were deserting a unit that was stationed there, possibly waiting to cross over and join the battle.

"Vasyl, find some wire or line and tie him up." I ordered.

The colonel started protesting, blustering that I could not tie up a senior officer of the Red Army.

"Colonel, I can shoot a senior officer of the Red Army if I so choose. I am empowered to do so by Comrade Stalin. If you would prefer me to shoot you, you only need to say."

"No, no!" the colonel capitulated, holding his hands up for Vasyl to fasten them with some thin electrical wire he'd ripped from the wiring of the jeep. Müller took out a greasy piece of rag and gagged the astonished officer.

"Let's move," I ordered. We started forward, herding the prisoner along. We reached the east bank of the Volga by nine o'clock and waited. At ten o'clock Müller got out his torch and flashed the recognition signal across. There was an answering signal, a few minutes later we made out the dim shape of a rubber boat paddling towards us. The bow hit the shore and four men jumped out with MP 38s pointed towards us.

"It's ok," I said to them in German, "we are on your side. Our orders are from Colonel Bernard Steinmetz, General von Paulus' intelligence officer."

They shone torches at us and inspected our faces, eventually they were convinced. We pushed our prisoner into the boat and Vasyl held him down on the floor while the troopers paddled us back across. We landed once more on the shore of the city at Stalingrad and found that Colonel Steinmetz had a jeep waiting for us, a Kübelwagen, to take us to HQ. We drove between the piles of rubble without incident and soon stopped outside von Paulus' headquarters. We delivered the Red Army colonel to the Abwehr office and then were ushered into Steinmetz's office to make our report. We were chatting to Steinmetz when the door opened. Steinmetz went quiet, stood to attention and there stood Friedrich von Paulus, General, Commander of the 6th Army, Hitler's warlord in Stalingrad.

"Are these the men?" he asked Steinmetz, who nodded. We did not look very prepossessing, filthy, tired and scruffily attired in Red Army uniforms.

"Your information must be wrong, Obersturmführer," he said abruptly.

"General," I began, but he held up a hand to stop me.

"I have conferred with Wehrmacht Intelligence in Berlin, the Abwehr and Führer HQ in Rastenberg. They are quite definite. Based on Luftwaffe reconnaissance and our own prisoner interrogations, there is no Soviet build up outside of Stalingrad."

I stared at him. He was pale, sickly looking, a tic constantly jumped in his right eye. This was the general in command of our 6th Army?

"You may submit a written report of what you observed to my office in the morning. Obersturmführer, I assume you are not a trained intelligence officer?"

"No, Sir," I replied.

"I thought not. But thank you for your efforts. You may be pleased to

know that we have just secured the area of Spartakovka, it now belongs to us. The Russians are in full retreat." He looked at me sardonically, "Which does not, of course, give much credence to your information. Good night, gentlemen."

We stared after him. Müller, Vasyl, Tatiana and myself looked at each other, open mouthed, aghast. He must have taken leave of his senses, or did he know something we didn't? Who needed to be an intelligence officer to count tanks?

"I'm afraid that the General has just pronounced the official verdict from Führer HQ. No tanks. I suggest you get some sleep, I will try and arrange a flight out in the next few days," Colonel Steinmetz informed us.

We exchanged salutes and left. I think it was at that moment we realised the madness, the delusion that occupied the minds of out leaders. We realised that the war was lost.

APRIL 1944

I looked at the lines of PoWs stood to attention in front of me. I recalled the troops that had fought on the Stalingrad front, on both sides, were probably amongst the toughest and finest that both Germany and Russia would ever produce. In contrast, these men in front of me looked neither fine nor tough. We were in Stalag XXI-B situated in Thure, Poland. The soldiers were principally British, and I understood that the camp had something of a reputation for being an easy regime. So much so that there appeared to be a kind of unwritten agreement between the prisoners and guards. Each kept a low profile. There were no prisoner escapes or excesses of brutality and discipline by the guards. Of course food was short, as it was across the whole of the Third Reich, but other than that these men had probably the best of the war. I gave them my stock speech as usual.

This time, however, I noticed several of the men looking at me with interest. Himmler's office had been very firm. They were increasingly disappointed with the poor results achieved so far in my prison camp recruitment drive. Personally, I couldn't care less which side these men fought for, or whether they fought at all. Quite obviously the war was lost. Out of the corner of my eye I could see the contrails of a bomber formation, probably American, returning from a terror raid against the shrinking German territories. It was nothing unusual, the British and American air forces seemed to have complete control of the skies and it appeared there was very little the Luftwaffe was able to do about it.

So why would any allied prisoner consider joining the German cause, the losing side? Boredom? Or perhaps they had some kind of a suicide wish. Either way if I could leave this place with several of them signed up it would at least keep Himmler off of my back for the time being. Müller and I dismissed them and went to the guardroom to wait and see if anyone volunteered. Within minutes the door opened and one of the PoWs stepped in.

"Your name?" I asked him.

"Henderson, Private Ian Henderson," he replied, standing at attention.

"I am Obersturmführer Wolf, as you already know, Private. Why do you wish to join the Waffen SS-British Freecorps?"

"To be honest with you, I'm fed up sitting in this camp. I joined Oswald Mosley's Black Shirts before the war and I always thought that he had the right idea. The real enemy has always been Stalin."

"Are you prepared to fight on the Russian front?" I asked him.

"Yes Sir. Absolutely."

I nodded to Müller, who led him away into the waiting room next door. The door knocked again and I had a similar interview with a Pioneer Corps corporal. Like Pte Henderson he had been a Black Shirt sympathiser and was keen to get out of the camp, where his fascist leanings had caused him to receive more than one beating at the hands of his unsympathetic fellow prisoners. By the time we got in the Kübelwagen to drive away we had six men waiting in the guardroom for SS transport to collect them and deliver them to our SS-British Freecorps barracks outside Berlin.

I thought back to Stalingrad, where returning to Berlin was something that was uppermost in my mind, in everyone's mind. The question of how to avoid a starving, freezing death in that war ravaged hell.

CHAPTER SIX

NOVEMBER 1942

We stood to attention, facing Himmler's hatchet man, Standartenführer Neurath. "The Reichsführer has read your report, Obersturmführer, you have had an interesting time on the Eastern Front. He wishes to know more about your assessment of General von Paulus. Your report suggests that he is not entirely as reliable as one would wish for in an army commander. Would you care to elaborate on that?"

Neurath was quite obviously looking for more ammunition his boss Himmler could use to play the power game that went on endlessly between the Wehrmacht and the SS. The winner, of course, would have immense power in the Third Reich, second only to Adolf Hitler. Each side fought relentlessly to gain influence. The stakes were high, complete control of the entire German armed forces for themselves. This was a very dangerous game and I was determined not to get involved!

"We only saw General von Paulus very briefly, Standartenführer. I really know nothing more than what I put in the report."

I remembered the pale, ill, twitching figure of von Paulus as we left his HQ. Personally, I wouldn't have given the man command of a supply company, let alone the 6th Army, but that was not my business. After we left the headquarters building we had spent a very restless night camped in a former stable nearby. In the morning a runner came and told us to get back to HQ quickly. A Junkers 52 with supplies was due at Gumrak airfield shortly and would be ferrying out the wounded. There would be space for us on the aircraft. Apparently Himmler had insisted that his SS people had priority and forced von Paulus to grant us seats on the plane. We rushed back and got a lift in a Kübelwagen that was just leaving for the airfield. Thankfully the artillery barrages had not yet started and we had a bumpy yet uneventful journey to the landing strip. Wehrmacht pioneers and Russian prisoners had rushed to repair the shell holes that pockmarked the tarmac. At the side I could see rows of stretchers loaded with wounded for evacuation. It was a pitiful sight, they were covered in bloody bandages, attendants hovering over them with drip bags, trying to keep them alive and as out of pain as was possible.

The city was still quiet and we were able to hear the sound of engines as the Junkers 52 approached the airfield. It circled once while the pilot checked the ground conditions. Then it smacked down on the runway, bouncing on the shock absorbers, the tyres smoking as the pilot applied maximum braking power before his aircraft went off the runway. The repair job had been carried out in record time, but the best they could do was to bring into service the runway that was much shorter than it had been before the fighting started.

The Junkers taxied up to where the rows of stretchers and their attendants were waiting. Immediately the aircraft door was flung open and two Luftwaffe personnel jumped out shouting to the stretcher bearers to load the wounded. The stretchers were quickly brought to the aircraft door and then lifted inside with as much care as tough, war hardened veterans were able to employ. No one cried out, the silence was eerie. I would have expected the men to be screaming in agony. Some of the wounds were terrible, missing limbs and huge wounds barely covered by the bloody bandages wrapped around them. The pain must have been intense. Yet the soldiers bore it stoically, perhaps the prospect of leaving the embattled city was enough of an anaesthetic for them. A Luftwaffe Feldwebel called us over.

"You are Obersturmführer Wolf?"

"That is correct, I am Wolf, this is Scharführer Müller. This lady is in my unit, as is Vasyl here, one of our Ukrainian allies."

He shook his head. "I'm sorry Sir. I only have orders for you, the Scharführer and the woman. Nothing about the Ukrainian, I cannot take

him."

"Feldwebel," I told him, "Vasyl is coming with us, orders or no orders. He is part of my group."

"That may be, Obersturmführer, but without orders he does not get on this aircraft." The man folded his arms and looked truculent, although a little nervous. We had seen a lot of action in the past few days, and it showed. Ragged uniforms, dirty, scarred, faces stretched with the stress of continuous action, we were armed to the teeth with a variety of pistols, semi-automatic weapons and wicked looking knives. We did not look like men to say no to. Still, he had said no. I cocked my PPSh, but did not point the barrel at him. Out of the corner of my eye I could see Müller had pulled his knife out and was moving to the side, ready to do what he did best. I caught his eye and shook my head, not this man, he was one of our own, killing him would get us nowhere.

"Feldwebel, I'll tell you once, and only once. We are acting on the direct orders of Reichsführer Himmler. The Reichsführer requires that we bring this Ukrainian back to Berlin with us. Either he comes with us or I will arrange for you to discuss your refusal directly with Prince Albrecht Strasser."

The man hesitated. I had to give him some credit. Most soldiers, indeed most people in Germany, would immediately capitulate when faced with a direct order from Hitler's SS supremo, police chief and head of the SS. But he was only human and realised where his best interests lay.

"Very well, Obersturmführer, the Ukrainian comes with us. Please hurry and get aboard, as soon as the wounded are loaded and the aircraft refuelled we are leaving straightaway. We have a flight of ME109s due over in about twenty minutes to escort us, the Russians seem to have increased their activity around here lately."

I told him about our last flight being shot down. He nodded, "It's getting very risky over Russian airspace these days, the sooner we can finish the job in Stalingrad and push on the better. The Führer has assured us that the Russian campaign will be completed shortly. Maybe the war can end. My wife and I are looking forward to the lebensraum the Führer is planning to offer us all. We want to take up a nice little farm, well a big farm, I suppose. I've seen a few nice places on the ground between here and Kiev, I keep a lookout as we overfly them."

I didn't like to tell the man that if he planned to take over someone's farm in Russia or the Ukraine, it would take more than Hitler's say-so to make the locals tamely give up their land and livelihoods to one of the invaders. The idea of lebensraum was the overriding goal of this massive effort in the east. It stemmed back to a dream to capture lost territory following the Great War and to also give space to the German population. This poor fool had swallowed the line dished out to all the German people about their destiny and their right to living space. I remember having read about Hitler's desire to grant the German people the 'lebensraum' they needed to breathe and thrive. It was always made clear that this vacant space was in the east, an area that offered massive resources and limitless land. We were beginning to learn that the land was going to carry a very heavy price.

We climbed aboard, the last of the stretchers was loaded, the door slammed shut and immediately I heard the roar as the pilot revved the engines. He taxied out to the opposite end of the airfield and immediately took off into the wind. The aircraft banked and took up a heading that would take us back to Germany. I looked out of the window and could see two 109s keeping station. That was reassuring, at least we stood some chance of leaving Russian airspace this time without being shot down. The four of us settled down to the long flight, finding spaces in the cramped and crowded cabin to lie down and doze. A scream startled me and I came to. It was one of the wounded who was experiencing terrible pain, probably due to the bumping of the aircraft in the chill air. He was alone so I went to offer help. The man was a Wehrmacht lieutenant, missing his right arm and his face covered in lacerations. With his remaining arm he was trying to comfort his stomach which was bandaged and causing him a great deal of distress. I gave him some water from my flask which he slipped gratefully.

"Thank you. SS?"

"A long story." I replied. "Is there anything I can do to help?"

"Persuade Adolf to get the 6th Army to pull back from Stalingrad to somewhere sensible," he said, trying to smile bravely through the pain.

"Like where? Germany?" I grinned at him.

"Good plan, yes Germany would be good. You know the situation in Stalingrad?" He asked.

I nodded. "Yes, I am well aware of the situation, it stinks."

"You know we'll lose," he said.

I looked at him long and hard. "Yes. We will lose."

I stayed with him while the aircraft droned on towards Germany. Eventually, he fell asleep but I sat by his side in case he needed help. Occasionally I held him as the plane bucked and bumped in the turbulent air, but he seemed to be managing to sleep. One of the Luftwaffe people announced that we had entered the airspace of the Reich, everyone cheered, thinking of their homes and families. A medic came over to check the lieutenant I was caring for.

"There is no need, Obersturmführer," he told me. "He's dead, probably been dead for the past hour." The medic turned to another patient. What a way to go I speculated, through the horrors of Stalingrad only to die when you were almost home. I hoped that when my time came it would be quick, not holding out a beacon of hope only to have it snatched away in the last agonised moments.

We landed at Berlin Tempelhof Airport, it was totally chaotic. The RAF night bombing and American day bombing had wreaked havoc on the airfield and surrounding buildings. It was not as smashed up as the airfield at Stalingrad but wasn't much better. We bumped into a slightly erratic landing and finally came to a halt. Several ambulances rushed out on to the tarmac and came up to the aircraft. Within minutes the casualties were being loaded into the ambulances for transfer to a hospital. A fuel bowser was already refuelling the aircraft ready for the return trip. I climbed out followed by Müller, Vasyl and Tatiana, who caused more than a few heads to turn.

On arrival in Berlin we had enjoyed ten days leave, during which I was able to show Tatiana the sights of Berlin, at least those sights that hadn't been flattened in the allied bombing raids. By day we walked around the parks and up and down the Kurfurstendamm, Berlin's once smart and prosperous central boulevard which was still putting on a brave but slightly shabby front in the face of the raids and the wartime shortages. We sat in cafes and drank coffee, talking endlessly about whatever subject came to mind. The war was taboo. We visited the zoo and laughed at the animals, any of which would have provided a banquet for the hungry soldiers that fought on in the Cauldron that was Stalingrad. Indeed, the troops themselves were now calling it the Cauldron. Tatiana admonished me for thinking about filling soldiers' bellies with the meat from the zebras and sea lions.

We had checked into a hotel close to the centre of the city. Despite the almost nightly bombing raids we both resolved to do our best to ignore them and let fate decide our future. If there was to be one! Tatiana made love like a tigress, passionately demanding everything I had to give her and giving everything of herself in return. It was one of the high points of my life, perhaps the highest point, this mad, reckless period living with a girl who seemed to be joined to me as much emotionally as physically when we made love. At some stage during those ten days we made a solemn pact. This was a country at war, embroiled in perhaps the most vicious and embittered war that had ever been known. When our leave was over, we would live again as separate people, for we had to fight as separate people if either of us was to survive. There was little place for passion and love in the midst of the savage fighting that Germany was engaged in. Afterwards, well, we'd wait and see the outcome of the war first.

Our leave over, we reported to Neurath at Prince Albrecht Strasser. Vasyl had been whipped away for interrogation by officers of the SD, the SS intelligence service, when we landed in Berlin. He was sat in the corridor outside Neurath's office, waiting with Müller. It was a pleasant reunion, I had been fearful that Vasyl may have been mistaken for a double agent and executed. Müller was, as usual, taciturn. I asked him how his leave went.

"Too quickly, Herr Obersturmführer," he replied.

"Did you have anyone to visit, Müller?" I asked.

"Yes, Obersturmführer," he grinned nastily, "every whore in Berlin."

I gave up, there was no conversation to be had with him. The red light outside of Neurath's office turned green and we took this as the signal to enter. We trooped in and unasked, sat down. Neurath fired a series of probing questions at us, clearly fascinated and distracted by the beautiful

Tatiana Medvedev.

"My dear, somebody like yourself with a good knowledge of languages as well as of the Russians themselves, could do no better than work here at Prince Albrecht Strasser. I could find a job for you as an analyst and interpreter, you would be on my personal staff and under my protection."

It was a transparent ploy for Neurath, a married man with four children at the last count, to get the beautiful Polish aristocrat in his bed. Sadly for him it was a ploy she had heard dozens of times in the past, she was expert at eluding the trap.

"Your offer is very kind, Standartenführer. However I wish to fight the Russians, I have offered my services to Obersturmführer Wolf and I am now working with him and under his protection."

Neurath inclined his head, accepting defeat gracefully. "Very well, Miss Medvedev, if that is what you wish I shall not object. Now, since you flew out of Stalingrad there have been developments. The Russians have launched a massive two-pronged counter-attack with several hundred brand new T34 tanks, supported by apparently limitless new divisions of motorised infantry. They caught us completely by surprise." Müller and I looked at each other. Neurath caught the look and grimaced.

"Yes, I know about your report, Wolf. What do you want me to say? Frankly, I think the high command of the 6th Army ought to be taken out and shot."

"They probably will be if they don't beat the Russians," Müller murmured.

"Thank you for your observation," Neurath said," it's a pity, Scharführer, that the SS is not running the operation at Stalingrad. Things would be very different. But we are not running it, the Wehrmacht is now aware of its mistakes and the Führer has instructed them to remedy the situation."

I was appalled, if von Paulus had taken the trouble to evaluate the intelligence that my group had brought back from behind the Russian lines, he could have anticipated the Russian counter-attack and even led it into an ambush. Instead, it seemed that he had been sucker punched by the Russian operation, which Neurath informed us was called Operation Uranus. And here in Berlin they talked of the 6th Army rectifying the situation! How could a starving, beleaguered army rectify anything? They couldn't even feed themselves, let alone fight.

There was still no detailed information on exactly what was happening, other than that the fighting had transformed from bitter street fighting to a desperate defence as a never-ending horde of Soviet troops hit the flanks of the 6th Army. A quick look at the map Neurath was showing us clearly demonstrated the problem. Our fears of a Russian counter-attack were proved true. Soviet forces had smashed hard into the Romanian, Hungarian and Italian units we had been using to guard the flanks. It looked like von Paulus was fighting back, counter-attacking fiercely along both flanks, but for how long could they survive?

"We're sending you back, Wolf."

"Back where?" I asked him. But I already knew where, back to the Cauldron of Stalingrad, the killing machine that was slowly destroying the might of the German Wehrmacht. I could feel the eyes of the three members of my group boring into me. Had we escaped by the skin of our teeth, only to be sent back?

"But surely, Standartenführer, we've done our bit? It's a Wehrmacht operation, they should sort out their own mess."

"The Wehrmacht high command has indeed been made to look very foolish by ignoring the intelligence provided to them by the SS. Reichsführer Himmler requires you to take your team back to Stalingrad and evaluate how the 6th Army can be rescued from the encirclement. You will be flying out at first light tomorrow morning from Tempelhof. You will have five days to evaluate the situation and reconnoitre the Russian positions, we need to know the enemy strength and if possible their immediate intentions. We've heard news of even more tanks massing. Are they planning an all out attack on our troops or do they intend to keep us under siege through the winter, and just starve us out? That's your brief, report to Tempelhof at 0500 tomorrow morning. Good luck."

We were shocked, to have come from the hell of Stalingrad and then spend a pleasant ten days leave in Berlin, we all expected the next posting to be anywhere but back to Stalingrad. But arguing with Himmler's representative was not an option. We saluted, I acknowledged the order, about turned and we left the office.

We walked out to the street, no one said a word. What was there to say? I turned to speak to them, but before I could say a word a black car screeched to a halt almost next to us. Four men jumped out, black leather trench coats and trilby hats, the uniform of the Gestapo. I wondered what the hell they could want with us, we had just left Prinz Albrecht Strasser. If they had business with us surely they would have done it there. But it was not us they were after. Instead an old man, he looked to be nearly eighty, was pasting a poster on to a wall proclaiming that Hitler had lied to the German people and the war was lost. As I was thinking what a bloody fool he was to put such a poster on the wall near to Gestapo headquarters, the four men grabbed him and started dragging him into the car. I could hear him shouting, "They killed my son, Hitler is a murdering butcher. The war is lost, he'll kill us all."

One of the Gestapo men hit him hard on the head with what looked like a rubber cosh. He went silent immediately and slumped into their arms, allowing them to drag him into the car and away. He was probably right, poor devil, Hitler was indeed a murdering butcher and the war was quite definitely lost. It was the right thing to say, but in the wrong place and at the wrong time.

"There seems to be an epidemic of deafness in Germany today," Vasyl said.

"You'd do well to remember that, Vasyl," I said. "Being deaf is definitely the healthiest way to live in Germany."

We found a bar and ordered drinks. Even the wartime schnapps seemed to be a pale shadow of what it was a few years ago, it tasted weak and insipid. I proposed a toast.

"To Stalingrad, may it be a quick visit," I said.

"I'm just hoping that the RAF bombs Tempelhof Airport in the night so we won't be able to take off," Müller said, to a chorus of hear hears.

The following morning we were bumping and droning our way across the endless Russian steppes in another Junkers 52, this time sharing the space with piles of boxes carrying supplies for the 6th Army. There were no replacement troops on the flight, the Wehrmacht had decided that sending in fresh troops to a besieged position was pointless. Except for us of course! I felt that we were some ancient ritualistic sacrifice to the gods of war, almost as if we were to be metaphorically tied to a stone altar and killed to appease the gods. We landed under fire, the Junkers hit the edge of a shell hole on the runway and nearly pitched over. Thankfully the pilot managed to correct in time and he brought us to a stop. Already men were shouting to hurry, hurry, hurry. They were hurling the crates out as fast as humanly possible. Alongside the aircraft I could see the familiar rows of stretchers waiting to be evacuated to the Reich. We jumped out, avoided the bustling troops loading and unloading and found a Kübelwagen that had been waiting for us. Less than an hour later after an uncomfortable ride, dodging snipers and shell bursts, we arrived at 6th Army Headquarters. Colonel Steinmetz was anxiously waiting outside to greet us.

"I'm sorry you had to come back," he said, "but Himmler was getting jittery about the situation here and didn't seem to want to trust Wehrmacht intelligence. No, no," he said seeing our grim faces, "I know we should have listened, I know we were wrong, but that's history. We need to get you on your mission and then you can return to Berlin. If Himmler wants to send some of his SS Panzer divisions to help us, I don't think General von Paulus will refuse."

"We'll do our best, Colonel," I replied. "Where do we jump off?"

"We want you back in the city, Obersturmführer. The Reds are still holding out in the factory complex, if we can finish them off it would give us a chance to turn and address the problem of the encirclement. At the moment they're snapping at our heels day and night and we need to finish them off once and for all."

I recalled the endless lines of boats crossing and re-crossing the Volga carrying Russian reinforcements and supplies and wondered if they could ever be permanently removed from the factory complex. I doubted it, but decided that Colonel Steinmetz would not be interested to hear of my doubts.

"Very well Sir, if you can show us where to stow our kit, we'll make a start at first light in the morning."

The Colonel had a private soldier show us to our quarters. It had been a long, cold flight and we wanted to get some rest before entering the heat of the battle of Stalingrad the next morning. The next day, we set out at six, it was still dark. By seven we were pinned down under the vicious crossfire from two separate Russian machine gun positions. We were still

five hundred metres from our destination, the factory complex.

As we lay sheltering from the machine gun fire, back in Germany Adolf Hitler gave a speech that was listened to all over the Reich. He shouted that "no power on earth will force us out of Stalingrad". I noticed German soldiers looking uneasily across at the Russian positions. That was on November 8th. On the other side the Russian General Chuikov gave his speech saying that, "time is blood". I wondered were both armies in Stalingrad doing exactly what Stalin wanted them to do, continue their attrition in the rubble of the city, buying time with their blood whilst the Soviet build-up of troops on our 6th Army flanks continued. I afterwards found out that General Jodl gave Hitler several intelligence reports showing that the Russians were assembling huge numbers of troops northwest of Stalingrad. There was reportedly a further build-up to the south of the city, where the Romanian 4th Army was assisting General Hoth's 4th Panzer Army. But in Stalingrad itself, von Paulus now claimed to have taken the city. Although he was planning yet another offensive against the factory district, which began early on the morning of November 11th. We had stood and watched the massive bombing raid of our 4th Air Fleet. The factory chimneys in the Stalingrad industrial complex, still standing until now, were sent crashing spectacularly into the rubble. Many of the troops cheered. But many, like me, were silent, wondering how the Luftwaffe creating still more barricades, trenches and defensive positions out of the rubble would help us. Soon, a total of seven German divisions were attacking on a three-mile front east of the Stalingrad gun factory.

APRIL 1944

I was thinking about those days in Stalingrad as I surveyed the camp of Stalag IV-D, located near Torgau in the Reich. This camp wasn't a PoW camp in the true sense, but rather a distribution centre for moving the prisoners between work camps. Those camps included mines, factories, railroads and farms in the area. We approached the large white structure that served as the main administration building, situated beside the railway line.

Another motley group of ragged British prisoners was assembled in front of me. My boss Standartenführer Julian Amery, the English politician's son who had volunteered to establish the SS-British Freecorps, had been quite firm, the recruitment drive was still not going well enough. Apparently, even Adolf Hitler had expressed his dissatisfaction with the small numbers that had come forward to fight on the Russian Front. Amery made it quite clear, either recruit more men or be permanently posted back to Russia. Even Müller, the icy SS assassin who had been assigned to me when I first joined the SS-Liebstandarte Adolf Hitler, was nervous. The Russians had begun to counter-attack in massive numbers. The terrible defeat at Stalingrad was almost a distant memory and it was clear that being sent back to Russia was tantamount to being sent to die one of the most hellish deaths imaginable.

"Sir," he said to me that morning, "you're British, surely you can get some of them to see reason, can't you just promise them anything to get them to join up? Never mind if they're bloody useless, the war is lost anyway. We just need a good result to keep us away from the Eastern Front."

"Getting cold feet?" I smiled at Müller. "Nervous about going back?"

"Nervous, no," he said. "But you know as well as I do that the war in the east is over. The Führer should build a high wall between us and Russia and keep the barbarians out of our country."

"Not much chance of that," I said to him. "Why don't you mention it next time we're in Berlin?"

He didn't reply. We both knew the score, neither of us wanted to go back although both of us had discussed many times the almost certain prospect of not surviving the war. Then again, although fate may have intended for us to be killed before the last shot was fired, why lend a hand? If fate wanted to kill us it could manage quite well on its own. I had promised Müller that I would do my best.

"And so, fellow Englishmen, I can promise you the very best of everything. You will get rank, first-class uniforms, first-class food and will be joining an elite group of soldiers to fight the Russian savages. There is no doubt that when the war has ended England will require you to fight on a new front against the Russians. We English need to join with Germany and its allies to beat back the Soviet hordes. You can be part of

this elite corps who will be in the very forefront of the fight, admired and valued by everyone you meet."

The war was turning. Sadly not only did the German nation no longer see the SS as an elite, they regarded us as Adolf Hitler's bully boys. As an organisation that was part of a repressive political apparatus, alongside the Gestapo, which seemed increasingly to be turning against the German people.

I finished my speech and we returned to the guardroom as usual, this time we didn't have long to wait before the first of the volunteers began arriving. By the end of the day we had acquired the eleven men to fight for the SS-British Freecorps on the Eastern Front.

"Rather them than me," Müller said gleefully. "I've had enough of fighting the Russians to last me for ten lifetimes."

"I agree with you wholeheartedly, Scharführer. Now, bring the Kübelwagen to the gate, we'll get loaded up and start back for Berlin."

We loaded our kit into the Kübi and Müller drove us away from the camp and in the direction of Berlin. It was a peaceful drive through the German countryside. The war seemed to be a million miles away. Farmers tended their fields, albeit helped in most cases by foreign prisoners who were assigned to work the land. We passed a couple of beautiful young women, proudly wearing the traditional German dirndl that was so favoured by the Führer as an emblem of the purity and wholesomeness of German women. To me, it was anything but. I had known plenty of German women who wore the dirndl by day and by night turned into insatiable and rapacious whores. Perhaps they were desperate to escape the hardships and misery of the war in a few moments of sweaty sex. It was a pleasant thought, tumbling these maidens in the hay. Those were the days, the good days.

Müller heard it first, the sound of an aero engine changing as it peeled off from its course and started its attack run. "Scatter, off the road," he shouted urgently. The Kübi driver, a private soldier, was evidently new to the sudden raids by Allied fighters. He slowed down slightly and turned round, mouth opening to ask us for more instructions. Müller and I had been through this a dozen times in the past. I was in the front passenger seat, he was in the rear behind the driver. We both tumbled out of the

vehicle and rolled across the ground in one smooth motion. The startled driver looked sideways at his passengers who had suddenly jumped out of his vehicle. Then there was the jackhammer sound of Browning machine guns as the aircraft opened up. Spurts of dust were thrown up off the road as the burst hit the ground just behind the Kubelwagen, climbed over it and tracked all the way through it. It smashed into the driver and continued forward through the engine compartment, leaving both vehicle and driver bloody wrecks that hurtled into a tree at the side of the road. The four machine guns suddenly stopped. Müller and I both stayed flat, keeping undercover and out of sight of the attack aircraft. I had seen it as it flashed past, an RAF Mosquito, clearly one of the many that crisscrossed Germany in nuisance raids designed more to destroy German morale than do any strategic damage.

The de Havilland DH.98 Mosquito was a twin engine fighter bomber made entirely from wood. The plane certainly shared similarities with our own BF110 twin engine fighter, made famous in the first year of the war. These Mosquitoes were very fast and becoming a common sight hurtling past on precision bombing missions and reconnaissance patrols. We had come to hate and fear their endless lightning raids.

Eventually the drone of the aircraft faded away, apparently the pilot was satisfied with the damage he had done and was not about to turn back for a second pass. We got up, dusted off our uniforms and went over to the Kübi. Thankfully, our packs were largely intact. Müller's had taken two bullets through the body of the pack that had punched holes in the cheese sandwiches he'd collected from the commissariat before we started on our journey. Mine had sustained one bullet that had lodged itself in an old copy of the complete works of Shakespeare, a book that I had carried around with me since the day I joined the Waffen SS. I don't know why, it seemed to be something quintessentially English, something that would be a link with who I was. I'd constantly reminded myself to open the book and read it but so far, apart from the Merchant of Venice, I had not made much progress with Mr Shakespeare's works. There was nothing else left worth salvaging.

Müller unstrapped the shovel and we took it in turns to dig a shallow grave for the driver. I ripped off his dog tags and put them in my tunic pocket, then we lifted his body into the grave and covered it up. Müller banged the spade into the ground and I fastened the driver's pay book and identification documents to it so that a grave digging party could come along later and give the poor devil a proper burial. Somehow, after all of the bloodshed we had waded through on the Eastern Front, it still seemed harsh that the man had died so violently within the borders of his home country. We then trudged along the road and within twenty minutes got a lift from a Wehrmacht lorry that was heading for Berlin with supplies for the city.

We made our way to the barracks where we reported to the commanding officer, Julian Amery. I was immediately startled to see how white and strange he looked. As well he might, when Germany lost the war, which everyone knew would be not too far into the future, the British government would deal very severely with Mr Amery. I would receive no lesser treatment if I was to wind up in their hands, but as I was in no doubt that fate would not see me to the end of hostilities, I was not unduly worried. I made my report to him about the more encouraging response from the PoW camp, as well as the bad news about the jeep and driver.

He nodded, "Very well, Obersturmführer, that's an improvement. You will need to do better though, you know that the war is not going well. We are in a critical phase. We need thousands, tens of thousands of volunteers to join the SS ranks to defend our western civilisation from the Russians. You are to increase your efforts, I want you on the road night and day," then he rose out of the chair and banged on the desk, his voice raising to a scream, "get me the recruits, Wolf, get me the recruits! You must get more men, we must not lose this sacred battle." He slumped back into his chair.

"Dismissed," he waved at us. We saluted and left the office.

An aircraft was flying low overhead, we both looked up nervously but it was only a Junkers 52, probably on a routine training flight from the nearby Luftwaffe airfield. I could not see one of those aircraft without thinking about those last desperate days and weeks in Stalingrad, the Ju52. It was the 6th Army's only real link with the outside world after the Soviet encirclement.

SS ENGLANDER

CHAPTER SEVEN

NOVEMBER 1942

Just three hundred metres away I could see our destination, the Barrikady. The huge industrial complex manufactured small arms and ammunition, and like all the factories in Stalingrad was smashed into heaps of rubble and broken machinery so that it had become a series of defensive positions their own right. The individual workshops themselves created additional layers of defences, making this a major strongpoint. To one side loomed the Tractor Factory, to the other the gigantic structure of the Red October Metal Factory. We were keenly aware that the Russians held the Tractor Factory and parts of the Red October Factory. Our intelligence had reported that the Barrikady was in German hands. Yet one of the machine guns had fired at us from either inside or very close to the Barrikady. It seemed like yet another intelligence failure to add to so many other failures that had combined to allow the Russians to devastate our forces inside the Stalingrad Cauldron. We crawled back a short distance to a mass of huge steel pipes that littered the ground.

"If we crawl through these pipes we should be able to get most of the way to the Barrikady," I told them. "What do you think?"

We check out the ground, the pipes were randomly scattered all the way up to the factory with no more than a ten metre gap at most where one ended before another offered further cover.

Vasyl nodded. "Yes, we could do it. There's an open space, though, about thirty metres immediately in front of the factory. If the Russians are in there they'll shoot us down like dogs."

"We'd better hope they're not in there, then!" I replied, with a smile to soften the words. "Müller, lead the way. Let's go."

We rushed towards the pipes and as we reached them a head popped out, startled by the sound of our approach. It was a Russian sniper, camouflaged in a collection of rags and strips of sacking. Müller's knife flashed and the man's last breath sighed as Müller rushed past him, barely halting to deliver the killing, slashing blow to the neck. We clambered into the thick steel tube over the dying body, now a twitching bundle of old, useless rags. We were in the first pipe, safe from the Russian machine gun fire. At least, for now.

We crawled through the end into the next pipe. There was barely a gap from one to the other, so we were safe. Then the next and the next. The gaps got wider but we dashed from pipe to pipe without giving the Soviet machine gunners time to take aim. Finally we were almost there, just inside the end of the final pipe with only the thirty metre gap between us and the relative safety of the factory building.

"I'll go first," I told them, "let me get into the factory and I'll get ready to give covering fire. Wait until I start shooting then come over together. Make it fast!" I added. They all nodded, they didn't need to be told to hurry. We would have a tiny window of opportunity before the Russians got the range. Then I was away, running, no time to crouch down to hide from the bullets, speed was the only factor that counted. I heard the clatter as a Soviet Maxim machine gun open up. It was soon joined by the faster, lighter chatter of the DP light machine gun as the other gunner tried to track his weapon onto me. Being the target of two machine guns certainly made me run faster than I would ever have thought possible.

The DP was an unusual looking machine gun. The magazine was circular and placed flat on the top of the gun, much like a gramophone. It was easily manufactured and like most Russian weapons was very reliable and solid. More importantly to us though, was that the pancake magazine only held forty seven bullets and took some time to fit a new one to the gun. That was the best chance to evade its fire, I kept that thought uppermost in my mind, trying to count the rounds fired at me.

The bullets clattered nearer and nearer. At the last moment I jinked to

the side, I was nearly there when the gunner switched aim and spurts of dust kicked up near my feet. With a last desperate jump I literally leapt through the opening in the factory wall and I was in, screened from the bullets. I found a good position where I could see the machine gun nest, checked I had a full clip in the PPSh and opened fire, seeing my bullets strike the steel shield of the Russian machine gun. The gunners ceased fire and ducked down. Vasyl, Müller and Tatiana rushed out of cover and ran across towards me. A helmet popped up above the machine gun shield to get a better view of the target. I switched aim and saw a patch of red appear on his helmet as he was knocked back by my burst. The others were running, Vasyl in the lead. Tatiana was behind him. I could see he was holding her hand, pulling her along. Müller brought up the rear keeping his PPSh ready to fire, watching for a further threat from the Russian machine guns. The machine gunner I killed had obviously given them pause for thought and before they had time to recover our group had arrived inside the cover of the factory building. Chests heaving, breathing heavily, panting with exertion, Müller and Vasyl immediately dropped into a firing position behind the masonry waiting for the Soviet reply, but none came. We had made it.

"Listen," Vasyl said. "Upstairs."

We stopped all movement and listened. Sure enough, we could hear, what, voices? Yes, it sounded like voices.

"Steinmetz said that the Russians had been driven from this area several days ago," I told him. "They could be our people. We need to make contact."

As I got up to go and find them Vasyl put a hand on my arm.

"Not Germans. Russians."

"Russians? Are you sure?"

"Listen again," he said.

Again we were quiet. I could hear the voices faintly. Then I heard a shouted 'Yob Tvoy Mat'. Fuck your mother, the common Russian curse. The Red Army was here, in this building on the first floor.

"Fucking intelligence," Müller snarled, "do they ever get anything right?"

"Maybe this time they did, Scharführer," I replied quietly.

"What do you mean?" he asked.

"Didn't they have a grudge against us for making them look like fools over the Soviet tanks we saw, which they denied were ever there? I'm wondering if this isn't their revenge. Himmler wants to show Hitler how useless the Wehrmacht is and isn't this just the opposite? Show Hitler that Himmler's people got themselves caught in a Russian ambush?"

There was silence. It was an appalling prospect, possibly sacrificed by our own side in the name of politics.

"What difference does it make?" Tatiana said. "We're here, the Russians are here. Whatever brought us, we need to deal with it. What do we do next?"

"I think surrender would be a good option," I heard Vasyl say.

"Surrender? What the hell…" I looked around. A group of Russians had quietly taken up positions around us. How they had moved so silently I had no idea, but they were sheltering behind abandoned wooden cases, crouched behind pieces of steel machinery and peering in from a smashed window frame. We had at least fifteen guns pointed at us, PPSh's, Mosin Nagant rifles and I recognised a DP light machine gun. Next to a rusty cast iron hydraulic press a man in the black jacket of a political commissar stood quietly, hands on hips. He had a thin smile on his lips, a smile of pleasure. His pleasure, not ours, of course. I looked at the others.

"That's it. We're done, put down your guns."

Müller looked around wildly, like a trapped animal. But it was clear we were finished, the slightest move and the Russians would have cut us to shreds.

"Very wise," the commissar smiled, speaking in German. Fortunately he had no way of knowing any of us spoke Russian. "Tie them up," he shouted to his men in Russian, "then we'll find out exactly what they are doing here."

A dozen Russians came up to us and tied our hands behind our backs with thin, strong line. We were searched and our weapons and documents removed. The commissar stood looking at them, leafing through the pages, clearly enjoying his victory. He lit a cigarette, one of the Russian style cigarettes with a cardboard tube at one end, tobacco at the other.

"So, you are in command, yes? An Obersturmführer?"

I nodded. He gave me a hard look. "We were not aware that the SS were in Stalingrad. What is your unit strength?"

"Four," I replied. "You're looking at it."

"I don't believe you," he snarled.

"Well, fuck you, Commissar, I really couldn't care who you believe. There are no other SS in Stalingrad. Believe it or not, that's the way it is."

I crumpled as a rifle butt slammed into my kidneys, then crashed into the side of my head. I managed to keep on my feet, but I could see stars spinning in my eyes.

"The small one, bring him here!" the commissar shouted.

One of the soldiers brought Tatiana over to him. He ripped off her helmet, letting her hair tumble down around her shoulders.

"So, a woman. You employ women in your army, SS man?"

"She's an interpreter," I replied. "Not a combatant."

"No? Why then is she carrying a rifle?" he asked.

It's my spare weapon, she doesn't shoot it."

"And the Walther? That too?"

I said nothing.

"Is she your woman then, Obersturmführer?" He casually slashed the barrel of his Tokarev pistol across her face, leaving a deep cut that began weeping rich red blood. I started towards him, only to receive another blow to the kidneys for my troubles.

"Oh, I see she is. Perhaps she can help with some answers to my questions. What is the SS strength in Stalingrad?" He asked her.

"I don't know, Commissar, I'm just an interpreter. I have been told that there are no SS in Stalingrad, just these men here."

"You're lying!" he shouted. "Strip her!" He instructed the men now holding her. They eagerly began ripping off her uniform using their knives and bayonets to slash off her trousers and underwear until she crouched naked, hands frantically tried to cover her breasts and genitals. I could see red cuts on her body where the eager knives of the soldiers had cut too deeply when they stripped her.

"Now, how many SS are there in Stalingrad? You will answer me quickly or I will give you to my men to help you with your memory. Our attack will be going in at first light tomorrow, not that you need to be concerned. Twenty of our divisions. We'll cut through your fascists like a knife through butter. You will not be there. But if you want to live long enough to get to one of our labour camps, you'll tell me how many SS we can expect to meet when we go in."

Tatiana was weeping now, shocked and terrified. "Commissar, I beg you, I just don't know, this man told me they were the only SS men in the city, perhaps it is true, I just don't know," she wailed.

"Gregory, take out your knife," the commissar ordered to one of his men, a gross, nasty-looking sergeant with what looked like a perpetual leer on his ugly face. The man pulled out a knife, it was almost déjà vu, we were seeing the Soviet counterpart of Müller. Was he their torturer and assassin? Undoubtedly he was.

"Gregory, I will ask her again. If she does not give me an honest answer, you will cut off her left nipple. I will ask her a second time, then you cut off her right nipple if she does not tell the truth. Is that clear?"

The soldier nodded, grunting. I got the impression that he was a mute. God only knew what terrible upbringing he had had in some wild part of a godforsaken Soviet republic, where probably torturing animals was the only way he could find any pleasure. Until of course the war came and gave him the chance to get his pleasure with enemy captives. He stood over Tatiana, knife ready.

"Now, how many SS are there in Stalingrad?"

I shouted, "For God's sake, leave her alone, she is telling the truth. We are on a mission here to gather intelligence for Reichsführer Himmler, nothing more. There is no SS presence in the city, none."

The commissar looked thoughtful, he was about to speak when one of his men shouted across to him.

"Commissar, this man here, I recognise him. He is one of ours, a captain in the infantry."

"One of ours?" He asked incredulously. "You mean he is an officer in the Red Army fighting on the German side?"

"Definitely," the man replied. "I remember him well."

The commissar walked over to where Vasyl was being held by two burly Russian soldiers. He brought up the Tokarev, I thought for one moment he was going to shoot him, but he slashed Vasyl across the face, then back across the other side of his face. Then back again, and again, and again, and again. Vasyl's face was a bloody bleeding mass, three of his teeth had been knocked out, his nose was broken and one of his eyes was totally closed. The other eye was half closed, he was a pitiful sight.

"So, a Soviet citizen that decides to fight for the fascists, yes?"

"Not Soviet," Vasyl mumbled, doing his best to speak through his broken and wrecked mouth. "I am Ukrainian, Ukrainian you hear, not a Russian barbarian. Ukrainian."

The soldier behind him smashed his rifle butt into the back of Vasyl's head, knocking him flat. I could see Müller looking wildly around, perhaps for any chance that we might grasp to get us out of this situation, but it was no good, we were totally helpless. Müller was clubbed over the head with the stock of a PPSh, knocking him to the ground.

"So," the commissar said to me, "what exactly have you reported to Himmler?"

"Nothing, so far," I replied, "we only arrived here from Berlin yesterday morning, this was our first mission."

"And your last, fascist," the Russian said. "We will show you how the Red Army deals with fascists that come spying on us in Stalingrad. Gregory, you can have some fun with the woman, when you are finished spend some time entertaining her friends. Leave the traitor until last. I want him to savour what is to come for him. You, traitor, are you a Christian?"

"Of course I am, all Ukrainian patriots are Christian, not communist animals like you." Vasyl replied, still defiant in spite of the terrible beating.

"Very well. You men," he turned to a group of his soldiers. "Fasten some of these wooden beams together, we'll make our Christian a cross."

The soldiers scrambled to carry out his orders. They quickly formed a rough cross, fastening two heavy beams together with ropes to hold them together. Then sickeningly, they dragged Vasyl to the cross which lay on the ground. It took twelve of them to hold him down while one took a hammer and a bunch of old, rusty nails. They hammered them through his hands, fastening him to the cross. To his credit, he didn't cry out, I couldn't be sure if it was shock or bravery that kept him quiet.

I looked around desperately for any prospect of an escape from this situation. The intelligence about tomorrow's attack, the words the commissar had inadvertently blurted out was priceless, exactly what we had come for. Then my own army came to our rescue, at least the Luftwaffe came to our rescue. It was clearly not a Luftwaffe plan to rescue us. Apparently some genius at HQ had decided it was time to bomb the Barrikady, for me it was the final proof that our presence here was part of a Wehrmacht scheme to discredit Himmler and regain some favour with Adolf Hitler. Still, it gave us some respite as bombs whistled through the air and began landing on the building. Russian voices shouted in chaos and confusion, giving orders, contradicting each other, running from one place to another.

The commissar opened his mouth to shout, then a piece of masonry fell from above and literally stove in his skull. He dropped to the ground lifeless while his men stared terrified at the chaotic scene. Under attack and their commissar killed, they would have much to answer for from the NKVD when they returned from their mission. The whole ground floor of the factory was enveloped in dust and smoke which blanketed everything and gave us a screen behind which we could try to escape. A soldier came up to me with a knife in his hand, I started thinking that I was about to be gutted when I recognised that it was Müller. He had freed his bound hands with a spare knife he carried in a pouch behind his back and was coming to cut us loose. I felt my hands free and rushed to help Tatiana while Müller went over to help Vasyl. I picked her up carefully but she was relatively unscathed, apart from the slash on her face and the shock of imminent torture that had left her trembling in terror.

"Tatiana, get dressed. Whatever you can find just get it on, we're moving. Müller, how is Vasyl?"

"He'll be fine." Müller replied, as he ripped out the nails that held Vasyl. The Ukrainian was in shock with the pain and blood loss but somehow he got to his feet, looking around for his weapons.

"We need to hurry, once the smoke and dust clears they'll open up on us with everything they've got."

I grabbed a PPSh and checked that it was loaded. The commissar still had the Tokarev automatic pistol in his hand and I prised it out of his lifeless fingers. I could see that Müller had picked up his own weapons and was helping Vasyl to arm himself. Tatiana had pulled on trousers, a tunic and boots.

"Get a helmet," I told her, "it's getting a bit lively around here. There'll be a lot of flying debris and shrapnel from the bombardment. Forget the rifle, just grab yourself an automatic, we need to get going."

The bombardment had intensified. Most of the roof and upper floor of the Barrikady had been blown apart and we could clearly look up through the gaps in the masonry to see the shapes of our Heinkel 111 bombers as they droned across the sky, unloading bomb after bomb. Thank God for the Luftwaffe, I thought, even if they were dropping bombs on top of us. I checked the group, we were ready, "Let's go," I shouted. Another line of bombs fell on the vast factory, exploding from left to right. After the fragments settled we ran to the left, hopefully out of the path of the marauding bombers.

The surviving Russians had disappeared, no doubt they had gone to shelter from the bombardment. I found a series of steps to an underground part of the factory. It seemed the best way to find solid protection. I led the way down into the semi darkness, lit only by holes in the ceiling where bomb and shell blasts had taken their toll. We rushed further along darkened corridors, punctuated with doorways, some with their steel doors still hanging smashed and broken from their hinges. Above us the ceiling was crisscrossed with pipes, apart from the numerous bomb and shell damage. Then we stopped, abruptly. A Soviet soldier stood pointing a rifle at us, a Mosin Nagant. He would have little chance against the all of us, but he could probably get one or two if he worked the bolt sufficiently fast. Not worth the risk, I decided. We needed to take him by stealth, not a frontal assault.

"Stop," the soldier ordered loudly, "or I shoot."

It was a woman's voice, as my eyes became accustomed to the gloom I could see that she was a Soviet lieutenant.

"You must put down your weapons."

"There are four of us," I said to her in Russian. "You cannot shoot us all. You must surrender."

She shook her head.

"Look, Russian, let's call it quits," I said to her. She was very young and beautiful beneath the filth and grime on her terrified face. I honestly didn't want a shooting match which she was bound to lose, neither did I want to lose any of my people. "Just back away and we'll pretend we didn't see you."

"Nyet!" she shouted.

We just stood facing each other, the terrified girl and the four of us. Then a bomb crashed down nearby and she shifted her glance. It was enough, Müller's hand moved slightly, there was a silver flash of metal whistling through the air and his knife buried itself in her stomach. She screamed, dropped the rifle and fell to the floor. Vasyl rushed forward, kicked the rifle out of her reach and checked her for more weapons, pulling an officer's Tokarev pistol out of her holster. She was sobbing quietly as she lay on the hard, concrete floor. Tatiana went over to check her wound.

"Wolf, this needs to be dressed, she's bleeding badly."

Müller walked up and pushed her aside. "I have the perfect remedy for wounded Russians. Here, let me show you."

He took the girl by the hair, tilted her head back so that she screamed in even more pain.

"Müller, leave her," I shouted, "let Tatiana deal with it."

Why was I not allowing Müller to finish it? We had no way to look after prisoners, besides this one was wounded. But she was a woman, and beautiful too. I had no idea how this would end, only that I could not allow her to be executed, not yet anyway.

"There's a good position just along here," Vasyl said, returning from checking out the immediate surroundings, "we can hide in there for a while."

"Ok," I called to them, "let's get in there. Müller, Vasyl, help carry the girl. Carefully," I warned Müller with a stern glance. They picked her up and carried her a few metres further along, then into the room Vasyl had found. It had a steel door, closed with strong clips like a submarine. There was a row of vats and boilers at the back of the dark space. Clearly it had been used for some sort of industrial process. When we were all inside Vasyl latched the door closed. It was a good position, the door would have stopped a round from a Panzer tank. The roof, sadly, had been badly damaged. Tatiana gave the Soviet girl some water. I could hear her murmuring to her in Russian.

"Her name is Olga, Olga Romanov," she told us. "I've given her some morphine to ease the pain, but she's badly hurt, Wolf."

"We're all in a bad way," I replied. "Look at Vasyl." The Ukrainians face was battered and bloody, his hands bore the bloody marks of his crucifixion, one eye was still closed, but he seemed to be managing with just one good eye.

"Olga Romanov," I said to her, she was awake and watching me, "we can't do any more for you. When we go we'll leave you here for your people find you."

Her eyes blazed with hate and malice. "You may as well kill me, fascist pigs. You'll all be dead yourselves soon enough."

Müller chuckled. "Proper little communist, isn't she. You should let me finish her."

"Yes," she blazed, "I am a proper communist and proud of it. I am proud of my country and proud of our leader, Comrade Stalin. He has made

Russia the greatest nation in the world."

"I thought that was Lenin," I replied, "and Trotsky who built the Red Army, until Stalin had him executed."

"No, that is not true, fascist. Trotsky was an enemy of the people."

"For creating the Red Army, your army?" I asked her. "Is that what you people believe?"

She looked confused for a moment then said, "He was a traitor, Comrade Stalin said so."

"So you believe everything that Stalin tells you, yes? What about the millions of Russians killed by the NKVD over the past few years, that's a lot more than our Adolf Hitler has managed?"

"Lies," she said. "There were no millions killed."

"And no Gulags either with millions of prisoners?" I enquired. She didn't reply.

I had to admire her. Despite the terrible pain she was a true believer. I reached down and took her papers out of her tunic pocket. Sure enough, she was a party member, a card carrying member of the greatest slave owning society the world had ever known. But she was no threat to us so I decided to stop baiting her. I heard her groan with pain and Tatiana began swabbing away a new gush of blood that was coming from her stomach wound. I looked at Tatiana, raised one eyebrow. She shook her head, no, she was beyond help. Well, that was one problem soon to be removed. Why was I worried about being callous, we were in the middle of a battle ground? I suspected that we were also on the losing side.

There was a sudden banging on the door, the Soviets were back. A voice shouted orders loudly and there was the sound of boots running along the corridor. There was an enormous crash as the Russians hit the door. They had found something to use as a battering ram.

"The roof," Vasyl called to us, "we can get out that way."

Of course, there was a readymade escape route. "Müller, help me stack some of these crates to make a step for us to climb on." We began to stack the boxes, aware of the increasing urgency as the banging of the battering ram kept crashing against the steel structure. Already the concrete and plaster around the door frame was beginning to crack, it was only a matter of time before they broke through, and very little time. We built a ramp with the boxes and I climbed on it to hoist myself out of the cellar and into the space above. Then a helmet appeared, a Soviet soldier's face peered over the hole and he raised his rifle, firing instinctively. There was a cry from below. My PPSh was strapped on my back so I snatched out my Walther, aimed and fired in one fluid motion. I hit him squarely in the chest, a heart shot, and he fell backwards.

"Who was hit?" I asked anxiously.

"It was the Russian woman," Vasyl replied. "She's dead."

We climbed out, one by one, there were no other Russians waiting for us. It was ironic, German bombers dropping their loads on us, German soldiers. Russian soldiers shooting their own wounded, an officer, a woman. If there was anything else more calculated to underline the stupidity, the senseless slaughter of this war, I found it hard to think of it just now. We were back in the Barrikady factory space. There was no sign of the Russians but in the distance, looking through the gaping holes in the brickwork, we could see a Soviet company forming up outside the Tractor Factory. It was time to move. We had what we came for. The factory complex, the three massive buildings that formed the pre-war industrial heart of Stalingrad was partially or entirely in Russian hands. And the Russians were due to attack at dawn. Twenty divisions deployed properly could be enough to throw the 6th Army back, even out of the city altogether, where they could be picked off at will in the frozen winter snows and unable to escape the encirclement. Then the Soviet artillery began firing, the start of what I presumed would be a long bombardment lasting through the night, prior to their attack. We were in luck. The smoke, noise and confusion were what we needed to escape.

We gathered in a deep bomb crater, just outside the Barrikady. It made an ideal jumping off point.

"Our artillery normally begins counter-battery fire after about an hour. When our guns start firing we'll start to move. We'll hop from crater to crater until we get to those buildings opposite. Look out for our people, if they see us coming from this side they may shoot first and ask questions afterwards."

We crouched down and waited. Sure enough after about an hour our guns opened fire. It was time to move. We climbed out of the crater and

161

began running towards the next one. Rifle fire started pinging all around us, coming from the direction of the Barrikady we had just left. We had obviously vacated the premises just in time. Müller and Vasyl turned and loosed off a fusillade of fire from their PPSh's. I turned to look, there were at least twenty Soviet infantrymen shooting at us from just outside the factory. Two of them went down under the storm of submachine gun fire, the rest dived for cover. We scrambled along to the next crater, then the next. Vasyl and Müller were pouring bullets into the Russians, who by some miracle did not seem to have anything heavier than bolt action Mosin Nagant rifles. A Maxim machine gun would certainly have made our flight impossible. We scrambled to the next strongpoint, a ruined tank that offered shelter from the Russian rifle fire. We got behind it, then a voice called out, "Halt!"

We were home. A Wehrmacht Major came out warily to meet us, heavily armed troopers flanked him. I could see an MG34 poking out from a nearby foxhole.

"SS? In Stalingrad?"

I groaned.

"Special mission from Berlin," I said abruptly. "Contact HQ if you've got any questions."

"You look as if you're in bad shape," he said. "Medic," he called to his men, "see to them at once." He turned back to us. "We'll get your wounds treated, then ferry you to HQ. What are we facing over there, any idea?"

"An attack, tomorrow morning at dawn, expect at least twenty divisions, we're going to make our report to 6th Army HQ."

"Christ," he blurted out. "We'll need to start preparing."

"A good idea, Major," I replied.

He looked at me. I could see the stress of the battle in his eyes. Doubtless mine were just as tortured. There was the unspoken question between us. After the attack tomorrow at dawn, would any of us be alive by the afternoon?

I didn't realise then, but on the evening of November 12th our attack immediately lost its punch when von Paulus called a halt. The Soviet 62nd Army followed up with a counter-attack. Our Luftwaffe commander, General von Richthofen, attacked the Russian bridgeheads at Kletskaya and Serafimovich on the Don River with his 4th Air Fleet. They destroyed several Russian pontoon bridges. The Russians built new bridges, with their platforms just below the river's surface, so that they were out of sight from the air. On that same day, General von Richthofen made a note in his diary that the Soviets were building up forces to attack the Romanians. He wrote that artillery pieces were now showing up in emplacements and questioned when the offensive would begin. Von Richthofen was not however unduly worried about the offensive, he was still convinced that the Russians were nearly finished.

The Luftwaffe was having problems getting air intelligence because of the poor weather, but on November 13th a reconnaissance plane flew at three hundred feet over a mile-long column of Soviet tanks moving west. General Chuikov and Red Army Chief of Staff Vasilevsky visited the buildup in the south and checked out General Vatutin's offensive capability on the Southwest Front. On November 15th Josef Stalin telegraphed Chuikov that everything was ready in Moscow and Zhukov could set the date for the beginning of the offensive from this point on. Chuikov and Vasilevsky had a discussion and agreed that the attack, Operation Uranus, should begin in the north on November 19th and in the south a day later.

When Hitler saw the Soviet build-up on the 6th Army's flanks, he urged von Paulus to continue to capture every part of the city.

"The difficulties of the fighting at Stalingrad are well known to me," Hitler told Friedrich von Paulus on November 16th, "but the difficulties on the Russian side must be even greater just now with the ice drifting down the Volga. If we make good use of this period of time we shall save a lot of blood later on. Therefore I expect that the commanders will once again fight with their usual dash in order to break through to the Volga, at least at the ordnance factory and the metallurgical works, and to take these parts of the city."

We got a lift back to HQ and made our report to Steinmetz. I wondered this time would it be acted upon, and how the High Command would feel now that their Machiavellian plan had failed. Would anyone in Stalingrad care, though? The city was doomed, all but a few senior officers had known it for some time. The Russians fought like lions, shoot a hundred of them and two hundred stepped forward to pick up their weapons and go on fighting. When would they learn that we weren't going to beat these people?

APRIL 1944
Another camp, this time Stalag X-B, located near Sandbostel in north-western Germany, nine kilometres south of Bremervörde, forty three kilometres northeast of Bremen. It had been a long, tiring drive to get here. When we arrived I wondered was it worth bothering with. My mission was to recruit Britishers for the SS-British Freecorps. Yet when we got here we found many of the prisoners were French, Belgians, some Greeks and even some Italians following Italy's surrender in September 1943. The Italians were treated badly, loathed by the Germans as traitors and turncoats. Being treated badly was a euphemism for malnutrition and torture. This camp was so godforsaken, situated on a damp bog in this forgotten corner of the Reich. Rations were frequently late arriving,

leaving the prisoners hungry and even more ragged than most, and the guards bad-tempered at this posting. The weather was drizzling rain combined with a cold easterly wind. But it was better than the Russian Front, I pointed out to one guard who grumbled about being called out to escort Müller and me.

Our SS-British Freecorps was growing, albeit slowly. I guessed we had enough men now for a couple of platoons, not a Corps by any means, but a start. This would hopefully be enough to keep Himmler off of our backs. The men were training at our Berlin barracks, they seemed enthusiastic enough. Certainly the SS rations were filling their bellies and helping them to recover the strength lost during their time eating just the starvation rations supplied to the prison camps. They were learning German, loved nothing better than strutting around Berlin in their walking-out SS uniforms, Himmler should be proud. How they would cope with the Eastern Front was another matter, where our SS divisions mounted attack after attack on the Russian hordes, often in the face of overwhelming and suicidal odds. Casualty rates of seventy five percent were common, sometimes whole divisions were virtually wiped out. I elected not to mention those figures during my recruiting talks. They wanted to hear about good food, esprit de corps, being part of an elite unit. The good of the cause, fighting the Russian savage before he dragged your woman outside in the street to be raped. About smart uniforms, good pay and living conditions, gifts of land and farms in the east when the war was won.

"Attention!"

The British Senior NCO brought the ragged band of men to attention. A miserable looking bunch, the worst yet. They looked as if they had already served on the Russian Front. The other prisoners, the French, Belgians and Italians, watched curiously from a distance. I opened my mouth to speak just as the French broke into a loud rendering of the 'Marsellaise', trying to drown me out. They should have saved their breath, the camp was a microcosm of the traditional feuds between nations, perhaps it was the constant squabbling for rations. The French were hated as much as they hated many of the other nationalities.

I continued with my speech requesting more men to join us in Berlin, more freshly pressed Stormtroopers to be prepared for the Reichsführer's plan of German European domination.

"Men, you have a unique opportunity to fight the Russian savages who threaten even Britain in their war for world communism. Join us and fight these animals. Hitler does not want war against Britain. Many times he has tried to make peace. Why, England and Germany are united in many ways, even your royal family are German. Why would Adolf Hitler want to make war against Britain when it is already ruled by a German King?"

I told them about the royal family's convenient name change from Saxe-Coburg and Gotha to Windsor, in 1917. I told them of the Prince-Duke of Teck, who became the Marquess of Cambridge and took that surname. The Prince-Count of Battenberg became the Marquess of Milford Haven and Earl Mountbatten of Burma, who took the surname of Mountbatten and was a prominent commander in the British army. It was all prepared by Prinz Albrecht Strasser of course, powerful nonsense, but it was also true even if totally irrelevant. Quite why a few aristocrats, British in every way except name, anglicising their names meant a damn thing was a puzzle to me, but it certainly helped to persuade some waverers.

I finished my speech with the usual exhortation to report to the guardroom if they wished to join up and we walked back to the camp office. Passing a long narrow hut, I felt a stone hit me on the shoulder. We took shelter as a storm of stones, clumps of mud and debris rained down on us from the other side of the hut. The guards saw the attack and ran towards the back of the hut. Several shots were fired and the rain of debris ceased.

Afterwards I found out that two Frenchmen and an Italian were killed, one outright, the other two died in the camp medical room, where there were almost no drugs and precious few dressings with which to treat their wounds.

We filled in the paperwork in the camp office and went to the guardroom where a total of nine recruits joined us. Some were buoyed up and optimistic to be leaving the camp and getting into action. Some looked sheepish, guilty. I glanced at Müller, he caught the look. SS training would soon sort them out. If that failed, the Eastern Front was an intensive course in motivation to fight to stay alive.

Except in Stalingrad, where many gave up the fight to live altogether. Starved, freezing to death and abandoned by their leaders, the German High Command, who persistently refused to listen to reports of Russian reinforcements, many literally lay down and died. Stalingrad, the man killer.

SS ENGLANDER

CHAPTER EIGHT

NOVEMBER 1942

"Excellent, Obersturmführer, excellent. I can assure you that this time your intelligence will be acted upon, immediately. We can catch the Ivans with their pants down." Steinmetz left his office to send the report direct from the radio room to Berlin. I reflected that actually it was the Russians that had caught the 6th Army with their pants down. It would take more than a besieged, starving army to dramatically change the situation. Of course the battle was lost, we all knew that. There was only one sensible option open to us, to evacuate the Cauldron of Stalingrad. Rumour piled on rumour about rescue missions that were on their way from the outside, but wiser souls elected to believe it when they saw it. The famous General Erich von Manstein was apparently on his way with the 4th Panzer Army, but whether it was true, or indeed if they would even get through, was by no means certain.

If anyone could do It, von Manstein could. Erich von Manstein was one of the most prominent commanders of the Wehrmacht and was held in high esteem by his fellow officers as one of the Wehrmacht's best military strategists. He had won decisive victories in Poland and France and was now being transferred here. Adolf Hitler had appointed him commander of the newly created Army Group Don. Sadly, though, this unit consisted of a hastily assembled group of tired men and armour and was tasked with the critical new plan, Operation Winter Storm. This required von Manstein to smash through to Stalingrad and establish contact with von Paulus. Once contact was made the 6th Army could withdraw, if necessary, under the protection of Army Group Don.

It was all nonsense. There was only one sane action to take and that was to leave Stalingrad immediately and break out of the encirclement, at whatever cost. The sooner the better, left too long it would be too late. Colonel Steinmetz returned, "Good news, I've passed on the information to Berlin. All our divisional commanders have been alerted, so we'll be ready for them, Haupsturmführer."

"Obersturmführer, Sir," I replied.

"Not any more, you've been promoted. Congratulations, Captain. We'll all be generals by the time this war is over."

I stared at him. "I think not, Colonel."

"No," he shook his head, "perhaps you are right. I think, Hauptsturmführer, that you and your group should get some rest. Dismissed."

"Thank you, Sir." I saluted and left the office to find my group. The three of them, Vasyl, Müller and Tatiana were in the sergeant's canteen, drinking strongly brewed coffee heavily laced with vodka from a bottle that Vasyl had managed to conjure up. They handed me a cup and warmly toasted my promotion. It meant little to me. In fact I had strong doubts that any of us would ever leave the city of Stalingrad. The Russian noose was tightening and I suspected that the coming attack with twenty divisions was just the first of many. The Russians seemed to have limitless resources. Probably the only thing stopping them storming the city with the vast reserves of T34 tanks was that the city itself was a natural tank trap, bombed and bombed again so that hardly a clear road remained along which any tank could manoeuvre.

When the bottle was finished Müller went off to find some more. He came back with four bottles under his arm. I wondered what had happened to their previous owner. Some things were best not to think about. We refilled cups with the vodka, not bothering with the coffee. We had one aim and one aim only, to get totally and hopelessly drunk, to shut out the horror and despair of what we had seen in this city over the past few days and what we knew would be coming in the very near future. Vasyl managed to swap one of the bottles of vodka for some cigars and we all lit up, even Tatiana made us smile when she eagerly took one of the cigars and puffed away at it like a veteran. When Vasyl and Müller were earnestly engaged in a deep discussion about the merits and demerits of Soviet and German armour, I took Tatiana to one side, out of sight of the others.

"Tatiana, my darling," I said to her. I kissed her hard on the lips, causing a few wolf whistles from the envious NCOs watching us in the mess. "We all know that the situation here is hopeless, we know there is no absolute certainty that any of us will escape from this place. But I want you to marry me, headquarters has a priest attached to it, we could get married straight away. I love you so much and I want you to be attached to me, and me to you, for the rest of our lives, no matter how short or long that may be. If I only have another day to live, or fifty years, I want to know that I can spend it with you as my wife. Will you agree to become my wife?"

She stared at me for a few moments, her eyes wide and a little frightened. The medic had done his best to treat her wound, but the scar on her face would take weeks if not months before it healed. It didn't matter to me how many scars she had on her face, I was totally in love with her.

"My dearest Wolf," she said tenderly. "I'm not blind either to the situation. None of us are in any kind of position to make plans. I love you too, I love you deeply. In any other circumstances I would say yes immediately, even while the war is still on. But I'm sorry I can't, not here, not in Stalingrad. Wolf, it's a nightmare, a living, waking hell. Yes, I want to marry you, but not here. Will you ask me again when we have finally left this place, never to return?"

"Of course, that's a promise, my darling." I was disappointed, but understood exactly how she felt. She had been brutalised by the Russians in the Barrikady and had come within a hair's breadth of being mutilated with a knife by the Russian psychopath. She needed time, and time is what I would give her.

I held her close to me, enjoying her soft female warmth in this place of such terrible hardship, pain and death. Then I turned when I heard shouting coming from our table. Müller was wrestling with a tough-looking Wehrmacht sergeant, gripping him with one hand, throwing hard punches with the other. The other NCOs were cheering their man on and the big sergeant was giving a fair account of himself, in most circumstances he would perhaps have been almost unbeatable. But this was Müller, the man who regarded psychopathic violence as a sort of cultural therapy. There was no need to intervene, this was not the officer's mess. I watched them slug it out, the sergeant gradually being worn down by the hammer blows that Müller dealt him. Finally he dropped, to the groans of dismay from his fellow sergeants. Sensibly he didn't get up, I had seen Müller kill men with his bare hands. He was not a man to fight with hand-to-hand. Fighting men like Müller would be best done with a gun, preferably at long range. He was a wicked fighter, cunning, clever, devious and very, very mean.

"What's it all about?" I went over and asked Vasyl.

"The sergeant called me a Russian pig when he heard my accent," the Ukrainian replied. "Your Scharführer took exception to his comrade being insulted by a member of the Wehrmacht."

"His comrade? Müller has a comrade? I'm astonished. Müller has never had a comrade in his life."

Vasyl shrugged. "He has now. He's a good man."

Fair enough, I left him and rejoined Tatiana, telling her about Müller. The sadistic Scharführer frightened her, she was just as surprised as me that he had defended Vasyl and called him a comrade. Perhaps if the war went on for long enough, some things would change for the better. We went back to the table, "Are you ok, Scharführer Müller?" I asked him. He looked pretty battered, the other man had landed a few good blows on him.

"I'm fine Sir, I just need more vodka. Let's drink up."

We picked up our cups and drank, refilled them and finished them off. By then we were all beginning to feel highly intoxicated, so I decided to call it a night and left with Tatiana. Some of the sergeants jeered again as we went off together, but Müller gave them a nasty look and they went quiet.

I was staggering a little. Tatiana was slightly less drunk than me, so she helped guide me back to the small room I had been allocated to sleep in. Despite the cold we stripped off all of our clothes and got under the coarse army blankets together. I held her to me, but the vodka was too much and I must have drifted off to sleep. I awoke to the sound of an explosion but Tatiana was already awake, she soothed me, telling me it was just a random shell. I held her to me, feeling the beginnings of a warm arousal. She smiled, and slipped her hand down to hold my organ, then gently began stroking it. I became hard almost instantly.

"You seem to have recovered from the vodka, Wolf," she said, I could hear the gentle amusement in her voice.

"We'll need to put it to the test," I replied. I cupped her breasts in my hands. They were soft yet firm, warm, alive. They were wonderful. I could smell the female musk of her body, the heady wine of woman-scent that drove men crazy. I was no exception. I slipped my hand down between her legs, massaged the area around her vagina, then sent my fingers exploring to find her clitoris. She gasped, telling me I had found the right spot. We kissed, caressed, loving each other in a way that seemed magnified, so at odds with the awful butchery that surrounded us. Soon, I shifted over and guided my penis into her. She reared, arched her back with pleasure and began moaning with delight as I gently seduced her. She shivered with each strong push that sent my hard organ driving into her, sending her to the same peak of pleasure that I too was climbing. Soon, too soon, I felt myself unable to hold back any longer. I came, spurting again and again inside her, feeling her stiffen and groan even louder as she reached a climax at the same time as me. We just held each other. There were no words we needed to say.

We lit cigarettes and lay there, happy and comfortable in to be together, touching one anothers' bodies.

"I thought they would kill me, Wolf," she said.

I had been afraid of the same thing but we could only live for the day in Stalingrad, even for the hour. So fickle was life in this benighted city, life held so cheaply by all sides, we had to grab even every minute. We were disposable, Russian and German alike. Shoot us down, and our warlord masters would find more from their hordes of fanatics to take our place. We only had the moment, we had each other, that was all and that was enough. Then the curtain on the door was pushed open and Müller walked in, "Sir, we have orders. We have been recalled to Berlin."

"Thank you for marching in on us, Müller," I complained.

"No problem, Hauptsturmführer," he grinned. He walked out, and we got dressed. We found the others waiting in the canteen where there was hot coffee waiting for us. I took a sip of mine and spat it out. God, it was disgusting.

"What is this shit?" I shouted.

"Ersatz, made from ground acorns," Müller told me. "It's all they can get, supplies are so short."

Unknown to me, the final part of the battle was about to be played out many miles to the west, the final encirclement of Stalingrad. Although the railway line had frequently been cut, and the airlift of supplies was repeatedly interrupted by the Russian fighters and fighter bombers, there had been some perilous routes in and out of the city. By November 21st the Soviet 51st Army reached Kalach on the river Don. On November 22nd as the combined German and Romanian Front broke up over its entire length, a distance of fifty miles in the north and thirty miles in the south, Chuikov poured six armies into the breach. The Russian cavalry cut the western railway line from Kalach in various places. The bridge at Kalach had been readied for demolition and a platoon of Wehrmacht engineers was waiting on November 23rd for the order to blow the bridge.

Late that afternoon the engineers heard tanks approaching from the west. Their lieutenant at first thought they were Russians, but then saw that the first three vehicles were Horch personnel carriers with 22nd Panzer Division markings. He assumed that they were reinforcements and told his men to lift the barrier. The personnel carriers stopped and sixty Russian soldiers leapt out. They killed most of the engineers, captured the bridge and dismantled the demolition charges. Twenty five Soviet tanks passed over the bridge and headed southeast, where later that day they made contact with the 14th Independent Tank Brigade from the Soviet 51st Army. The Russian armies had joined. A quarter of a million Germans were trapped in the Cauldron.

"Good morning," a voice called to us. It was Colonel Steinmetz, looking tired and haggard.

"Apparently we are to go home, Colonel. Do we have seats on a Junkers yet?"

"Past history, I'm afraid. Our airfield at Pitomnik has been taken by the Russians. We lost a lot of aircraft, over seventy. The rest flew out of the Cauldron to escape the Russian tanks. Gumrak is still open, but for how long, who knows?"

"When will our aircraft be returning?" I asked him.

There was a silence. "Returning?" he asked. "Pitomnik is in Russian hands, Gumrak is under constant shelling and bombing, flights are limited, precarious at best. Besides, the Heinkels and Dorniers can't land at Gumrak, it's too short, even the Ju52's struggle at times."

"But how do you get supplies, ammunition, fuel, food? What will you fight with if we are surrounded and the airstrip is lost?"

Steinmetz shook his head. "Frankly, I don't know. I have no doubt our staff are working on it."

He looked me in the eyes, I could see the truth revealed there. He was resigned to never leaving the Stalingrad Cauldron. Their fate was sealed. Steinmetz had seen his own death written indelibly on the destroyed tarmac of the Pitomnik airfield.

"So, we have no means of escape?"

"Not at present, no, spaces on any flights we do have going out are reserved exclusively for casualties. I'm sorry. I will notify you if there is a change in the situation. Good luck." He turned on his heel and left the canteen.

"So that's it?" Müller asked truculently. "We're totally fucked, no way out?"

"There is a way." We looked around. Vasyl stood with a map in his hands. It was an old pre-war survey map.

"I was issued with this when I arrived here with my Red Army unit. There's a network of drainage ditches, culverts and some tunnels running cross-country. It's part of the drainage system that was installed when the farms were collectivised."

Collectivisation was part of the Soviet Union's ambitious programme of food production. This was conducted by the consolidation of individual land and labour into collective farms. The theory was that this would immediately increase the food supply for urban populations, the supply of raw materials for processing industry, and agricultural exports.

Everything that we had seen so far seemed to confirm what we had heard back home in Germany, that this uniquely Bolshevik idea simply deprived the population of their ability to provide for themselves and their families. Once more, the peasants starved, just as they had under the Tsars.

"Will it take us all of the way?" I asked him. "We would need to get all the way to Rostov, it's a fair distance."

He looked at the survey map. "It will take us most of the way, the last few kilometres we'll just have to to manage as best we can. At least we'll be away from the main battlefields."

I checked out the map, Müller looked over my shoulder. It was certainly possible. Risky yes, but staying here was a certainty of capture and death by the Red Army.

"We could do it," I told them. "Vasyl is right, if we stay in the drainage culverts we could slip right past the Russians. It's by no means certain, but probably the best hope we have. I suggest we leave tonight, are we all agreed?"

They all nodded, there was really no need for discussion. Any hope, no matter how small, would be better than waiting for the mercy of the Red Army. Müller went off to scrounge up supplies, anything we could eat on the way. It would be difficult, the German army was slowly starving to death in the Cauldron, especially now that the supply flights had been cut off.

When asked by Hitler, Göring had replied, after being convinced by Luftwaffe General Hans Jeschonnek, that the air force could supply the 6th Army with an "air bridge". This would allow the von Paulus to fight on while a relief force was assembled. This air bridge would need to fly in at least four hundred tonnes of supplies a day. This was insane, the 6th Army was the largest army we had, the idea that we could fly in everything they needed to one tiny airfield was the lunatic scheme of a madman. In reality we would be lucky to get more than a hundred and twenty tonnes a day and that was when the planes could actually make it here and land. There were already thousands of men that were simply incapable of fighting. They huddled in the ruined buildings or at the roadsides, slowly starving or freezing to death. Von Paulus, in yet another of his shameful orders, had decreed that the twelve thousand wounded men that were unable to fight would forfeit their rations. Even the ones who could fight, however, could not count on the weapons and ammunition to fight the battle with.

If anyone could locate scarce food supplies, Müller could. He was a very persuasive man. I took Tatiana and Vasyl to find ammunition and weapons. We were in luck, we had come to use the Soviet PPSh's, the ubiquitous submachine gun that was the backbone of Russian infantry firepower. We found the Russian guns more reliable in the mud and snow of Stalingrad, the ammunition was plentiful, often taken from dead enemy soldiers, so they were our preferred choice. Many Germans preferred to keep their tried and trusted MP38's, so we were able to beg and borrow several ammunition drums for the guns, together with spare clips for our Tokarev automatic pistols. In a pinch, the ammunition was interchangeable, the 7.62mm round could be used to load magazines for both weapons.

One tired quartermaster swapped a bag of German stick grenades for two bottles of vodka that Vasyl seemed to mysteriously produce like magic when the occasion demanded.

"Going to fight a war?" he asked. We didn't reply. "How about some Russian winter uniforms?" he offered. "We've got a few on the shelf, no bloodstains."

"How much?" Vasyl asked him. "Four bottles," the quartermaster tentatively said, wondering how much more of the precious, warming, mind deadening spirit he could bargain for. In the end he settled for two bottles in return for four of the Soviet white winter camouflage uniforms together with four pairs of warm winter gloves. Our own winter uniforms had started to arrive, albeit in small quantities, a reversible garment with Wehrmacht field-grey on one side, winter-white on the other. But we wanted to look like Russians, it was our best hope. We had already pulled off the masquerade on more than one occasion, there was no reason to think it would not work for us again. We returned to the canteen. Müller was back already, carrying a heavy backpack loaded with food. We had five hundred kilometres to travel to reach relative safety in Rostov, a total of three hundred miles! I left them and went to see Steinmetz, he was sat in his office, drinking quietly from a hoarded bottle of schnapps. He had pictures of his family spread out on his desk. I made no comment about them.

"Colonel, we need transport to the western edge of the Cauldron."

I told him that we would be attempting to sneak through the lines, but no details of the drainage culverts we planned to travel along. We didn't want half of the 6th Army using the same route.

"Yes, I can arrange for a Kübelwagen to be made available to you this evening, Hauptsturmführer. Do you think you can get through?"

"Maybe," I told him. He understood I didn't want to broadcast our route.

"Very well, good luck, Wolf. Perhaps we'll meet again one day."

"Good luck to you, Sir. Yes, maybe one day we'll all see the sun shining on the coffee houses in Berlin."

He smiled and shook my hand. I saluted him, he returned the salute, then I left. Back in the canteen we spent the rest of the day smoking, chatting, cleaning and oiling our weapons. Everything was neatly and carefully packed into the backpacks. The Soviet winter camouflage was rolled up and tied to the packs. It was almost time to go. The tension rose. We managed to persuade the cooks to give us as much hot soup as they could spare, we would need it out in the open where the temperatures dropped to thirty degrees below zero.

The cooks grumbled mightily, they had better things to do than fatten up the SS, they said, didn't we know the army was going hungry, and so on. Vasyl parted with another bottle of vodka and the grumbling stopped.

"That's the last one, I'm afraid," he told us. But it had been sufficient currency to gain us the supplies that would give us a fighting chance of breaking out to Rostov. I checked my watch, it was nearly six o'clock and the sky was dark. A private soldier entered the canteen, wrapped in at least two greatcoats that we could see, together with scarves made of rags wrapped around his head. He saluted.

"Colonel Steinmnetz ordered me to report here Sir, transport to the western side of the Cauldron."

"Thank you, Private, we're ready now," I replied.

We looked at each other, this was it. Four of us. Two Waffen-SS, a Ukrainian former officer of the Red Army and the daughter of a Polish aristocrat. God help us!

"What are you smiling about?" Tatiana asked me. I told her.

"Wolf, Vasyl told me there are only two Soviet tank armies between us and Rostov, so it'll be fine," she laughed gaily, infected by the warmth of the canteen and the excitement of the escape attempt. Müller and Vasyl looked at me. No it wouldn't be fine, every hand would be turned against us, if they caught us we would be tortured and executed as spies. The weather threatened even the best prepared soldier with severe frostbite, and we had no doctors or drugs to treat it. The food would last us four days, at best, in these sub-zero conditions. The journey would take us at least ten days if all went well, much longer if it did not. If we were to factor in packs of wolves that roamed the steppe feasting on the thousands of corpses that littered the countryside, and bands of partisans that patrolled the area looking for stray Germans to pick off, it was anything but fine. It would be a bloody, desperate business. But we were bloody and desperate, so we had a chance. A very small chance!

We climbed into the Kübi and sat hunched inside our greatcoats as protection against the freezing night. It was no time to take a ride through the Russian steppe in an open top vehicle. The driver cautiously edged his way west away from the city, driving without lights so as not to attract a wandering Soviet night fighter. The night was brightly moonlit, reflecting off of the snow so that it was not too difficult to stay on the track. The ground was frozen, but the Kübelwagen managed to stay on the road without sliding off into a shell crater or ditch. It took us four hours to reach the western edge of the Stalingrad Front, the Cauldron. Our artillery was pointed to the west, waiting for the inevitable Russian attack that would attempt to smash through at any time. Why the Russians delayed was difficult to fathom, they could have sent a troop of boy scouts in here and the army would probably have surrendered. We passed rows of Panzers, guns again pointed west waiting for the Russians.

"Why don't they break out?" I asked the driver, puzzled. It was a formidable force.

"No fuel," the driver replied. "They used the last drop of petrol just getting here, now they're just being used as gun emplacements."

What a monstrous, stupid waste, I thought. The might of the German Wehrmacht, the very means to punch through the Soviet armies that encircled them, rendered impotent through a simple lack of petrol. Someone should be shot for this fiasco, but they probably already had been! With the failure of the airlift to bring in sufficient supplies the tanks and other working vehicles had barely enough fuel deploy, let alone to fight a battle and reach out across the steppes to link with von Manstein's relief effort. If they were to break out our soldiers would have to make the trip on foot whilst fighting the encircling Soviet troops and armour. Above us the Soviets had almost total air supremacy, meaning that moving out or manoeuvring in daylight was guaranteed suicide. It was hard to imagine how the promised air bridge could supply even a fraction of what this vast army needed.

The Kübelwagen stopped. I turned to Vasyl who was looking at the map.

"Is this the place?" I asked him.

"Near enough," he replied. "If we jump off here, we need to head south for half a kilometre, then duck down into the first culvert."

"Fair enough, let's go," I ordered.

We climbed out, shouldered our packs and began moving off, Vasyl leading. We had decided not to wear the white winter camouflage uniforms yet for fear of being shot by our own side as Soviet infiltrators. We intended to change into them just before we hit the Russian held sector. We marched through the snow, the ground crunching underfoot. Pockets of our troops huddled in foxholes, sheltering from the cold. The cold! It was fearsome out here in the countryside, at thirty degrees below it cut through us like a knives. We wrapped scarves around our heads, so that we looked almost like a group of mummies stumbling along wrapped in dirty bandages. There were more parked Panzers stuck without fuel, helpless to manoeuvre if the Russians attacked in any strength. Then we reached our start point. It was a low bridge over a small frozen stream. We climbed down into the culvert, put on the white winter camouflage and began walking west. Soon we could see the lights of Russian campfires. They had no fear of our artillery zeroing in on them, by now they had realised how desperately short our guns were of ammunition. We came within two hundred metres of a Red Army camp. Now we crouched down, crawling along the culvert on all fours to keep out of sight of the sentries. We got past them without incident, stood up and walked on carefully.

It was a quiet night, a pity about the moonlight. I would have preferred it to be darker but at least we could see our way forward without stumbling. We pressed on further. Another Russian camp loomed in front of us, this time it was much bigger, it looked like a divisional HQ. We dropped down to a crawl again and pushed on slowly. The going was difficult, the intense cold made every effort, even breathing, harsh and painful. We got past the main camp and continued on, there were only isolated pockets of camp fires now, we were nearly clear. Then I heard a nearby shout. "Halt!" We stopped and I waited for a shot, but none came. I looked up, a sentry was leaning on the rail of a small bridge over the culvert, staring at us suspiciously. We still had a chance. We all spoke fluent Russian and were dressed and armed as Soviet soldiers.

"It's ok," I shouted. "Commissar's department, we are conducting a surprise inspection. These soldiers are NKVD, my escort."

"No one told me of an inspection," the sentry grumbled.

"Of course not, soldier. You were not told because it is a surprise inspection. Only your general knows. You can put down your gun. Do not dare to point your weapon at one of Comrade Stalin's personal representatives. Quickly, man!" I shouted. "You have done well to challenge us, I will mention it in my report. But if you do not put that rifle down now, I will have you shot!"

I had raised my voice to a threatening, bullying tone, as a commissar would be expected to do. They were the slave masters in Stalin's communist paradise. This man was only human, he lowered the rifle.

"Advance, comrades," he said. "Comrade Commissar, may I see your papers? It would be expected of me."

"Of course," I told him. "Sergeant," I snapped at Müller, "show the sentry here our identification. Hurry man, I don't want to be here all night."

Müller nodded, his eyes took on that vacant killing gaze that I had come to recognise. He marched up to the sentry, put his hand inside his camouflage jacket and swept the knife out and under the man's throat in one perfect, almost balletic movement. He caught the soldier as he fell, only a slight gurgle sound in the quiet night.

"Bury him under the snow," I ordered, "we don't want them to see his body until we are a long way away from here. Vasyl, give him a hand."

The Ukrainian ran forward, between them the men dragged the body fifty metres away to a mound of snow and quickly buried him in a shallow grave. They came back and we moved on. Vasyl came up to walk next to me.

"Wolf, I'll take the lead, we don't want to run into any more sentries. If I bump into one, you'll be warned in advance. We may not be so lucky next time as we were with that fool. If we meet a suspicious party member or an officer, they won't be so easy to kill."

It was a good idea, one I should have had myself before we were challenged by the sentry. The Ukrainian moved off, we waited until he was about fifty metres ahead, then we followed. We were nearing the outer perimeter of the Russian Division, soon we could no longer see the camp fires. The culvert disappeared into the black hole of a tunnel that ran underground. We crawled inside, the darkness closed around us, freezing, damp, claustrophobic. Vasyl crawled ahead, I followed, then Tatiana with Müller bringing up the rear. The crawl seemed endless with the ever present fear that the end of the tunnel may be too tight to squeeze through. But after half an hour the blackness of the tunnel began to lessen, we were near the end. Soon we emerged under the harsh, freezing moonlit sky. There were no Russians in sight, so we stood up, picked up the pace and marched forward.

Suddenly, I saw Vasyl hold up his hand. "Stop," he whispered.

We crouched down and waited for him. Soon, he was back with us.

"Partisans," he said, "about ten of them."

"Are we clear to get past them?" I asked.

"Yes and no. They've got prisoners, Germans, two of our soldiers. One of their women is torturing them."

I could tell by the tone of his voice that there was something more. "And?"

He hesitated for a moment. "She's flaying them alive, peeling off their skin with sharp knives."

183

I heard Tatiana's tiny cry of horror. I think even Müller was surprised at the barbarity of these Russian partisan women. Then there was a loud, screaming shout of agony and despair.

"Right, we can't just leave them. We'll crawl forward along the culvert, use the PPSh's. Open fire when I start firing. Don't stop until they're all dead. Is there any hope for the prisoners?" I asked Vasyl.

"I think not," he replied. "They're too far gone to survive. Maybe a hospital, but otherwise," he shrugged.

There was only one decision to make. "We'll finish off the prisoners too, it's all we can do for them. But make it quick, kill them and move on. The noise could bring a Soviet division down on our heads. Let's go."

We crawled forward until we were only ten metres from the partisan camp. The two German soldiers were stripped almost naked, whimpering in terror and pain, their bodies bloody. I made sure that all of the partisans were in sight then pulled the trigger.

MAY 1944

I was thinking of that day, one of our last in Stalingrad, when I realised that I was again daydreaming. We were in Schwerin, Stalag II-E. From the camp I could see the castle of Schwerin, located just outside the city, capital of the Bundesland of Mecklenburg-Vorpommern in the very heart of the Reich. Another batch of dismal dispirited British prisoners, spending their fourth year in German captivity.

Müller and I were doing our best to get results, results at any price that would satisfy our masters and keep us away from the Eastern Front. The war was going from bad to worse. The Russians had launched attacks on several fronts with their seemingly limitless tanks and reserve troops. Our propaganda ministry kept issuing proclamations about forthcoming miracle weapons that Adolf Hitler would be using to swing the tide of war back into Germany's favour. But many people were now wondering why these weapons were not already being used to halt the Soviet attacks. I was about to start my standard speech when a soldier detached himself from the group of prisoners and marched up to me in a demonstration of parade ground precision and swung his arm up in a perfect salute.

"Regimental Sergeant Major Oakeshott. I would like a word with you, Captain, before you speak."

"It's Hauptsturmführer, Sergeant Major, I replied. "Captain is a Wehrmacht rank, I am a member of the SS."

"I know what your rank is," he spat out. "I also know why you are here and that you are an Englishman. You should be aware that under the terms of the Geneva Convention it is against the rules of war to try and recruit men to fight against their own country."

"Thank you, Sergeant Major," I replied. "I have examined the rules of war. I have no intention of asking any of these men to fight against Great Britain."

"Great Britain or any of her allies," he said firmly.

He was a decent man. I could hardly imagine what being cooped up in this camp for four years had done to his morale. Yet he had clearly retained much of the dogged determination that would have taken him to the most senior position that a non-commissioned officer could aspire to in the army. Most soldiers thought of regimental sergeant majors as the real leaders of a fighting unit, nothing I had seen contradicted that view.

"Sergeant Major, I have a job to do, you have a job to do. Your comments are noted. Please will you rejoin the ranks."

"Why are you fighting for the Jerries?" he asked. "Don't you know that Germany has lost the war? You know what we'll do to you when it's all over."

I had heard this conversation many times in the past from almost every one of the prison camps I had visited. I wondered at the sanity of Heinrich Himmler in sending me on this mission, hoping that Englishmen would respond well to another Englishman. It hardly took a military genius to know that they would instinctively hate and despise me for fighting for the enemy, for being a traitor. It was not a good way to go about recruiting them.

In the event, we recruited four new men from that camp. The RSM was right of course. Germany had totally lost the war. Like everyone else, I was just going through the motions, waiting for the bomb or bullet that at any time would end the nightmare my life had become since I had killed that man in a bar fight long before the war had started.

The only way most of us got through it was by drinking as much alcohol as possible when we were out of the battle line, doing our best to temporarily forget the horror of the war and the terror of what lay ahead.

CHAPTER NINE

NOVEMBER 1942

The night calm was torn away by the vicious sound of our PPSh's firing long, continuous bursts. We peppered the camp with clip after clip of ammunition, the partisans were caught completely by surprise. Their bodies jerked spastically as the bullets struck, tearing into them, ripping flesh and bone apart. We must have hit them with nearly two hundred and fifty rounds, five drums of ammo. I shouted to stop firing and went out to inspect the bloody carnage. They were all dead, including the two poor devils who had been partially flayed, they had at least found some peace. The partisans, eight men and two women, were shredded and almost unrecognisable. We found several fully loaded PPSh drums to replenish our ammunition. I looked around, but there were no obvious troop movements in our direction. They could come, however, at any time.

"Move on!" I shouted.

We dropped back into the culvert. Apart from the ammunition, we had helped ourselves to some hot pieces of meat that the partisans had been cooking on their fire. We ate the food as we went along, the warm feeling in our bellies easing some of the horror that we had seen in the camp. Stalingrad always seemed to surprise us, as if the depths of this particular hell had no bottom. The night grew colder, but I made them push on. Surprisingly Tatiana didn't protest, although I could see she was very, very tired. Vasyl and Müller grumbled a little at the pace, we were all worn out. I felt as if the life was slowly draining from my body into this endless, frozen waste. But if we stopped, we died. Then I saw the first signs of dawn breaking, piercing the night sky with streaks of lighter colours. I ordered them to carry on until we reached the next tunnel. By then it was nearly light. We slumped down to make camp, spending the day just outside the entrance of the tunnel. We could quickly crawl in if we needed to hide from any Russian eyes.

"What a night," Tatiana sighed. "I hope it won't take many more of those to reach Rostov. By the way, how many nights do you estimate to get us there?"

"Ten," I replied. She looked shocked. Ten nights of frozen marching and crawling along the drainage ditch, through cramped dark tunnels, constantly on watch for the enemy. Ten days of making camp on the bitter tundra. Sleeping only fitfully through the bitter sub-zero temperatures and ever present terror we would be discovered by the Soviets. Or even worse, by the partisans. I neglected to tell her that ten nights was optimistic, it could take a lot longer if we hit trouble.

It was a terrible day. Even though we were exhausted we found it hard to sleep. Several times we heard the squeaking rumble of tank tracks, T34's, heading east towards Stalingrad. Those poor bloody bastards of the 6th Army. Once a motorised rifle regiment came close, lorries packed with infantry, again heading for what would surely become the final resting place of von Paulus and the pitiful remnants of his army. No one came near to our camp, though. By late afternoon darkness had descended, it was time to move on. We put on our packs, adjusted the scarves around our heads to keep out the worst of the cold from our faces, and departed. It seemed even colder. Without the scarves to muffle the freezing air, it would sear in the throat, causing a terrible burning feeling to add to our problems. The night was uneventful, we passed no further enemy positions and by next morning we had made good time. Everyone cheered up and that day we got some real sleep, as much as anyone did sleeping outdoors in this arctic land.

And so we carried on night after night marching along the system of culverts, dropping out of sight if we saw the enemy, sleeping by day next to one of the numerous tunnels that punctuated the ditches. We travelled for seven nights before we encountered any Russians. But we were growing weak, the food had run out the night before. With at least three more days to travel before I estimated we might reach the German lines in Rostov, we were in trouble. Travelling through the bitter cold with no food, and only interrupted sleep through the day, nervous that at any moment we could be discovered by the Russians, we were debilitated so much that I doubted our ability to survive for three more nights outdoors on the Russian steppe in the depths of this exceptionally cold winter. The human body needed food to survive, just to keep the heart pumping and the brain working. We had nothing to replace the reserves of body fat we were now using up, squandering fast, just to keep alive and keep moving. We had reached a simple equation; we needed food, warmth, shelter, or we would die. Then we saw the village.

It was a dilapidated collection of huts, probably quite large by local standards in this desolate steppe. There were perhaps forty or fifty buildings in all, probably some were stables. Didn't the peasants share their homes with the animals in places like this, though? Or had I read it somewhere? No matter, it was food and warmth.

"Vasyl, flank to the right, check it out. Müller, go to the left. I'll go forward in the centre and stop just short of the village. If we hear any shooting, we'll know where to head for. Go now, try and keep quiet. It looks peaceful enough, but there could be a company of Russians camped here. If we do see any soldiers, we'll see about moving on. But we need the food, if there are not too many to deal with we'll try and kill them without waking the whole village. Get moving!"

They moved off, I went forward with Tatiana behind me. We reached the first line of huts. I couldn't see anything to worry us. Then further in, we crept forward until we were in the village square. There was a well there, a ramshackle collection of old planks with a rope and bucket stood next to it. And a Russian military GAZ jeep! Damn, of all the luck, why couldn't we just find a village with no troops? Yet there was no obvious evidence of a strong Russian force. It looked as if the occupants of the jeep had just stopped here for the night. There was not even a sentry. Just then I heard someone whistling. We stood back in the shadows then I crept forward again. Peering around the corner I could see a Soviet soldier whistling away to himself as he urinated against the wall of a hut. Perfect. I drew my Tokarev, stepped forward and behind him. Then I spoke to him quietly, "Don't move Comrade, or I'll blow your balls off. Stand still, that's right, keep hold of your dick. Let go and I'll put a bullet in it. Understood?"

He nodded vigorously, terrified.

"Who are you?" he asked in a tremor.

"We are on a visit from Berlin," I replied. "Adolf Hitler sends his compliments."

The man shook with fear. "Tatiana," I said. "Go and find the others, bring them here."

She ran off to find them. Soon she was back with Müller and Vasyl.

"Müller," I said to my Scharführer, "ask him how many soldiers there are in the village. Use any methods you like."

He smiled.

Five minutes later the Russian was dead, but not before he told us that the village was being used as a billet for a unit of NKVD infantry. No sleeping under the stars for Comrade Stalin's political police.

"The kitchen is that building across the square," Müller pointed. "They're all asleep, why not just grab some food and then get on our way?"

I considered for a moment. We had to eat to give us the strength to fight off the bitter cold and keep moving to Rostov.

"Very well," I replied. "Let's go."

We got to the kitchen hut. The door had a flimsy lock and Vasyl just bent it back with his bare hands.

"Soviet craftsmanship," he grimaced.

In the kitchen we found food. A couple of loaves left over from the day before, sausages, a large vat of stew presumably for the following day, and strips of beef or horsemeat. Also a large circular cheese and even a large jug of milk. It tasted foul, like curdled goats milk, which it probably was, but we were starving so we found some enamel mugs and drank it down. Müller explored the shelves and came back with a large tin, I checked the label. Rat poison, obviously to keep vermin away from the food. He looked at me questioningly. I nodded, "Put it in the stew, then put the tin back on the shelf. We don't want them to know we were here."

We stuffed ourselves with the precious food then filled out packs with as much as we could carry. Müller emptied the poison into the stew, then we cleared up and left. Of course they would know that their food stores had been raided, but that was normal in wartime. It could have been hungry peasants, partisans or a military unit. Either way, after they ate the stew, they would not be doing much investigating.

We left the kitchen hut, Vasyl and Müller carried the dead soldier with us out of the village and we buried him in the snow. With any luck, we could wipe out a unit of Soviet NKVD troops. At least it would be some payback for the bloody debacle we were leaving behind. Besides, it was one body of men less to come looking for us if our presence became known to the Russians. Back in the culvert we marched on, I was determined to get as much distance between us and the village as possible before dawn. I pushed the pace hard, but there were no protests this time. They all

191

understood the urgency. Besides, we had full bellies to march on. It was enough, for now. Then everything went wrong. It started with a massive roar, hundreds and hundreds of Soviet T34 tanks, most with a full complement of tank riders, the infantry who rode into battle actually riding on the hulls of the tanks. Behind the tanks were lorries packed with motorised infantry, so many it was impossible to count. It looked as if we were caught in the middle of the Soviet final buildup prior to their attack on Stalingrad. Within two kilometres of us the tanks manoeuvred across the steppe. Hundreds of lorryloads of infantry were laagered, ready to make camp, fleets, literally fleets of aircraft roared overhead, more planes than I would have thought existed in the whole of Russia.

"We can't get through this lot," I told them.

Vasyl nodded in agreement. "My friend, this whole area will be crawling with troops, possibly within hours. Our Russian disguise will not get us through that much security, we need to find somewhere to hide until these units move past."

"Any suggestions?" I asked.

"Obersturmführer, I have an idea," Müller said. "The village. We could go back there and wait. We need to shelter somewhere, we can't survive out here."

"But we left the food poisoned, the NKVD bodies will be there."

"Exactly, Sir, we could go back, hide the bodies and garrison the village as NKVD. They will have papers with them, orders from their HQ. We just take over their mission."

It was an incredible idea, mad enough to work. Besides, we had no choice. We retraced out steps and entered the village cautiously. We needn't have worried, they were all dead. Müller and Vasyl dragged a dozen bodies out and hid them in a snowdrift. If we weren't out of here by the time the thaw came, we would be beyond help anyway. Tatiana and I had searched the uniforms of the officers. We'd found a packet of documents in a pouch, maps and identity papers for the whole contingent. Apparently the NKVD didn't trust their men to carry their own personal papers.

Then we settled into the village and acted for the next six weeks as an NKVD garrison. Amazingly no one came to question our authority. All we had to do was check the papers of passing units and keep a lookout for deserters.

It was six wonderful weeks that Tatiana and I spent building a relationship which we promised each other would last for our lifetimes. Christmas came and went, Müller had found a tree outside the village and we celebrated with vodka and home baked bread, together with a couple of chickens we roasted, we had found them half starved in a peasant hut. Then the armies moved on, an incredible sight, hundreds of thousands of men, vehicles and tanks sweeping towards the doomed city of Stalingrad. That night, we left the village, picking up the route back through the culvert.

Once more, just before dawn, we camped next to a tunnel. When the dawn blossomed in the sky the sun shone and I could hear birds singing. We must have been close to Rostov, possibly no more than twenty or thirty kilometres away. For the first time I began to feel that we night make it. In truth, when we set out I thought we had no chance at all of getting through. It was just that trying was better than the slow death by cold and starvation that was surely the inevitable fate of the 6th Army. Yet now, things were different. We had nearly made it. I took out my binoculars.

"Rostov," I told them. "We're nearly there."

They laughed, hooting with joy.

"Wait," I told them, "that's not all. It looks like a Soviet force camped outside of Rostov, besieging the city. It's not going to be easy. Vasyl, we're about twenty five kilometres outside of the city, how much further does the culvert run?"

He checked the map. "A kilometre, maybe two," he replied.

I checked my binoculars again. "The ground is pretty hilly, lots of cover. We can do it. We'll start slipping through their lines as soon as it's dark. We need to do this in one go, we may not find any cover for another night. Let's eat, sleep, then have a good meal before we set off. We need to travel light, so we'll ditch everything, including the food before we leave. They'll have plenty in Rostov, and if we don't make it…"

I didn't need to finish. If we didn't make it, we wouldn't need the food!

"Wolf, there's a group of huts to the south, about a kilometre." Vasyl was scanning the surrounding area with the binoculars. "It may be worth me taking a look, they'll assume I'm with the Red Army, no cause for alarm. But they may have some knowledge of a route past that Soviet army. I can be there and back in a couple of hours."

It was risky. The sun shone in the sky, he could easily be spotted by a roving Russian patrol. Who would, of course, assume he was another Russian in their winter camouflage. I decided to take the risk, getting past that Soviet army to our lines in Rostov was going to be difficult, if not virtually impossible. He went off, fortunately having the presence of mind to saunter. A man running from cover to cover would stand out like, well, a German soldier on the Russian steppe.

We dropped our packs and rested after the long night march. Müller handed out some rations that we ate greedily. We needed calories, lots of calories, to enable our bodies just to survive in the vicious climate. Then we dozed while Müller took the first watch. I awoke to a commotion, ripped out my Tokarev and looked up, but it was Vasyl with a woman. She was in rags, a pitiful creature at first glance. But then, through the filth and the grime I could see she was in reality magnificent, a woman who properly dressed and cleaned up would have turned heads in any city of the world. Not pretty, perhaps, like Tatiana, but her face had an animal vitality that shone through the filth like a beacon. She must have been six feet tall, almost as tall as Vasyl. He stood next to her, but he was not holding her and she was unarmed. I relaxed and holstered my automatic.

"Who the hell is she?" I asked him.

"She is like me, a Ukrainian. The Russian pigs were billeted in that hamlet and they had her in chains to stop her escaping. They kept her to service their officers."

He put his arm around her shoulders as if to soothe her. I doubted that this woman needed soothing from anyone, she looked very capable. Very feminine but very tough, a strange combination, a strange woman. It was obvious that Vasyl was already smitten.

"Can she help us find a way through the Russians?"

"She can, Wolf," he replied.

"What about the officers that were billeted there?"

"They went back to their unit. If they return to the hamlet tonight they'll only see that she has escaped, they're not going to go after her, not in the middle of a war zone."

"True. Very well, Vasyl, she comes with us. What's your name?" I asked her.

"I am Nataliya," she replied.

"Right, Nataliya, where will you go after we reach Rostov?"

She looked at Vasyl, then back at me. "I will return to the Ukraine, to my home. This man has said he will help me."

Vasyl nodded, "Her home town is less than fifty kilometres from where I was brought up, I will get her home."

Another stray woman I had collected along the way, another woman brutalised by the war. Brutalised by the Russians, brutalised by the Germans, it made no difference. These women were innocent victims caught up in man's savagery.

"You'd both better try and get some rest, we'll need to start working through the lines towards Rostov tonight. We're going to need every ounce of strength and skill we possess. Even then, it may not be enough."

"We'll get through, Haupsturmführer," Vasyl said, a determined note in his voice, his eyes fixed on Nataliya.

Well, well, so that's the way it is, I thought. Love at first sight, and in the middle of a war zone. Vasyl elected to take the next watch, and I got my head down to take some rest. Tatiana lay down next to me, Müller found a space just inside the tunnel and before I dropped off to sleep I saw that Vasyl and Nataliya were sat next to each other, talking earnestly and each holding the other's hand. Obviously Vasyl thought Nataliya was in need of comfort and reassurance, I thought wryly. Twice during the day I was woken to take my turn on guard. Once, I could have sworn that Vasyl's clothing was rather more untidy than normal, as if he had dressed in a hurry. Well, I thought, if he wants to freeze his bare arse off in the Arctic climate it was no business of mine. We all needed some comfort and reassurance, especially in wartime. Except for Müller, of course, other than prostitutes I had never seen him close to anyone. Apart from the people he killed when he seemed to go into some kind of erotic, climactic haze, almost like the final act of sex. I knew that for him killing was a type of sexual gratification. He was a man to be watched, a man for whom killing was as much pleasure as sex. I was shaken awake for the last time, the daylight was fading rapidly. It was time to get ready.

We took food out of our packs and ate quietly.

"Sir, we need to head south west, the bulk of the Russian army is directly to the south between us and Rostov. To the south west the terrain is fairly wild and we have the best chance of getting through," said Nataliya.

While I had been asleep, Nataliya had taken the opportunity to clean herself up. I suspected that she and Vasyl had taken other opportunities too, but that was another matter between them. She was truly a very attractive woman, strong, magnetic and vital in every way, almost like an athlete in training. I thought briefly of the Russian brutes that had chained her for sex. To tie down such a unique woman seemed a truly abominable crime.

"Very well, let's clear everything away. We're too close to the Russians to leave any evidence of our being here, so make absolutely sure that you hide everything in the snow."

We trekked south west as Natalyia had advised. Vasyl took the lead, Natalyia walked beside him, showing him the way. There was no talking now, it was night and any sound would have carried a great distance. We needed to keep listening for any signs of the enemy. Vasyl constantly stopped, held up his hand for us to halt and went carefully forward to check out possible dangers. Although the diversion meant that we would have to travel about five kilometres further than the direct route, I still hoped to travel the whole distance in one night. By midnight we were making excellent progress and I estimated we were no more than twenty kilometres away from the city and the safety of the German lines. Then I saw Vasyl hold up his hand. He came back slowly and quietly.

"What's the problem?" I asked him.

"I'm not sure," he replied. "I can smell smoke just ahead, cigarette smoke, Russian cigarette smoke. It looks as if it may be a Soviet checkpoint, probably looking out for deserters from the army outside Rostov, but they're going to be difficult to get past."

"What do you suggest?" I asked him.

"We have to take them, Wolf," he replied. "Provided, of course, there aren't too many of them. I'll scout ahead with Müller if you don't mind."

"Müller," I said quietly, "go with Vasyl, see if we can dispose of them without making too much fuss."

He nodded and drew out his knife. The two men crept forward quietly. Ten minutes later they came back. They had reconnoitred either side of the Russian position. There were four soldiers, probably regimental police. Obviously they were an observation post to watch for deserters, as we had thought.

"Can we take them without any noise?" I asked. "We have no idea how many there are nearby, we don't want to start a firefight that'll bring the whole Soviet army down on our heads."

"I think so," Vasyl replied. "It'll need the three of us, the girls can stay here."

I spoke to Tatiana and Nataliya. "Keep quiet, keep low and stay out of trouble. The best advice I can offer you if we run into trouble is to head due south away from the immediate battle area, find a village to hide up in."

They both stared at me, I was proud that neither showed any fear. I was touched by their faith in us three being able to pull it off. I hoped they wouldn't be disappointed, for myself as much as for them.

We crept carefully forward. Like Vasyl, I smelt the cigarette smoke before I could see any sign of the soldiers. Then Vasyl pointed to some dark shapes, the four Russians were concealed in a shallow depression in the ground, so that only their shoulders and helmets were visible. As we crept closer, I could hear them talking to themselves quietly. They were all smoking, the four cigarettes ends dancing backwards and forwards in the night like fireflies as they puffed at their tobacco. As far as I could see they were armed with only Mosin Nagant bolt action rifles, there was no evidence of any automatic weapons at their position. I guess that if their only task was to deal with deserters, a rifle would be more than enough to stop and possibly shoot a couple of wayward soldiers. Vasyl whispered to us he would take the two in the centre, myself the man on the right and Müller the soldier on the left. We carefully laid our PPShs on the ground and drew our automatic pistols. I had no need to tell them that a single shot would give the game away. The pistols were only to be used, if necessary, to threaten. I took out my knife, a Swiss hunting knife that I carried in my jackboot. Vasyl pulled his knife from his belt, Müller's knife was already in his hand, and we went silently forward. Closer and closer we came, until we were no more than a metre behind them. I could even smell the strong odour of onions mingling with the tobacco, presumably from their most recent meal.

Vasyl lept across the gap and landed squarely on top of the two soldiers in the centre. Simultaneously I rushed forward and took my own target, gripping him around the neck with my left arm, choking off his airway and preventing him from shouting out, then I stabbed down with my knife into his stomach. Again and again I stabbed, desperate to kill the man before he had the chance to cry out. It may not have had the graceful elegance of Müller's sweeping slash that ripped open the man's throat it in one curving cut, but I was not an expert knife fighter like him and was content to just make sure of the kill. I felt a hand on my arm and whipped round, but it was Vasyl.

"You can stop," he said quietly. "He's dead, you don't need to do any more. They're all dead."

I looked down. The four men had not stood a chance. I shivered with passion and rage, but my target lay butchered at my feet. The two soldiers Vasyl had targeted were sprawled together, almost as if in some kind of an embrace. Müller's target lay neatly on the ground, as if asleep. It was too dark to see the expression on Müller's face but I knew his eyes would have that post-coital look, the lips with that satisfied smile. We went back and retrieved the women, then continued on our way. Our group detoured further south for twenty minutes to lay a false trail in case anyone tried to follow us. I wasn't too worried, I was certain that the Soviet authorities would assume their men had been killed by a band of deserters and would look for the attackers in any direction other than that which would take them in the direction of their own army. Eventually we got back on course. Now the lights of Rostov were more visible to guide us, the occasional beam of light shining up into the sky, probably vehicle headlights. As we got nearer to our lines, I dared to let my hopes rise, but I knew we were still a long way from home.

We marched on through the night. The Russian positions were now clearly visible, which made it easier for us to see them in advance and skirt around them. I had taken the lead, Müller was behind me and Tatiana walked in the middle. Vasyl and Nataliya brought up the rear, no doubt whispering sweet nothings to each other, I smiled to myself. I checked the distance and made an estimate that we were less than ten kilometres from the city of Rostov.

Rostov-on-Don was a major Soviet city positioned at the mouth of the Don River where it flows into the Sea of Azov. The city was the gateway to the oil rich Caucuses and one of the main targets of the original Barbarossa campaign. Since its capture after a bitter to and fro battle that lasted until July 1942 the city had been held by the Germans, but only just. The Soviet units we had seen were already on their way to finish off the defenders at Stalingrad before turning to launch a series of major spearheads towards all the remaining cities, including Rostov.

We would probably get clear of the Soviet army in around five kilometres, before we made our way through the final few kilometres of no man's land that was the inevitable bloody, disputed demarcation of any battlefield, ancient or modern. The snow crunched under foot as we marched on through the bitter cold. The snow blanketed the bleak desolate landscape, as if nature was trying to hide the scars of violence that marred this vast region. I was lost in a reverie, lost to the pure, white beauty of this smooth white land we walked through, so that when it came it was a shock.

"Halt! Papers!"

I came rapidly awake. Standing in front of us, flanked by three men either side, stood a major of the Red Army field police. Two of the men were armed with PPSh's, the others had rifles. The major had a Tokarev in his hand pointed at us.

"Who are you, where are you going?"

I rapidly came to my senses.

"Captain Sokolov, NKVD, Major. We are returning to our headquarters."

"NKVD? Your headquarters are not in this direction, Captain. Please show me your papers, now."

"Very well," I replied, fumbling in the breast pocket of my tunic. I was desperately trying to gain time. Then I heard a shout, Vasyl calling to us in German. "Get down on the ground, now!"

Müller, Tatiana and I threw ourselves down. The Russian major hesitated, confused by the sudden movement. Then Vasyl's PPSh opened up from behind us. The bullets smacked into the Russian soldiers who were open mouthed, too stunned to react. The major got off a shot before I saw him struck by the burst of firing, which seemed to go on forever. Vasyl emptied the whole fifty round clip into the Russians.

"Thank God, I thought we were finished," I said. Müller knelt down, checking the Russians, two were still breathing. He looked satisfied as he brought the knife down.

"Vasyl," I called, "well done, a brilliant job. Let's press on before anyone comes looking to see who was shooting."

There was no reply.

"Vasyl?"

Then he loomed up out of the night. He was carrying Nataliya in his arms. She was limp, dead. A bullet had entered her head just under the eye. I looked at Vasyl's face. He was totally, utterly grief stricken.

"I'm truly sorry," I said. He looked at me. "One shot, the bastard fired one shot. She stood up to help me, she thought I'd stumbled, it just hit her, knocked her down. She's dead."

Tatiana went up to him, put her hand on his shoulder. Müller, surprisingly, took Nataliya from him and laid her gently down.

"It was such a short time, Wolf, so short. She was Ukrainian, she should not have been here. I was taking her home."

Tears had formed in his eyes. "I know, Vasyl, I know. She was a wonderful girl, I know. Vasyl, we really need to move on, those shots will have roused the whole countryside. The Russians could already be on their way!"

He looked at me, shook his head. "I don't want to go on. I'll stay, hold them off while you push on."

He wanted to die. I understood how he felt. We had taken shock after shock, pain built on pain until the agony became so unbearable that death would be preferable to life. A blessed release from the non-ending torture. But I needed him alive. We were in a desperate situation and I needed his solid strength, his shrewd intelligence and instant reading of battlefield emergencies. He was both a blunt instrument and a second set of brains that would help us to stay alive between here and the city. Eventually I persuaded him, and we scooped a grave out of the snow and buried her. Vasyl paused for a moment, I could see him quietly speaking a prayer. Then he nodded at me, it was done. We shouldered our packs and carried on, the lights of the city guided us. We saw no more Russians that night. Just as dawn was breaking we reached our lines. We had taken off our Russian winter camouflage so that we would not be mistaken for the enemy, but I still had to talk quickly to a Wehrmacht colonel who came to see who the new arrivals were. Eventually he reluctantly let us pass into the city.

"You will find other SS units in the city, Haupsturmfuher, so you will be among friends. Where are you going next?"

"Berlin, I hope," I told him.

"Lucky man," he smiled. "Is this girl staying with you?"

I nodded. "Then I wish you good luck," he smiled. "She is very beautiful. If she was mine, I would take her far from here and never come back."

I thanked him and we moved off. The city was yet another victim of both Russian and German bombing and shelling. First, we bombed and shelled the Russians until they left. Now they were bombing and shelling us to push us back out of Rostov. We found an SS communications unit. Eventually I managed to get through to Berlin, Prinz Albrecht Strasser. Neurath came on the radio.

"You have done remarkably well to survive, Wolf. You know that von Paulus has surrendered?"

"Surrendered? That's incredible, he had a quarter of a million men! When did it happen?"

"We got the news this morning, the Führer is furious."

"Sir, there were a quarter of a million men on the Stalingrad Front, the whole of the 6th Army, as well as the Romanians, the Italians, the Hungarians. Could they not have been rescued?"

"The Führer said they disobeyed orders," Neurath said dubiously.

I thought of the huge body of men, a whole German army. Starving, frozen, low on fuel, low on ammunition, abandoned.

Neurath described the last days of the 6th Army as we listened in disbelief. Apparently the Soviets attacks had forced the survivors back into the city so that the 6th Army ended up defending the same areas that the Soviets had previously been defending against the Germans. They had been pushed to the Volga and fought in bitter street fighting battles in the factory districts. Von Paulus had been offered surrender terms, but refused out of duty to the Führer. Only after even more desperate combat did Hitler finally promote von Paulus to Field Marshall, assuming he would not surrender if promoted. No Field Marshall in German military history had ever surrendered. Von Paulus refused to take the hint, the following day his army laid down their arms. Over ninety thousand starving prisoners were taken. It was astounding.

The radio crackled again. "You are to return to Berlin, where you will be debriefed on the Stalingrad situation, the Reichsführer is looking for an explanation to give the Führer for the debacle. A whole German army surrendering to the Russians, it's unheard of. The 6th Army was the largest military formation in the entire Werhmacht. It's astonishing!"

Neurath went quiet for a few moments, then evidently decided to say no more on the Stalingrad situation. "Make your way to the railway station, I will have the SS-Feldgendarmerie notified that you are coming. You will have priority on a train returning to Germany. Good luck Hauptsturmführer. Out." The radio clicked off.

"Right," I said to the others, "we're going back to Germany. Tatania, you'll be able to shop for some clothes. Müller, you can get some good hard drinking in, I might even join you. I daresay you'll have other things in mind, too."

"Oh yes," he smiled. "I can think of a few. Vasyl, I must show you to the delights of Berlin."

Vasyl shook his head, "No thanks."

"You'll change your mind," Müller laughed.

Four hours later we climbed on a train, bound for Berlin. The train was packed with people, Wehrmacht, SS, all going back to the Reich, on leave or for transfer to other units. Maybe some were running before the oncoming Russian juggernaut. Our passenger coach was one of only two reserved for passengers.

"What are the others?" I asked a Wehrmacht major.

"Casualties," he replied, "casualties from all over the Eastern Front. I suggest you stay away from them, it's not a pretty sight."

But my curiosity was aroused. After the train had left the station I walked back to see the first aid wagons. It was horrific, like the very worst of Stalingrad enclosed in the cramped, dark, smoky space of the railway car. Men broken, bloody, moaning, some were screaming in agony. They were virtually heaped one on another, the first aid orderlies desperate to get as many of them as possible out of Russia and back to the Reich for hospital treatment. But there were too many casualties and not enough drugs, bandages or doctors. I helped give water to several men, some clearly dying, then helped two orderlies hold down one screaming soldier, ripped apart by a shell burst, while a doctor amputated his right arm. I had had enough.

I went back to our coach, but the horror was not over, I was to see much more before we reached the capital.

JANUARY 1945

I thought of those two brave, beautiful women, Tatiana and Nataliya, as we waited behind a wrecked Tiger Mk IV, just outside the Deli railway station, in the city of Buda, part of the twin city of Budapest. God knew there was little enough beauty in this destroyed city, like that former German and Russian battleground, Stalingrad. My unit, the SS-British Freecorps, had completed their training outside of Berlin and had immediately been sent into action to help repel the Soviet hordes. From my initial contingent of thirty men brought to Budapest, I was reduced to only seventeen, two had deserted, others refused to fight, some had fallen victim to the Russian shelling that was daily pulverising the city to dust.

We had been transported to support the defence of the city from the Russian armies that constituted Malinovsky's Second Ukrainian Front. Our 4th SS Panzer Corps had initially begun an offensive in the direction of the airport, trying to recapture that vital supply line back from the Soviets.

Retreating from a series of disasters in the east, we had already blown up all the Danube bridges to try to hold back the progress of the Soviets. Just like at Stalingrad we had found ourselves in yet another bloodthirsty siege that slowly but steadily reduced the entire city to rubble. The defences were assigned mainly to the Hungarian army under German leadership to defend the city, stiffened with a variety of German units including the Waffen-SS. There was even a unit of Deutsche Jugend, German youth, who were assigned to guide and direct the gliders being used to bring in supplies.

We had yet to hear whether or not our latest attack had been successful, but in the meantime we were part of several makeshift units positioned between the Deli station and Chain bridge to guard against a major Soviet counter-attack. So far we had twice been attacked by units of Russians, who charged at us in small groups, undoubtedly to test our defences. I noticed amongst the attackers several women, uniformed and armed identically to the men, rushing our positions with the Soviet battle cry 'Urrah' on their lips. Like the men, they died exactly the same, some dropped instantly as our MG 42 machine guns cut them down with precision bursts. Then a third group of Russians leapt out of cover and charged straight at us.

Thank God for the MG42's. More numerous than the MG34's, they were deadly accurate and had a phenomenal rate of fire of about 1200 rounds of 7.92mm per minute. Every burst fired sounded like one loud buzz and they burnt though the ammunition at a frightening rate. The psychological effect of this gun was so powerful that follow-up waves of infantry often scattered at the mere sound of this gun. I hoped that these Russians would run out of men before we ran out of bullets, but I has seen the Russian hordes, they seemed to be inexhaustible. It was a forlorn hope.

Some dropped dead, shot through a major organ. Others screamed and writhed in agonised terror, left on the hard icy ground outside the Hungarian capital while their comrades continued with the attack. The women soldiers may not have possessed the classic beauty and magnetism of Tatiana, but these Russian women were brave, incredibly brave. They were like lions, often charging into battle and taking insane risks, whilst the men shrank back in fear or were forced to attack with the women out of shame. The attack got closer and I saw two of my men fall, hit by the rifle and submachine gun fire before our MG42's scythed the Russians down, stopping the attack dead. A few survivors running back to their positions, I ignored them and checked my casualties.

SS-Schütze Williamson, formally an airman in the RAF, and SS-Unterscharführer Roberts, formally a corporal in the Royal Corps of Signals and stalwart of Oswald Mosley's Blackshirts. Roberts had been captured at Dunkirk. Williamson parachuted out of a stricken Stirling twin engine bomber, shot down by a Luftwaffe Junkers 88C nightfighter, the aircraft that were wreaking havoc with the RAF during the long, dark nights. The Junkers had originally been designed as a general purpose fighter bomber but had found its perfect place as a heavy night fighter. Equipped with powerful radar detection equipment and heavy weapons, usually at least three machine guns plus heavy cannon, it was no wonder that it brought down Williamson's Stirling together with hundreds of other Allied bombers.

These men had counted themselves lucky to be alive, afterwards, lucky to get the chance to escape the monotony and poor rations of prison camp life. The prestige and comradeship of like minded men in the SS-British Freecorps. Good food, smart uniforms, a girl on your arm on frequent nights out with your comrades. But everything had a price. Roberts and Williamson had now paid that price. I checked the rest of them, fifteen left, thugs and thieves all of them, but they were unquestionably good fighters. They waited grimly for the Russians to come again, two of them clutching Panzerfausts, the single shot anti-tank weapon, ready to launch at any Russian armour that came at us. Surely they no longer believed in the possibility of German victory, so what were they fighting for? Or like me, were they trapped, with no place else to go? My men had been ecstatic when they were told they were going to fight the Russians, the job they had trained to do. Infected with the myth of SS invincibility, they were confident of easy victory. None had seen the endless trains that carried the enormous casualties back from the Eastern Front.

I saw no need to enlighten them. They would find out soon enough that the Russians were hard and bitter fighters, more than a match for the German forces that they met in battle after battle across the blood soaked land of the Soviet Union. We fought off yet another attack, then a Wehrmacht lieutnant arrived and announced we were pulling back to new positions inside the city. We picked up our weapons and followed him, glad to be escaping the open ground and endless attrition of the Russian attacks. I counted off the remnants of my SS-British Freecorps unit. Fifteen men, myself and Müller.

The faithful psychopathic Müller, who always brought up the rear, watching carefully for any signs of the Freecorps men trying to desert. I suspected he wanted someone to try it, I could almost sense him gripping the knife, waiting for a chance to give it a new sacrifice of human blood.

CHAPTER TEN

FEBRUARY 1943

The train rattled across the endless Russian steppe. For the first time I began to feel warm, although I couldn't escape the stench coming from those poor devils in the medical carriages. Vasyl disappeared into the next car, another carrying troops returning to the Reich. Ten minutes later he returned carrying two bottles of vodka, which he opened and began passing around. There was little talking, we each had a feeling of guilt that so many troops were not returning to Germany, nor was it ever likely that they would. Tens, hundreds of thousands of men left to rot and die in the snows of Stalingrad. Would it ever be enough to slake the bloody thirst of our Chief Butcher, Adolf Hitler, or his equally bloody opposite number, Josef Stalin? I doubted it. They were men whose epitaphs would be etched in the slaughter and blood of millions. Soon, though, the warmth of the train and the vodka combined and I fell asleep, oblivious.

The train must have stopped, but that wasn't what woke me up, it was the stench. Far worse and far stronger than the smell that came from the carriages of wounded. I looked out of the window. We were stopped at a station, the sign on the platform said Wroclaw, Poland. I got up and opened the window, another train had stopped alongside us and that was where the stink was coming from. Cattle cars, all locked closed. Animals, that would explain it. Then the high pitched wail of an air raid siren sounded, the signal to take cover. How on earth could thousands of wounded men take cover in such a short time? It would be impossible. I looked at the others.

"I'm staying here, too much warmth and vodka, I'll risk the air raid. Besides, the train has red cross markings, we should be safe from attack."

Technically, we should not have been travelling in a train marked with red crosses. It was totally against the rules of war. The German authorities, however, didn't seem to be taking an undue interest in these rules since the Red air force had recovered their strength and were attacking our military communications in increasing numbers. Would the Russian pilots take notice of the red crosses? I was dubious, I imagined that some might, others would not.

We heard the whistle of bombs falling, perhaps about half a mile away. They got nearer and there was a high pitched whistling, "Down!" I shouted. We flung ourselves on the floor. I lay on top of Tatiana, protecting her from the blast if a bomb hit us. There was a huge explosion rocking the carriage on its springs, several of the windows blew in with the force of the explosion, but we were unhurt. The bomb had struck directly between two of the cattle wagons opposite leaving them half-wrecked, the roofs blown off, so that I could see inside. They were not animals inside, they were people. I saw the survivors panicking, jumping off of the train, some trying to help free wounded from the carriage. They were in a pitiable state, emaciated and ragged. Russian prisoners of war, perhaps? But there were women and children mixed in with the men, so clearly they weren't military.

I slid the window fully down and shouted across. "Do you need help?"

Several of them looked up, one replied, an old man with a long beard and black homburg hat which he clung on to. "We are beyond help, SS man." He looked to me like a Jewish rabbi.

Guards rushed along the platform shouting orders, "Back, back in the carriages, do not leave the train!"

"Are you Russian?" I shouted across to the old man. "No, we are Germans, German Jews," he replied wearily.

One of the guards dashed over and smashed the butt of his Kar98 rifle down on the old man's head.

"No talking, get back on the train, hurry. You two," he grabbed two of the pathetic looking prisoners, they looked as if they had not eaten for weeks, "pick up that piece of refuse, throw it back on the train." He was pointing at the old man.

I was speechless. These were Germans. Jews, yes, Hitler had called them 'untermensch', subhumans, but they were still Germans. The old Rabbi was a German citizen. I called across to another guard, an SS-Sturmmann, who had run up and stood guard with his MP38 pointed at the Jews.

"What's going on?" I shouted. "Are all of these people prisoners? What have they done?"

"They are Jews, Hauptsturmführer," the man shouted back. "Done? They've done nothing. They are Jews, that is enough. We are taking them east, to a camp. For selection."

"Selection?"

"Certainly. Those fit enough can work, those not will be disposed of."

"How do you dispose of those not fit enough to work?" I asked him.

The guard crossed over the tracks and came up to my window.

"Herr Hauptsturmführer, perhaps you have been in Russia too long, you do not know what is happening. Jews too useless to work are sent to the gas chambers for extermination, it is the Führer's plan to rid the Reich of the Jews. It's all done properly. Afterwards, the bodies are hygienically burned. The plan is to exterminate them all, millions of them. But Sir, I have told you this because you are an SS officer. It is for your ears only. This whole operation is being run secretly on the orders of Reichsführer Himmler. Non-SS personnel must not learn of it. Now, I have to go."

He turned and walked back to the other train, then began herding and marshalling the terrified prisoners back aboard.

Müller, Vasyl and Tatiana had been listening next to the window. They looked grey, shocked. Even Müller, the killer, the man who had explored every aspect of torture and death was for once appalled and astonished at the horrific suffering of his fellow man.

"Wolf," Tatiana spoke first, "what on earth is going on? Why are they murdering those poor people? What will they do to me? I am so frightened."

I shook my head, I too couldn't speak. Is this what I was fighting for? To murder thousands, even millions, of innocent old men, women and children, just because of their religion?   What could I do, though? What could any of us three do? We were just tiny, infinitesimal cogs in the vast German war machine. We had even given our oath of allegiance to the Führer. It was not an option to say we didn't sign up to be a part of this savage war on innocent German civilians. That would be a certain route to a bullet in the back of the head, we knew the penalties for any kind of opposition to the party line. Of course we knew that Jews received rough treatment in the Reich, were despised and hated by the Nazi regime. But this? What the hell were they thinking of?

Eventually our train pulled out of the station, continuing its journey back to the Reich, to Berlin. We had nearly a day to travel, but there was little conversation. The stations whistled past, we didn't stop again. Neither did we come under attack. Was it the red crosses painted on the roof? Were we just lucky? Or were the Russians marshalling their forces for something unpleasant. There was the appalling business of the German Jews on that train. If the guard was to be believed, the SS was part of a machine that had declared war on its own people, treating them worse than animals. Was it really planning the extermination of millions of Jewish civilians? Could I keep Tatiana safe? I looked down at my uniform. Suddenly it seemed soiled, coated with the filth and dishonour of what we had witnessed.   I asked Müller for his opinion, he just shrugged.

"We're all going to die sooner rather than later, Herr Hauptsturmführer. This war will kill us all before it ends."

"But those people…" I began.

"Sir, you heard the guard. It's a state secret. That means Gestapo. I suggest you leave it well alone. They are not nice people to deal with, believe me."

"Did you ever consider joining the Gestapo?" I asked him. "You sound as if you know something about them."

"I was seconded to a Gestapo unit during the invasion of Czechoslovakia," he told me. "We rounded up suspected partisans."

"So you didn't wish to join them permanently?" I asked.

"Too much paperwork," he laughed. "Besides, they didn't like my methods, said I was too harsh on the prisoners!"

There was no sensible reply to that statement. I felt Tatiana and Vasyl watching me, fascinated and appalled. Was this the country to which they had given their loyalty? Compared to the barbarities they had seen committed by the Soviets, the episode at the railway station seemed to plumb to new depths of human horror on its fellow man. All we could do was exactly what the rest of Germany did, become deaf, dumb and blind. That was the key to survival in the savagery that often passed for justice in the Third Reich. We trundled over a long railway bridge then pulled into a station, Frankfurt An Der Oder. We had crossed the Oder and were back on German soil. Despite everything, we smiled at each other. Vasyl broke out one of his innumerable bottles of vodka and before long we were swapping jokes and stories. We were home, at least our temporary home. And we were out of Russia. We shook hands, Tatiana kissed me warmly and passionately. I felt sorry for Vasyl's loss, for the brave girl killed by the Russian officer out on the steppe. But Vasyl would survive, we were all survivors. Even after Stalingrad we had survived!

Outside Berlin our train came under attack. We heard the sounds of sirens wailing and then the train lurched to a stop. "Air raid! Everyone out, take cover!" a railway official shouted. We climbed out of the carriage and walked to the side of the tracks. There was a deep gully, the four of us climbed in and lay down.

"No, no, you need to go to the air raid shelter, it's half a kilometre away," a railway policeman shouted at us. "That's the rules."

We could hear the distant drone of heavy bombers. Müller stood up and took hold of the man's jacket.

"You go fuck your rules, Grandad. Before we get to the shelter the bombers will be over us, so you bugger off. We're staying."

There was a loud whistling noise, Müller grabbed the policeman and dragged him down into the gully. A bomb exploded two hundred metres away, hitting us with a monstrous shock wave, showering debris and earth over us. A second bomb hit the steam engine that pulled the train, causing the boiler to explode with a shattering roar that sent out clouds of steam, throwing the engine off the tracks and over on its side.

It was the third bomb that caused the most shocking damage, hitting the carriages of wounded at the exact spot where two of them joined, shattering the cars and sending stretchers, wounded, doctors, nurses and orderlies hurtling into the air, then crashing down to the tracks and the surrounding area. The screams were terrible, I could take it no more. I ran out to try and help the wounded. They were lying amidst the twisted remains of the carriages, moaning and screaming in agony. Vasyl and I dragged some of them out of the wreckage, carrying them to a clear space near the tracks. Bombs were still falling nearby but I couldn't care less, these people needed help. Unlike the Jews at Wroclaw, we were at least able to do something here. I could see Tatiana bandaging a wounded nurse who was bleeding badly from the stump of an arm that had been blown off in the explosion. Müller was trying to hold her down so that the wound could be dressed.

We stayed for several hours until there were dozens of rescuers bustling around tending to the wounded. I saw doctors administer what I knew were lethal doses of morphine to very severely injured casualties. One looked at me as he saw me glance at him. He shrugged, what could he do, then turned away and carried on with his gruesome, grim task. When there was no more we could do, we hitched a ride on a Flak regiment lorry carrying ammunition into the city to resupply the towers that were supposed to defend Berlin from the bombers. The driver seemed cheerful enough, "It's better than going to the Eastern Front, although we get our share of action here in the city. Where are you headed?"

"Prinz Albrecht Strasser, I replied. "Reichsführer Himmler's Headquarters."

His cheerful demeanour lessened instantly. "Yes, Herr Hauptsturmführer, I'll take you there straight way."

The mention of Himmler's HQ stopped all further conversation. This was the Germany of the deaf, dumb and blind, after all. He dropped us outside and drove off hurriedly without a word. We entered the building guarded by two SS troopers in steel helmets. They came to attention when they saw me, an SS officer, entering the building. We reported to the security desk and showed the clerk our documents. An SS Sturmmann came down and showed us to Neurath's office.

"Gentlemen," he smiled, "welcome back to Berlin. Miss Medvedev. Vasyl, I didn't get your surname?"

"Just Vasyl," the Ukrainian replied.

"Very well. The Reichsführer has been impressed with your reports. He has used them to show the Führer how the Wehrmacht bungled the campaign badly at Stalingrad, it means more resources for the Waffen-SS."

"That was not my intention in sending the reports, SS-Standartenführer Neurath. The 6th Army fought magnificently against overwhelming Russian forces. They needed supplies, reinforcements and petrol, not criticism."

"It's academic, Hauptsturmfuher, now that they've surrendered. The Führer has decreed that the 6th Army was poorly led by its officers, they were cowards. Von Paulus was promoted Field Marshall by the Führer, within days he repaid the honour by surrendering his troops to the Russians. Cowards!"

I remembered in time that I was in Berlin, the city of the deaf, the dumb and the blind.

"Yes, Sir," I replied.

"Excellent. The four of you are to be allowed a well earned rest here in Berlin, you have a week's leave. We have reserved rooms in the Hotel Adler on the Kurfurstendamm. Enjoy yourselves then report back here in seven days. Vasyl, Miss Medvedev, I cannot technically order you to do anything, but may I take it that you will be happy to remain under the orders of Hauptsturmführer Wolf?"

"Where he goes, I go," Tatiana said. Vasyl nodded. "For the time being, yes," he agreed. "I will fight the Bolsheviks, with or without German help, until my country is free again."

"Very well. Scharführer Müller, I am authorised to promote you to the rank of SS-Sturmscharführer." Müller smiled delightedly, the army equivalent of Regimental Sergeant Major. It was the highest rank an NCO could hope to gain within the SS.

"Vasyl, in view of your rank in the Red Army, I am awarding you the rank of SS-Untersturmführer." Vasyl just nodded silently. We were all aware that this was just a ploy to get him on to the unit strength of the SS-Liebstandarte Adolf Hitler. That way his loyalty would be assured, once in, it was not an option.

"As for you, my dear Miss Medvedev," he said, turning to Tatiana, "I understand you wish to accompany Hauptsturmführer Wolf as his assistant, is that correct?"

She nodded. "Very well, you are to be given the rank of SS-Helferin. Welcome to the Waffen-SS. My orderly will sort out your paperwork and administer your oaths as you leave."

"Oaths?" Tatiana asked sharply. "What oaths?"

"All SS personnel are required to swear an oath of loyalty to the Führer, Miss Medvedev, it is a simple formality."

"And if I do not wish to swear loyalty to Adolf Hitler, what then? I am fighting the Russians, not joining the Nazi cause body and soul." Her eyes blazed with passion. It was clear she was remembering the Jews on the train at Wroclaw.

"If you wish to leave Prinz Albrecht Strasser, Miss Medvedev, then I suggest you have no choice. I trust I make myself clear? Or should I look further into the period you spent with the Russians in Stalingrad?"

I stepped in quickly before she got a ticket to the Gestapo cellars. "That is totally clear, Herr Standartenführer, I will make certain the oaths are all properly sworn."

"Excellent." He smiled. "Welcome to the SS, Helferin Medvedev and Untersturmführer Vasyl. Please report back here in exactly seven days from today, shall we say at 09.00? I will have your assignments ready. Nothing too arduous, I assure you."

"Thank you, Sir." I saluted, Müller did the same. I looked meaningfully at Vasyl and Tatiana. Reluctantly, they followed suit. We trooped out to the orderly's office, while we were waiting, Tatiana whispered to me. "Wolf, you know that some of my family were Jewish, I'm scared. I feel sickened by this whole thing. I can't forget those poor Jews on the train at Wroclaw. What are these monsters doing? I just can't do it. It would be like swearing an oath to the devil."

"Tatiana, my love," I whispered back. "I understand, believe me, I fully understand. These people will be dealt with when the war ends, I'm certain of that. In the meantime, there is nothing we can do, especially here. For me, my love, just for me, grit your teeth and swear the oath. Do it for the love you have for me, the love we share. It is our only hope."

She looked very pale and tense, angry to be caught up in this situation.

"Very well, Wolf, I will do it. But only for us. The oath will be a lie. You understand?"

"Perfectly, my darling," I murmured, relieved. "Thank you."

Then we were ushered into the office where the oath of allegiance to Adolf Hitler was administered.

'I swear by God this sacred oath that I shall render unconditional obedience to Adolf Hitler, the Leader of the German Empire, supreme commander of the armed forces, and that I shall at all times be prepared, as a brave soldier, to give my life for this oath.'

Tatiana was pale during the ceremony, but had enough sense to know that there was no alternative, other than the Gestapo and possibly a concentration camp. She and Vasyl received temporary papers and identification, then we left the building and found a nearby bar.

"Now that I am a SS-Sturmscharführer, I should be leading a regiment, you know," Müller laughed.

"Of course, Sturmscharführer, the SS-Liebstandarte Adolf Hitler is currently on the Russian Front, I'm sure they would welcome you."

He looked rueful. "But on the other hand, you do need me to take care of you and your people, Sir. I think I'll stick around."

"Excellent, Müller. How are you spending your leave?"

"At the Hotel Adler, where else? It's all paid up for seven days. That's seven hot baths, seven decent dinners and the rounds of the nightspots. Paradise! Vasyl, why not join me?" he asked.

"Thank you Sturmscharführer Müller," the Ukrainian replied. "I have no one in Berlin, I would be happy to try and help you drink Berlin dry. And you, Wolf?"

I looked at Tatiana. "I'm sure we'll find something to keep us busy," I smiled. She grinned back. It was a pleasing prospect.

When we finally said our goodbyes to Vasyl and Müller we went back to the Hotel Adler. We had a hot bath together then literally fell into bed. I was very tired after the journey, it would have been enough just to be with Tatiana. But it was not enough for her. As my eyelids began to droop, the said sternly, "No, Hauptsturmführer, now that you are my SS commander, I expect you to command me! Or at least," she giggled, "a part of you to command me." She took hold of my penis, began massaging it gently.

"Ah, you're waking up, Sir," she said happily.

Then she leaned down and took my penis in her mouth, sucking and rubbing it with sweet, warm tenderness. My organ shot upright like a Hitler salute, I put my hand between her legs and felt the moist heat that was the very essence of her womanhood. Her body quivered.

"I order you to move around so that we can make love, Helferin Medvedev."

"Oh yes, Sir, anything you order."

She turned her body around, pulled me over her then guided my penis inside her. It was like an electric shock, all trace of tiredness left me as I allowed her hot passion to engulf me. She gasped as I drove hard into her, "More, my darling Wolf, more, oh, do it harder."

We sweated and writhed, gasped and moaned for what seemed like an endless voyage of bliss, smothered in the clean smelling sheets of the Hotel Adler, until we finally came to a shattering climax. Her first, then I felt like a fighter plane taking off as I pushed deeply inside her for the magical ecstasy of blissful sexual release.

Afterwards we lay there, quietly smoking. In the distance we could hear the sirens wailing. Soon the bombs would start to drop. Without discussing it, we both knew we would not want to go to the shelter. This night was magical, we may never experience another one like it while the war lasted.

"I hope Vasyl and Müller are having a good time. Wolf, these past few weeks have been terrible. Vasyl especially, he never got over that girl's death."

"They'll be drunk in some sleazy bar. Their pay in their pockets and a girl on each arm, I've little doubt," I smiled.

"Where will Neurath send us next?"

"I've no idea," I told her. "The problem is he sees us as experts on the Eastern Front with our knowledge of fluent Russian, as well as Vasyl being a citizen of the Soviet Union. Unfortunately we're very useful to him. I suspect Standartenführer Neurath may want us to be involved in prisoner interrogation. Apart from the languages, it's Müller's speciality."

"I am aware of Müller's speciality, Wolf. Are you happy with his brutal treatment of prisoners?"

"It gets the job done," I replied. "No, I'm not happy, but this war is brutal, probably the most brutal in all of history. Müller is just a symptom of it."

"Well, I'm sure that…"

She was interrupted by a banging on the door. I wrapped a towel around me and answered it. It was Müller.

"Hauptsturmführer, you need to get out now! A bomb hit the east side of the hotel, it buried itself in the rubble and it hasn't gone off."

"Tatiana, get dressed fast," I shouted, "we have to get out."

I threw on my clothes and we rushed out into the corridor where Müller and Vasyl were waiting.

"If we take the west staircase we'll be furthest away from the bomb," Vasyl shouted as we ran along the corridor. We got to the staircase and hurtled down the steps, taking them two and three at a time. At the bottom we ran straight out of the front door and onto the street which was packed with evacuated guests from the Adler, some in their pyjamas. As we watched a TENO truck, the Technische Nothilfe, the Nazi rescue organisation, arrived carrying the bomb disposal technicians.

TENO was the technical unit of the paramilitary Freikorps. Throughout the Third Reich the TENO focused on civil defence, disaster response and air raid rescue, general disaster response and relief work. They wore the green uniform of the police and were often referred to as the TENO Police.

"Move back, move back," a Berlin Luftschultz officer shouted, he wore the armband of the Air Raid Warden Service. TENO men were setting up barriers, pushing us back further and further from the threatened building. Everyone went quiet as the bomb disposal technician entered the building. The all clear sounded and arc lamps suddenly came on, flooding the surreal scene with the unearthly glare of artificial light. Wisps of smoke drifted in the night, blown by the gentle night breeze. People started to talk quietly, as if the bright lights had restored some normalcy to the Berlin night.

The minutes passed, people started to grumble with the cold, "When can we go back inside?" one haughty sounding woman demanded of the Luftschultz official.

"We need to wait for the…" he was lifted off his feet, the rest of us were thrown back on the ground by the tremendous pressure of the blast as the bomb exploded. Milliseconds after the sound hit us there was a vast roar that seared the ears leaving people deaf and bleeding from the head. I shook my head. I couldn't hear anything, my eardrums temporarily disrupted by the blast. I stood up feeling dizzy, staggering to try and get my balance. The air was thick with dust. I found Müller, indestructible Müller, helping Vasyl to his feet.

"A taste of Stalingrad for the Berliners, Hauptsturmführer," he grimaced.

"Yes. Where's Tatiana?"

"Over there, she's fine."

I ran to Tatiana, she was kneeling down and talking quietly to an old woman. I could see the poor woman had lost a leg, it was lying on the ground several metres away. She shut her eyes in the terrible pain, then opened them and screamed, a haunting, wailing, cry.

"My husband, where is my husband? I don't want to die. Help, please help me, aahhhh," she sighed, giving her last breath. Tatiana laid her down gently and closed her eyes.

"Wolf, can we get away from here? I've had enough of blood and death. Somewhere away from the war?" Her beautiful face was etched with stress and misery, a reflection of the pain and suffering all around her.

"I'm afraid we can't, Helferin Medvedev. Not while the war continues."

"But it will never end," she protested.

"It will, my darling, it will," I soothed her. "Let's grab Müller and Vasyl, we need to find a new hotel. We have a few days leave left to us, we can still enjoy it. We've lost our personal possessions so we'll find a shop tomorrow and get you some new clothes. We'll need uniforms, too."

"You mean SS uniforms?"

"Of course, it will be expected of us."

At the end of our week we reported to Neurath at Prinz Albrecht Strasser. We wore our new uniforms, bought to replace the clothes we lost in the hotel blast. Tatiana managed to make the SS-Helferin uniform of a severe black tailored skirt and jacket worn over a white shirt, look positively elegant. The rest of us wore the usual black SS-Liebstandarte Adolf Hitler dress uniform, the sinister black edged in silver, and the jackets bearing our new badges of rank. The Standartenführer looked impressed.

"Excellent, your uniforms look rather different to the clothes you wore when you arrived here a week ago. Now, I have your orders. No

Stalingrad this time, Herr Hauptsturmführer. This time, it is the Reich that is pressing the siege. Once again, the Wehrmacht though has made a hash of it, so the Führer believes. Reichsführer Himmler requires a report from you, with a view to sending Waffen-SS divisions to break through the Soviet defences. We need to know can it be done, is it practical, and what mistakes are the Wehrmacht making, as usual. My God, these army generals. The Führer despairs of them. Do they know nothing?"

I didn't reply to that. Hitler had described many of these same generals as geniuses when they were winning victories. Had everyone forgotten so soon?

"Where is this operation taking place, Sir?" I asked him.

"Leningrad, on the Eastern Front. You are to report to Tempelhof Airport tomorrow for your flight out."

We were going back to Russia. To the bestial cruelty of a war that had explored man's potential for constantly surpassing himself in inflicting ever increasing depths of cruelty and horror. I thought of Stalingrad, the benighted city on the banks of the Volga where von Paulus had surrendered the whole of the 6th Army? A quarter of a million German soldiers dead and wounded, the survivors throwing themselves on the cruel mercy of the Red Army, of Stalin's avenging minions. I wondered about their fate. It would not be a good one.

We heard that after the surrender the Russians set fire to the old Soviet military garrison building, which our forces were using as a hospital. Hundreds of the wounded were burned to death. In the city Russian soldiers had wandered around taking prisoners, stealing their valuables, killing and maiming unarmed German soldiers. In a cellar near the centre of the city, fifty wounded German soldiers were soaked with petrol and turned into human torches.

Hitler had been furious when he learned of Von Paulus' surrender. He swore that he would never create another field marshal because no general could be trusted. In Stalingrad however General Strecker, the commander of German XI Corps, had held out in the northern part of the city. The Russians were furious at their resistance. Many of Strecker's men were not allowed to surrender when they ran out of ammunition, but were just ruthlessly shot down or even clubbed to death.

Before the XI Corps command post was taken by the Russians, General Strecker had sent a message to Hitler: "11th Corps and its divisions have fought to the last man against vastly superior forces. Long live Germany."

Goebbels of course had a field day with this display of German loyalty and heroism, I was just sickened at even more useless loss of life.

JANUARY 1945

We waited in the dugout, sandbags protecting us from the Soviet shelling that had razed much of Budapest to the ground during the siege. An SS-Sturmbannführer crawled out of a nearby communications culvert. The narrow trenches the city engineers had introduced us to were proving useful to move from place to place, without becoming a target for the Russians. With typical German ingenuity we had created a unit called the Europa Flying Squad Battalion, which used and regarded the Budapest culvert system as their own personal fiefdom.

"Hauptsturmführer, I need you to take out a fighting patrol and try to knock out that Soviet machine gun nest that's hitting us from the old police station across the square. Take three of your SS-British Freecorps people. That should do it. We'll give you covering fire."

"Do we have any tank support, Sturmbannführer?" I asked him.

He gave me a thin lipped smile. "We did, until the fools got too close to a group of ammunition wagons. When the Russians fired on them the wagons blew up, took out nine of our Panzers. No chance of replacements, so we use the Panzerfausts. But we have the 8th SS Cavalry Division on our flank, as well as, apparently, the 9th SS Mountain Corps. Although God only knows where they are, I'm still trying to locate them."

"Very well, Sturmbannführer," I replied. SS-Sturmbannführer Werner Stecher commanded our Waffen-SS units in this part of Budapest, a loose collection of mainly Freiwilliger, volunteer SS units drawn from countries across Europe.

Freiwilligen units were regiments created consisting of men who volunteered to join the German SS from an occupied country. Some of the most famous units include the 5th SS-Panzer-Division Wiking and the 11th SS-Freiwilligen-Panzergrenadier-Division Nordland. Some nationalities and units were better than others. The Wiking Division had an excellent track record and was known for hard fighting. Other units though were less than impressive and were obviously placed here as cannon fodder. My SS-British Freecorps was certainly part of this second group!

I gave orders to Müller to get the men ready. The rest of the SS-British Freecorps was in Berlin, helping to prepare the city for the Russian juggernaut that was rolling ominously towards the outskirts. I had been sent to help defend Budapest with Müller and thirty men, many were veterans of Oswald Mosely's Blackshirts. They looked as nervous as I felt. I only had fifteen men left following casualties and desertions. If Germany was defeated these men, like me, had nowhere to go except to the gallows. Unless of course we were not there so see the final defeat, which seemed most likely. The Red Army had swept across eastern Europe, destroying much of the German armed forces in the process. Now they were swarming across the very borders of the Reich.

"We're ready to go, Hauptsturmführer," he reported to me.

"Not you, Müller. I need you here to look after the other men." He smiled ironically. "Yes I know, it's not much, but it's all we have. If I go down, they're all yours."

It was quite normal in the Waffen SS for officers to lead from the front. In this case I interpreted my orders as meaning exactly that. Sadly, it also meant that casualties amongst SS officers were disproportionately higher than in regular army units. Perhaps this was to be my final battle. To end on a smashed and rubble strewn Hungarian street, riddled with Russian made bullets. Then I cursed myself for morbid thinking. I had come through this far, perhaps I would see it out to the end. Did I care?

If only my darling Tatiana has been alive to be with me here at the end. Instead I had lost her when she was buried beneath a heap of rubble in Berlin. She had fallen victim to a daylight B17 raid when an American bomb had flattened our apartment block. She had just been busy cooking dinner.

"Yes, Sir. Good luck."

"Thank you, Sturmscharführer. Men, when the covering fire starts, follow me fast. Müller, anyone who hangs back, shoot them. Clear?"

They all nodded. The covering fire began, quickly building to a furious crescendo.

"Now," I shouted, "follow me!"

We burst out from cover, zigzagging across the open ground, finding cover wherever we could, near piles of stones, an abandoned car. I saw SS-Rottenführer O'Neill, previously IRA, Brixton Prison and the Queens Infantry Regiment, captured at Dunkirk, hiding behind an upturned wheelbarrow. I shouted at him to move, "A bloody wheelbarrow won't stop Russian bullets you damned fool, move or I'll shoot you myself!" I saw two men go down, SS-Schütze's Wilson and Graham. Then we reached cover behind a thick stone wall. Across the street I could see the hotel that until recently had been Gestapo headquarters. The machine gun was only thirty metres away, but it was thirty metres of totally open ground. Already the Russians were looking our way, several had rifles and submachine guns covering where they expected us to break out and attack.

"Davies," I shouted, "I need you, now!"

SS-Schütze Davies came up to me. He was veteran of the Welsh coal mines, then the Spanish Civil War where he was captured serving in the International Brigade and then imprisoned in Germany. A natural sportsman, he lived only to compete. Equally adept in both rugby and football, he had joined the SS-British Freecorps following the frustration of endless, unending years of boredom. He was superb at throwing a ball. In football games he could almost score a goal from a throw-in thirty yards from the goalposts. He was equally deadly with a hand grenade.

"Can you do it, Davies?" I asked him.

He peered over the wall and checked the position of the machine gun, then ducked back quickly as one of the riflemen saw him and got off a snap shot.

"I think so, Hauptsturmführer."

He picked two grenades from his webbing and stood ready to throw.

"As soon as the grenades hit, we charge. Get ready men, we're all going together. Davies, do it now!"

He ripped out the first pin and threw the grenade, sending it in a massive arc over the wall towards the Russian position. He was already pulling the second pin when I heard the first Russian shouts of alarm. Then he bent his whole body backwards and flung his arm forwards, an almost graceful movement. His grenade followed the first one which we heard explode, then the second one exploded.

"Charge!" I shouted and ran out, shooting my PPSh from the hip.

The Russian machine gun had been destroyed, the crew were dead or wounded. In the distance a group of Russians had seen their comrades blown apart by our grenades and started shooting at us, but they were too far away for any accuracy.

Then I felt a massive thump to my chest and my legs flew from under me. The noises of battle gradually diminished, my world went dark and for the first time in a long time, I slipped into peaceful oblivion.

When I came to, I was on the back seat of a car, speeding along a dark bumpy road. Müller sat next to me.

"Welcome back to the land of the living, Herr Hauptsturmführer."

I blinked several times.

"Tatiana, where are you, my darling. Answer me, Tatiana, where are you?"

"She's not here, Herr Hauptsturmführer," Müller said quietly.

"Not here, where is she then?"

"Sir, you've had quite an injury, you must be in shock. Tatiana died in an air raid in Berlin, two months ago."

It all came flooding back to me, like a nightmare. I had just returned from a visit to a British PoW camp. The wrecked apartment building was all that remained of our home, no one had survived. I went and found the mass grave for the victims, Tatiana was just a name etched into a wooden sign erected next to the gravesite. I went and got drunk that night, the next day I went and begged for assignment to active duty. Soon after that, I was to lead my SS-British Freecorps unit into action for the first time.

Then I remembered the street battle in the city of Budapest.

"Where are we, Müller?"

"Austria, Sir."

"Austria? How long have I been out?"

"Four days. You took a bullet to your chest, the doctors got it out but

223

said it would be touch and go whether or not you survived. The Russians were all over us, so I got you out of the city. I found a Kübelwagen that still had some petrol in the tank."

I reflected that the Kübelwagen probably still had a driver as well, poor devil, but Müller had worked a miracle getting us out of there at all.

"The rest of the men?"

"Dead, Sir, all dead. All that's left now is a few SS-British Freecorps stationed in Berlin. Some may have already escaped, deserted, maybe gone over to the Russians, I don't know. But anyway, they're surrounded by the Russians, they're not going anywhere."

I was silent for a few moments. My SS troopers at Budapest were thieves, scum and traitors perhaps. But they had put on their uniforms, picked up their guns and fought bravely enough at the end.

"Where are we going now, Müller? And who is driving the car?"

"The SS organised our escape. All of Germany is collapsing, the Russians are camped outside Berlin. The SS has an escape organisation, the ODESSA. They're taking us across Austria to Italy, then by ship to Spain. Franco won't let us be extradited, we'll be safe there."

Spain. So it was all over. And I was alive, so was Müller. I thought of all of the people we had lost. Of my Tatiana, killed in Berlin. And Vasyl. Had he ever made it home? Despite being given rank in the SS, he soon learned of the brutal treatment meted out by the German occupiers to his Ukranian countrymen. He had come to us to say goodbye.

"Where will you go?" I'd asked him.

"The Ukraine, of course, home," he smiled. "Where else? I am a fighter, Wolf, there is a battle going on in the Ukraine, so that is where I go. Good luck my friend."

We had shaken hands and he left.

There were so many I had fought with, all good people, most of them lay dead on battlefields all across Europe.

I trusted that our warlords, Stalin and Hitler, had drunk their fill of blood.

END

Lightning Source UK Ltd.
Milton Keynes UK
28 July 2010

157481UK00003B/2/P